new life

sharmistha mohanty

IndiaInk
ROLI BOOKS

IndiaInk

© Sharmistha Mohanty, 2005

First published in 2005
IndiaInk
An imprint of
Roli Books Pvt. Ltd.
M-75, G.K. II Market
New Delhi 110 048
Phones: ++91 (011) 2921 2271, 2921 2782
2921 0886, Fax: ++91 (011) 2921 7185
E-mail: roli@vsnl.com; Website: rolibooks.com
Also at
Varanasi, Bangalore, Jaipur

Cover : Arati Subramanyam
Layout :   Narendra Shahi

ISBN: 81-86939-21-0
Rs. 295

Typeset in Perpetua by Roli Books Pvt. Ltd. and
printed at Press Tech Litho Pvt. Ltd., New Delhi

~

For Kabir

~

List of Acknowledgement:

— "What Jesus Runs Away From," *Say I Am You,* by Coleman Barks, copyright Coleman Barks, 1994, Maypop

— "Ode to Autumn," by John Keats, *John Keats, The Complete Poems,* Penguin, 1978

— *"Meghnad Badh Kabya,"* by Michael Madhusudhan Dutt, *Madusudhan Rachanabali,* Sahitya Samsad, 1985

— Translation of *Heer* by Madan Gopal Singh

— Speeches of Macaulay, *Macaulay: Prose and Poetry,* Selected by G.M.Young, Rupert Hart-Davis, 1952

— *"As if it were my native land,"* Michael Madhusudan Dutt, same as above

— Speech by Rammohun Roy, *Asiatic Journal, Vol.II, New Series,* May-Aug 1830

— Macaulay, same as above

— Letters, Michael Madhusudan Dutt, same as above

— "Crisis in Civilization," Rabindranath Tagore, *The English Writings of Rabindrnath Tagore, Vol. Three, A Miscellany,* ed. By Sisir Kumar Das, Sahitya Akademi, 2002

— "Do Not Go Gentle Into that Good Night," by Dylan Thomas, *Oxford Anthology of English Literature, Vol. II,* OUP, 1973

— Translation of *Panther Panchali,* Bibutibhushan Bandopadhyay, by Sharmistha Mohanty

— The Second Elegy, The Duino Elegies, *The Selected Poems of Rainer Maria Rilke,* translated by Stephen Mitchell, Random House, 1982

— "Naina katoriya zulfan kale dang…" *Pahari Masters,* by B.N. Goswamy and Eberhard Fischer, OUP India, 1997

— Third Brahmana, Brihadaranyaka Upanishad, *The Thirteen Principal Upanishads,* translated by R.E. Hume, OUP India, 1985

acknowledgements

To my family: Dr. P.K. Mohanty and Mahmooda Mohanty, Munir, Sara, Subhashis, and Rajeshwari, for being a collective spine, and protecting, through everything;

To Monica Chowdhury, Chitra Singh, Dr. John D. Rodrigues, Vijay Jamdade, and Sunita Menon, healers and guides all, my deepest gratitude;

To my teachers, James Alan McPherson and Mani Kaul, from whom I will always continue to receive;

To the Akademie Schloss Solitude, Stuttgart, Germany, for a fellowship, generous in more ways than I can say, during which parts of this novel were written;

To Dr. Eberhard Fischer for his generosity with miniature paintings.

ragini todi: a prologue

She stands with a veena in her arms. Three deer, two on the left, one on the right, look up at her face.

Beyond her is a pale, green landscape, very pale, with a few small bushes and even smaller undulations. There are no trees, no flowers, and the grass is sparse. Above all this is a pale sky, perhaps of first light.

Her lahenga is the same pale green as the landscape behind her. But on her lahenga there are flowers, diminutive flowers, not too many, not too few. The eye moves from the flowers to the landscape, wishing to bring some to the bareness outside. From the landscape, the eye moves back to the lahenga, wishing to bring the land's vastness to the flowers.

The landscape and the flowers, they desire each other. This desire keeps them in movement, going towards, coming back. The point of meeting, of that who can speak? Each time the possibilities change.

What can be whole only within itself?

Everything is broken somewhere, deeply, inexorably, and through this place of brokenness it leaves itself.

It lets itself be entered.

ONE

"I love a dark girl in a large house," said the man. Both precise and vast this description, not colliding with its object, but looking at it and through and beyond, leaving spaces.

How dark was she?

As dark as the rich brown soil of the Bay of Bengal where the Ganga meets the sea. The soil at the mouth of the Ganga was clay and silt, with barely any sand. It was ever changing because it was made of what the river brought and what the ocean took away.

When she was born her grandmother peered into the crib and loved her because she was the daughter of her only son. But she saw the child's dark brown skin that shone when rubbed with warm mustard oil, irrevocable skin, and was silent. She put out a wrinkled, life roughened hand, the fingers gently pointing in different directions, and placed it on the child's head. The girl did not look like her mother who was pale skinned and beautiful, she looked like her father, the dark one, and she was overjoyed to look like him, the person she loved most in her life.

How large was the house?

Large enough to hold the sufferings of a civilization as well as its gestures of joy. What overflowed went to the edges of the balcony and then, controlled itself. As she ran along this long balcony, her mother bathed. The water poured for hours as she washed herself and could not stop, till her hands and breasts were wrinkled from so much moisture, and the water seeped out from a crack below the door and flowed through the rest of the house to form a pool near the puja room where the gods sat speechless among red and yellow flowers, baffled by this unexpected offering.

She grew up slowly in that large house where the flowers in the garden changed with each season, but the water did not stop. She began to run from one room to another in that large, long house, flinging doors open and shutting them behind her, heavy wooden doors made from trees that had left the forests of Burma, but she could still hear the sound of the water falling. How far would she have to run? Sometimes, when her mother emerged, her beauty somehow still intact, it was almost evening.

She ran out of the house one evening, down the flight of stairs and onto the street. She ran down the street, past large houses with balconies open to the twilight sky. At the end of the street, there was a stallion, sprawled dead in the middle of the road, with staring eyes, and a thick black liquid flowing from its open mouth. She had never seen a horse here before. She touched the black liquid with three fingers. It burnt her hand. What could the horse have been doing on this quiet street of homes? She stood still, amazed. Then she sat down, between the horse's twisted legs, on the asphalt still warm from the afternoon sun. She reached out and touched the horse's dark brown flank and saw it was a shade darker than her own hand, but with very little life.

She looked closer and saw the body rising and falling, with a minute movement. Her hand stroked the flank, the still warm flesh. The black liquid from the mouth was flowing down the asphalt towards her and it came and touched her bare legs, creeping up to the edge of her dress. She continued to stroke the horse till the last light had gone from the sky and it really was evening. Suddenly, the horse began to stir. She took her hand away for a moment, but brought it back again. Then the horse moved, and though it moved gently, her hand was thrown off its body. It stood up, still awkward, steadied itself, and then slowly began to gallop away, gathering speed as it turned the corner to the next street, moving towards the main road filled with cars and buses and trams.

She did not know that she had stroked the horse back to its life and that in return it had given her its own strength and its power to run. But it was from that moment on that she learned to run, not only from but towards. As she ran the power taught her about distances. She learned that pain increases the distance between things, joy closes it, but both are sight. She savoured the taste of running. She would learn that the world holds many countries, and also, landscapes. She would learn that the body holds the soul's light, a fluttering, diminutive, overwhelming illumination, impelled only by itself. Her name was Anjali. There was a darkness under her eyes like the darkness of forests.

In the beginning, they say, the mountains had great wings. They flew through the air and alighted on the earth when they wished, causing the earth to tremble. But Indra cut off the mountains wings. He fastened them to the earth to steady it.

Maybe.

Maybe the mountains stood fast on the earth to see what it was like to hold still. Like the most courageous of human beings they desired to know not only the one but also the other.

Maybe they never flew at all, for where is the sense of loss in a mountain? They may have risen out of the ground with all the strength of the ground's desire to be closer to the sky.

When Anjali looked at beginnings, the light in her eyes and the darkness under them, created the most profound shadows. Through them she saw that each thing has several beginnings, and the one a person sees depends on how much the light and shadow choose to reveal, and of course, the angle of a person's gaze. When she asked her father what she was like when she was born, he said, "When you were born, my little golden one, my other heart, you saved me from dying."

There are as many beginnings as the changes in a heart and that is why stories of origin are always created anew. What is unchanging is the desire to find the first moment.

"But you wanted a son," said Anjali. She was fifteen and things had begun to reveal themselves.

"Who told you that?" he asked her, suddenly angered. "Who?"

Fathers like hers were doctors, lawyers, engineers, robust men helping the nation to move forward. The sorrow of having a daughter now had to be held inside, with dignity.

"Everyone," she said.

His face quietened. 'Not any more," he said.

"Why?"

"Because you've already taken me forward."

Anjali stands on the balcony of her dead father's house, in the afternoon sun from which she no longer desires to escape. Instead, she takes in the sun completely, enjoying the sweat in her armpits, the dampness above the lips, the way it suffuses her sari with a moisture. There are potted plants on the balcony that are withered, broken and covered with the street's dust. The ledge is discoloured by pigeon droppings that have hardened in the sun. She has sold the house, this house of long balconies and many windows, on a quiet street, this large house of her beginnings.

For days she has emptied it of things till there are only the walls and floors and ceilings. Yet, when she enters it she feels it is more full than ever. As she stands on the balcony she sees a man below, looking up at her. Like years before, when she wanted to see something on the street more closely, she walks down the stairs and onto the burning street in her bare feet. Her soles shrivel on the hot asphalt.

She sees him, as she wanted to, up close. He is perhaps a little older than her, his body bare to the waist, and with long, slender hands. His hair is knotted and falls below the shoulders, his beard till the beginning of his chest. The large eyes slant not upwards, but down, like an animal she has seen somewhere in the mountain woods. A dhoti of leaf brown Bengal malmal as light as wind falls to his bare feet, and trembles when the breeze comes, a dhoti like she has never seen before, like the ones which are never more made, because their makers are all gone.

Anjali stands before this man and she puts her hands on his dark chest covered with the softest hair. First the hands, and then she puts her head on it, and he puts his arms around and holds her. She wants to weep but her tears have all been used up. In his embrace she turns, she twists, she kisses and bites his chest and the soft hair on it. Under her mouth she can feel his blood rising, his muscles turning imperceptibly towards her, but he does not touch her in return.

She remains in his embrace till evening comes and she senses the evening star exactly above them. She looks up and only when she is ready does he let her go out of his arms.

"Listen," he tells her. "I have come to give you three things."

Anjali remembers the number three, the auspicious number.

"Hold open your palms," he says.

She holds them before him.

"Time. Always enough of it," he says, touching her right palm. "Perhaps even too much. So you can see."

"Aloneness," he says, touching the left palm.

"But I'm already married to the man I love, and so many, many friends—"

"Aloneness," he repeats, almost harshly "so you can see further."

"And where will you put the third one?" she asks.

"In between," he says, looking at her with the greatest tenderness. "Join your palms."

She joins her palms together. He touches the place where the palms join. She feels something heavy falling into her hands.

"What is it?"

"Imbalance," he says. "So your actions can always go beyond your sight."

As she looks up at him under the moonlight now, the darkness reveals what day had obscured. This man has in him the men she has already known, going all the way back to her father, and the men she would know in the future. She recognizes those slender hands, does she not, and perhaps the width of those shoulders? The eyes she has not yet known, nor that barely perceptible moving of the muscles.

In the very next moment he comes closer to her. He arranges her windblown hair, taking it away from her forehead and gathering it behind the ear. He says, "You had to lose the first man, your father, to gain the second, your love. Each man will have to be sacrificed in this way for you to know the next one.

And every ten years of your life, at the exact point where the decade turns, there will be a man who will destroy everything that exists and bring you a new world.

And you will always be prepared to receive him.

You will recognize him by his mark, however deep it may be hidden, of fearlessness.

Though you will travel the world the man will always be dark skinned, from a civilization nourished by the sun."

He looks at her once, a long look, and then he turns and walks away. She does not call him back.

That night Anjali lies down on the empty terrace of the house she has sold, on an old chatai, smooth as silk, made thirty years ago in Medinipur where it was once an art. Above, there are stars. She remembers that even when she was a child, the long balcony was where the home met the world. Suddenly, the present and the future recede and it is the past that enters her most completely, perhaps because it is the only time that cannot be redeemed.

In the morning came the sellers of fruit, vegetables, rice. Flowers were also sold but only flowers for the puja room, the hibiscus, the marigold. Those for a woman's hair would be sold much later, after evening fell. "Baas-mati," said the rice man, "Baas-mati." Each seller had a different pitch and tone, a different place where he would break the word in two, a personal rise and fall. Basmati, the special rice, incredibly fine, long grained, so special that it was eaten at weddings and pujas, and it came from far away, from the hills in the north. The cry brought people out to buy. But everything has more than one consequence, and the cry often brought with it a landscape, a particular light, a most necessary expansion of space. There were shawls from Kashmir, saris from Dacca.

Upstairs, the women stood on the balcony and looked down, meeting the upward looking eyes of the sellers, probing the baskets on their heads. The maid would go down to the gate and sift the rice in her hands. New or old, too fine or too coarse, had to be decided by touch and smell. The sellers were always men, wiry and strong. But when they put their baskets down outside the main door of the house and sat down, they let out a soft sigh, grateful for the shade and momentary rest. When they got up again, wiping the sweat from their foreheads with their palms, the body's ache and exhaustion passed like a fleeting shadow over their faces, before they went on their way again, back and neck completely straight, the large, heavy basket balanced on their heads.

You leave, and a thing you love stays where it is.

In the fire of mid afternoon when the hawkers rested, came a madman with nowhere to go. He wore a dhoti and over it a faded black blazer. On his head there were clumps of hair like monkey fur, with bald spots in between. "Everything is burning," he would scream. "The sky, this street, all these houses, the world. Burning. Burning…" Some days, after this he would sit in the middle of the street and weep loudly. If any windows in the houses were still open, they would shut at this time. On some days came a madwoman, her hair cropped very short like a man's, a brown cloth tied around her waist and falling to her knees, her chest bare. Her breasts drooped on a thin chest, but the nipples were always hard and full. She walked down the street like a child at play, curving one way and then the other, from right to left, till she reached the end and turned the corner, always smiling to herself.

When the sun was still strong but the children were already outside, came the animal shows. The sad dancing bear on a long chain that danced, the snake man with a black cobra coiled in his cane basket, the monkey man.

The monkey man came, and without rattling his drum, would dress the monkeys for the show. He dressed them with a great carefulness. Gently he raised their arms to pass them through sleeves, lifted the male and slipped his legs through the small trousers, and wrapped the female's tiny dupatta around her delicate neck. All this time a monkey child watched this ritual of dressing. It was thin and delicate, with a neck that could barely support its head, and when sitting still resembled a half formed human embryo.

There were the jugglers and the acrobats. A hard faced little girl vaulted from a tall pole and strong bodied men did impossible somersaults. The children who performed on the street were always different from the children who looked down from their balconies. They had a look of adulthood about them which removed them far from the children above. It led to a strange shyness on both sides. There came a sadhu lost in himself. A baul with his ektara, singing,

"*Moner katha balibar aage, chokher jal bahia jaye...*
Before I can speak my mind, tears flow..."

In the late afternoon came a fruit special to the season, a fruit which could be savoured in that particular idleness before evening came. In summer's peak and as the rains began it was mango, at other times jamun that made the mouth red, and guava, to be eaten with salt and pepper as the light fell.

Sometimes, when you leave never to return, that thing you love arrives, in its own time, at its own ending.

More than fruits and vegetables changed with the seasons. In spring came Krishna, with his body painted blue, and his Radha in golden clothes. Krishna was gentle and loving and standing next to his Radha he played long, never ending notes on a bamboo flute. Those notes filled the children with an unknown longing. They craned their necks to watch till the pair had disappeared around the next street corner. When Shiva came, his body covered in ash and his hair in a knot on his head, he arrived with an energy that had rarely been encountered, an energy which could destroy things and create them anew. Sometimes Parvati came with him, dressed simply, and sometimes he was alone, with his trishul. As they watched Shiva they became stilled, lost in something far larger than themselves. Radha and Krishna, Shiva and Parvati, and sometimes Ram and Sita, they all spoke in verses, they sang, they danced. At the end the coins were collected in a large stone bowl.

As the sun went down and the cars began to come home, the ice cream man rolled his cart down the road. After that the balcony remained empty, lit unevenly by streetlamps.

The last vendor of the day was the seller of jasmine. He came in the late evening darkness, with his cry of "Bel-phul, Bel-phul," his voice rising on the first syllable and falling on the second. As he came closer, the cry unmuffled itself and floated up into the evening. Then his thin, wiry figure slowly appeared, in a long white shirt and dhoti, strings of the whitest jasmine falling from his hands. When he was very close, the street filled with the scent of jasmine. He always walked looking straight ahead, as if walking and holding the flowers was all he had to do and selling was an unnecessary distraction. Sometimes a young woman ran down and bought a few strings for her hair, and perhaps one to tie around the wrist of a friend. Other days he walked on, never waiting to sell, into the pool of yellow light that the streetlamp threw down, and out of it, into the darkness.

And what if you did not love the thing then but love it now? Then you must know that you love something that no longer exists outside yourself.

One last man came down the street when the evening was turning into night. He was not a seller, and he asked for nothing. In a faded old shirt and trousers, a slim young man, he sang in the way of street people whose voice has a great throw and reach without ever being too loud.

> *"Oparete Shyam ache, eparete ami,*
> nayan mele dekho Radha, nadi bhara pani
> *On the other bank is Shyam, on this bank I stand,*
> Open your eyes and look Radha, the river is full of water."

And why do you love it now suddenly?

There were three things that took Anjali forward, three things that grew her up. The number three, again, the number of times that a deity in a temple was circled by the worshipper.

The first thing.

Outside the bathroom door stood her grandmother, always saying in the gentlest voice, "Come out, Pratima, come out. What about Anjali, what about Nayan?" There was no response. Her grandmother, after waiting a while, would walk away quietly on swollen feet.

Anjali's father had married Pratima for her beauty, a beauty that people would stop on the street to look at. But how could it ever be that simple, thought Anjali, even as she was growing up. Did daughters know some things that fathers did not? But what a daughter did not know, could not know, is that after you married that woman, and discovered that only her beauty was whole and everything else in ruins, you could still love her.

What about Anjali? She had been born into this, into the sound of water running. When she was four, the neighbour next door asked her one day to call her mother out to the balcony.

"She can't come right now," Anjali said.

"Where is she?"

"In the bathroom, where else?" she said.

"What do you mean?" the woman asked.

"That's where she is most of the time."

For the rest of the day, her mother did not say a word to Anjali. She couldn't understand what was wrong and begged her mother to speak to her even one word. But she didn't. She maintained her cruel silence. The ayah who looked after her, a woman widowed at fourteen and with no other family in the world, took her away to her room and comforted her. The next day Anjali broke down and pleaded with her mother.

"You were talking about me to the neighbours," her mother said. "I heard you."

"What did I say?" the little girl asked, bewildered.

"That I'm bathing all the time."

Anjali learned then that one could not always speak the truth.

"I'll never say it again," she replied, because she would have done anything to have her mother speak to her again.

"Good," said her mother, and took her hand.

Growing up, and into a young woman, she had never ever envied her mother, her beauty, even when the women who visited the house said, "Oh, poor little girl. Didn't have the good fortune to be born with a face like her mother's."

Every day she watched what this beauty covered, like flawless skin stretched over a body of disease.

Her mother woke up and went straight to bathe. There she stayed for two or three hours. Then to the puja room, for three hours. Here the gods were bathed and cleaned. Then fruit was cut, put onto tiny brass plates and placed in front of the gods. Flowers were counted, three for each god, arranged in small, perfect circles. Then the prayers were recited under the breath. It was only in the late afternoon and evening that she was ready to face the world, friends, relatives, neighbours. In between there were a few baths, an hour for each. At night, the routine began again.

By the time Anjali was grown enough to understand what it meant her parents had stopped sharing a bedroom. It was she who slept with her mother on their marriage bed. Her father slept in his study in the corner of the house, the room farthest away from this one. Although she had once asked her father whether she could sleep in her own room, where her books were, and her clothes, he replied, "Someone has to be with her at night." Anjali did not say, "Why not you?" She understood that it was even more unbearable for him than for her, and she did not ask him again.

At night, perhaps because there was nowhere else to turn, the rituals eroded Anjali, broke her down slowly as she lay in bed watching her mother, praying, washing her hands, praying again. Then as she lay down in bed, before she closed her eyes to sleep, fatigued by the repetition of ritual, her mother reached out and touched Anjali's face. Three times. It was not the touch of a mother, but of a woman who wants to keep destruction at bay.

When even the borders of ritual were crossed, something had to be done. It happened every few years. When Anjali was fourteen her mother began to scream out songs in the still heat of afternoon, songs of love, songs of devotion. She also chose a long knife from the kitchen and brought it to her dresser in the bedroom. Every once in a while she would glance at it quickly, then turn away. If anyone went near it she would shout, "Leave it there, it's mine." Then, once when no one was with her she took the knife and made a deep gash on her right arm. The blood spurted out onto the mirror and dripped down like paint, staining all the lipsticks, powder and perfume bottles below it a dark red.

The next day the three of them drove to the outskirts of the city to meet a guru, a saint renowned for his powers. He lived in a decrepit building with very narrow stairs, and an open drain flowing outside in which the water ran green. They climbed four floors and reached a small room filled with people, and without even a fan to cool the air. The guru was seated on one side on the bare floor, wearing a dirty white dhoti. He was a large and fat man with a face of rare compassion. He was talking to a young girl of perhaps seventeen, whose entire body and face seemed to be covered with large black warts. He spoke to her very softly, and then reached out and touched her head. The girl touched his feet and left.

Everyone turned to look at them, especially at Anjali's mother, they could not turn their eyes away, men and women. Her father said something to the guru. He looked at Anjali's mother for what seemed like a very long time. Her mother did not meet the guru's eyes. While he looked at her she looked around the room, at the walls, windows, and shelves. The guru got up and chose a book from a cheap plywood bookshelf, opened it at a specific page and gave it to her.

"I want you to go up to the terrace. I want you to stay there alone and read this poem aloud, to feel everything that is said, and I want you to weep, and weep, and weep."

Anjali knew this man had been able to look inside her mother.

"I won't do it," her mother said.

"Why not?" he asked, calmly.

"I can't. I won't." she said. Her mouth began twisting sharply to the left, as it always did when someone had upset her.

In a moment the guru became enraged. "Leave this room right now," he shouted, and everyone looked at them. "I don't want to see you here again."

Anjali's mother, a little taken aback, but without losing her eternal grace and composure, went out.

The guru asked Anjali and her father to wait.

"She will have to be left to her misery," he said. "If she changes her mind bring her back. What can I say?" He put his hands first on Anjali's head and then on her father's.

"But is there nothing..." said her father, his voice shaking just a little.

A look of compassion such as Anjali had never seen appeared on the guru's face. He began to speak and it took them a moment to realize that he was reciting a poem, in English. The pronunciation was flawed but he knew the words perfectly.

"I say the Great Name over the deaf and the blind,
    and they are healed. Over a stony

– 27 –

> *mountainside, and it tears its mantle down to the navel.*
> > *Over non-existence, it comes to existence.*
> *but when I speak lovingly for hours, for days,*
> > *With those who take human warmth*
> *and mock it, when I say the Name to them, nothing*
> > *Happens. They remain rock, or turn to sand,*
> *where no plants can grow. Other disease are ways*
> > *For mercy to enter, but this non-responding*
> *breeds violence and coldness toward God."*

They were silent on the way home.

The next time she threw her jewels out of the window, one by one, emeralds, rubies, gold, and the crowd of insatiable curiosity gathered on the street below as the servants ran down to gather the scattered earrings, necklaces and bangles. The time after that she attempted to strangle herself while bathing and was pulled out.

The doctor arrived in a suit and tie to examine her. He gave her medicines. He told her father, "Perhaps she has nothing really to do. You are a wealthy man…"

"Not so wealthy doctor," her father replied.

"Even so, Mr. Sen, you have servants, a cook, a car, a driver, and only one child. What is there for her to do?"

"Others survive very well, don't they, the wives of my friends…"

"You don't know that really, do you?" said the doctor.

Her father was quiet.

The medication always helped. It brought her back to her life of rituals.

Anjali wondered if anyone knew what *she* did. That even these extremes were not really extreme, they only seemed to be so, that her mother's attempt even at strangling herself was not genuine, she did not have the strength to kill herself or to truly live, that was the real truth, that she would forever remain suspended in between. She lasted through the power of ritual, given to this land for some greater purpose and perfected for centuries till it also turned into misery. It was her life's anchor, her reason for living. And they, her father and she and her grandmother, lasted through resilience, also a thing so much of this soil, and that most cruelly ambivalent of ideas in this land, acceptance.

For things to change, someone, somewhere, had to act, to help her father's helplessness, to suggest something, show them at least a small, narrow way, for what was madness but grief without limits? But there was no one.

And nothing would cure her, not doctors not saints. Anjali heard that the girl with the warts had been cured, her skin now flawless and beautiful, but in this country brimming with saints and miracles nothing would ever transform her mother.

The only thing to do was to last, for everyone.

Anjali grew into a young woman never speaking about this to anyone outside the house. She grew up using the antidote of her father's incredible love and he, she later realized, lasted by using hers. The love that bound them, father and daughter, made her mother more alone.

On a good day, when her mother sang under her breath songs of love and happiness, Anjali would feel hope assaulting her. It never went away, this outrageous hope, but remained hidden in unexpected places. Inside her it said, maybe from tomorrow my mother will bathe a little less, be kinder, and even, maybe she will become a mother.

"Ma, tell me, what is it that happened to cause you so much pain? What happened before you were married?"

"Nothing, nothing at all." She would stir the dal on the fire and her mouth would twist to one side.

She would tell her father in the evening, "I asked her again today."

"Did she say anything?" her father would ask, with eagerness, even after so many years, and Anjali would recognize the same hope in him that was inside her.

"No," said Anjali.

After a few such times she understood that her mother was incapable of speaking it, whatever it was. If she could speak it she might have been freed. But the thing that had to be spoken was too large for language.

When Anjali got dressed to go to college, her mother would stand next to her. She watched Anjali as she pleated her sari, put the anchal in place, drew a bindi on her forehead, lined her eyes with the darkest kajal.

"You're beautiful," she would say.

Anjali would look at her. "Ma…"

"No, my daughter, you are the beautiful one. Look at your eyes. And look," she said, lifting her arm and hitching the sleeve of her blouse up to her shoulders. "Do you see my arm? It begins from the shoulder and then there's a bump going in and out, like a man's. Now look at yours. Rounded and straight all the way down to the elbow." The mirror gave back their reflection, with their arms stretched out, one dark, one fair.

When Anjali had finished dressing her mother would say, "So, now you're going to go away and leave me alone. Every day, put on your sari, dress up, and go away. A kiss on the cheek while you leave, just to keep me quiet."

"I have to go now Ma," she says, and leaves the house.

"Black deer eyes," she hears her mother say behind her.

One day, she comes back home in the evening and sees an ambulance parked outside the house. Upstairs, her grandmother sits quietly on her chair by the large wooden desk. Her two aunts have come and they hover around, taking care of the small things, because no one, no one knows how to take care of the large ones. She looks for her father and finds him on the balcony, with his arms and chin on the ledge.

"Your mother has locked herself in," he says. "It got worse today. Ten hours inside, bathing. I had to call the hospital and the psychiatrist. They say if she's treated for two months she'll be better. But she won't go. She's run in and locked the door."

"Can't we force her ? Shouldn't we?"

"No. No, I can't do that."

They sit there under the falling evening and Anjali cannot seem to even recognize everything that rises inside her. She wants her mother to go, to perhaps get better, if there is a hope of that, hopeless hope, yet she also wants her to stay because that is at least the known, both for her and her mother, and her heart makes a small movement, after many, many years, towards this woman who has brought them all so much grief.

She goes to her mother's closed door and says, "Ma." There is no response. She waits a long time. She raises her hand to knock, but only touches the polished, smooth surface of the door made from trees that grew in the forests of Burma. For some things, natural human knowledge is not enough. Some greater knowing is needed, some greater experience. Perhaps from another life if not from this one. Anjali turns away from the door.

When she goes back to the balcony her father is talking to the doctor. Finally, the doctor, with his eyes full of pity, walks down the stairs, climbs into the ambulance and goes away.

They sit there on the balcony and after hours have passed her father says, "Anjali."

She turns to look at him. He is looking down at the street below.

"I know," he says, and clears his throat. "I know you're still very young." He pauses. "My little golden one." He becomes silent again.

"But… you are growing up."

He turns towards her. "Will you take this pain from me now?"

How could Anjali refuse him?

Was all of this auspicious? Yes. It would always enable her to separate the merely normal and the truly sane.

The second thing.

Anjali has to throw the sounds out with her teeth and tongue, rather than letting them fall, drop, slip. The "o"s are always difficult. If she doesn't try hard enough she will say the wrong kind of "o", produced by a careless opening of the lips. To make them perfect she sucks in her cheeks, keeps her tongue down and forms a small circle with her lips. By the time she is seven this new language emerges from her with confidence, so that later she can say, "Lord Cornwallis introduced the Permanent Settlement in India…" with all the accents in the right places, or "The Battle of Trafalgar…"

"How wonderfully she speaks," says her father, "she will go far, my little girl." Even her grandmother, whose greatest knowledge is in loving, gathers Anjali in her arms with pride.

In the very first years at school, the nuns assemble them together and say, "You must never speak here in anything but English, is that clear?" The little girls, and they are very little girls, bend their heads back, look up at the nuns with their large eyes and say, "Yes."

At the end of every school year a photographer comes. The entire class of little girls sit in rows on the white marble steps. On the top step is their teacher, Mrs Dasgupta, in a printed silk sari, looking confidently into the camera. Behind her rises a large closed door with rectangular stained glass windows. The little girls are all in their skirts and blouses, with their arms folded over their still flat chests. The skirt ends at the knees and the girls try to bring their knees together. But when the photograph is printed they see that many of the girls, including Anjali, have not brought their knees close enough to each other. Their white panties are clearly visible between their legs. Anjali is taught how to sit with her knees together, but it is not easy to learn. It is not naturally there in her child's body, nowhere part of her physical inheritance, for she, like every other little girl there, is the first generation in her family to wear a skirt. In a land of drapes and saris, the holding together of the knees has never been a necessity.

When Anjali goes to school each morning, her body changing, her tongue turning, she walks through the white arches, and sees the church steeple gathering in the new sunlight. Beyond the arches are long stemmed white lilies in the garden, marble statues. Further in, behind the church door are the Sisters, smooth faced and kneeling on their spotless robed knees, saying their morning prayers. Everywhere the colour of alabaster and swans. England she always thinks of as a wide expanse of white, with a little blue for sky, a little grey for clouds, and perhaps a patch of green for meadows.

That is how white becomes for her the primary shade, the beginning and ending of all colour. The spurting of colour all around, of the bright blue in the sky, the deep green foliage lit by a blinding sun, the saris leaping out of their fabrics in red and purple and orange, the jewelled gods covered with sindur, are all somehow loud and strident, like the languages of this land. White is gentle, muted, like ladies in ivory dresses and Belgian lace.

When Anjali begins piano lessons with Sister Mave she is six years old. The first thing she notices is her own dark fingers next to Sister Mave's incredibly pale, white ones. She cringes inside, seeing how brown her fingers are, like soil, like mud. But the piano enchants her. When the music fills her little girl's heart she slowly begins to forget about the colour of her fingers. How many countries are there where you have to learn, slowly, to love the colour of your own skin? Growing up, Anjali does not know. Those are the countries they never seem to learn about at school. Her dark fingers are eager, they learn how to play tiny little minuets from Bach, a Sarabande from Handel, a waltz from Schubert.

"Esho…" the purohit says.
    "Esho…" says a hundred people together.
    "Sachandana…"
    "Sachandana.." they say.
    "Bilyapatra pushpanjali…"
    During the Durga Puja they recite prayers to Ma Durga in the

large parks where the pujas are held. Those five days are when Durga, the bride of the great Shiva, comes to her father's house, just as women, once they are married, visit their parents' home sometimes, and only sometimes, Anjali is told. Durga comes to be loved, indulged by her parents and by all of us who pray to her. See how beautiful she looks, how sweetly she smiles, bringing such joy to us all. Her husband's house is so far away and our hearts fill with sorrow when she leaves because she will not be here again until another year has passed.

"Bilyapatra..." says Anjali, repeating the Sanskrit that she will never fully understand, looking hard at Ma Durga, her tall, strong, ten armed form, her large black eyes, the serene smile, the long flowing black hair, the demon on which she has placed her foot. There is something there, she can feel it, a power, a strength, a violence, and all of this related to the compassion in the smile, but it eludes her, she is distracted by the crowd at her back pushing in the heat of the morning, and already the flowers are flying above her head towards the goddess.

"What about mahisasura?" asks Anjali. "Why does she kill him? She's strong, isn't she?"

"Because he's evil, and Ma Durga is good. She protects us from harm."

Every year each puja returns, without fail. Durga, Saraswati, Lakshmi, Kali. They are the best things to mark time with, because they are themselves constant and changeless.

As her mother lights a hundred flaming candles for Kali on the long balcony, Anjali asks, "But why does Ma Kali stick out her tongue?"

"One never asks *why* about a goddess. Ma Kali is the way she is."

Isn't there something more? thinks Anjali, as she grows up and questions begin inside her. Isn't there something more? Outside? Inside? What is known returns again and again, what is unknown never reveals itself. The women pray every day in their puja rooms, for hours, repeating mantras, offering flowers, incense and fruit. In her home, prayer changes nothing. Not her mother, not her father's grief that grows daily. The only time that the pujas are interrupted is when someone in the family dies. Then comes the time of ashaucha, and no worship is permitted. The family is "unclean" then.

"Why?" Anjali has to ask again. She does not receive an answer.

It is only when her grandmother tells her stories, of princesses and kings and rishis and gods that no questions arise inside her. On the roof, sitting with their legs crossed on a chatai, her grandmother's soft, crumpled sari blowing in the evening wind, the stars just beginning to appear above, Anjali listens to the oldest tales, as old her grandmother says, as the world.

"So one day," says her grandmother, "Hanuman was sitting on a rock in the mountains, chanting the name of Rama, when Narada, the great musician of the gods came by with his tanpura. "Why don't you sing a song?" asked Hanuman? Narada, pleased by the request, proud as he was talented, immediately agreed. He sang an enchanting song, showing his complete mastery over his art. "That was the most beautiful thing I have ever heard," said Hanuman. "Why don't you sing a song?" asked Narada. "Oh, I have an awful voice," said Hanuman, "I am only a monkey after all." "But sing anyway," said Narada, as one would to a child. So Hanuman began to sing a song about Rama. It was much, much more beautiful than what Narada expected. The song rose and floated over the mountains. Narada slowly saw animals coming out from behind rocks and bushes and trees. Little squirrels came and sat at

Hanuman's feet without moving, the birds stopped their flying and landed on the trees nearby, the deer and antelope left their leaping and running and stood absolutely still. A little further on the peaks came the lions, the panthers and the cheetahs, silenced by wonder, listening to Hanuman's song.

"That was wonderful," said Narada, as he bent to pick up his tanpura, moved himself by the song. But he could not pick it up because every hard thing around had melted. Even the rocks had turned into liquid at the sound of Hanuman's song, and where boulders were, rivers now began to flow. Then Narada finally lost his pride and bowed before Hanuman. "Forgive me," he said, "for thinking I am greater than you. The faith and passion in your song are greater than my greatest techniques."

Sometimes, in return, her grandmother asks Anjali to tell her about the convent. She too, unlike other grandmothers, has been to a school herself, but not to a college. Anjali describes the convent as best as she can, a place without dirt or heat or noise, she says that the Sisters, especially Sisters Teresa and Miriam are exceptionally kind and always soft spoken, gliding through the quiet corridors in their white habits, she describes the way that assembly is held, with all the girls entering the hall in a straight line with their shoulders back and their heads held high, and then arranging themselves in rows, while a nun plays a march on the piano. When the whole school has arrived, the piano stops and everyone recites together:

> "Our father who art in heaven
> hallowed be thy name..."

Her grandmother listens carefully to what Anjali describes, and like Anjali she too asks no questions. When Anjali shows her how to sit like a lady, with the knees together, her grandmother adjusts her softly crumpled sari on her shoulders and smiles.

Outside the Victoria Memorial in Calcutta, on the emerald lawns, is a great, big bronze statue of the Queen on her throne. The Queen has a rather swollen face, strong yet vulnerable, with large pouches under her eyes.

Inside, the sun cannot penetrate the enormous marble halls, the high domes, of the Victoria Memorial. Anjali is grateful for the cool darkness. They are all in their uniforms of white and blue. The white shirt, always crisp and starched, is buttoned as close to the neck as possible. The perfectly pleated skirt is not allowed to have a waistband so as not to reveal a shape, and begins suddenly from somewhere around the waist and stops only where the socks begin, that is, at the calves. The old tailor with callused hands who makes Anjali's uniforms has to force his fingers away from cutting a shape, making a flow, from doing what he wants and what he has learnt for many years from his master. Miss Walters, their history teacher, wears a red skirt that ends well above the knees.

The Memorial is sixty-four acres of green lawns, ponds and marble in the centre of Calcutta. They say William Emerson, when he built the Memorial, was inspired by the Taj Mahal. But who can control the nature of the silence that a building will enclose? Inside these marble halls topped by great domes there is the silence of huge old paintings that depict long ago battles, dust, unstoppable dust, marble busts of proud men often covered with grime, the shuffling feet of a few apathetic visitors from small towns and villages. The high, thick walls and the small windows were made to keep the cruel tropical light at bay but so many, many years later they create only a thick and gloomy afternoon darkness. The girls wander through the echoing halls quietly.

"Look," says, Miss Walters, "the Queen on a palanquin." They all turn their heads. Amazing, the Queen on a palanquin...In the half light and shadow, they look at portraits. Lord Curzon, Bentinck, Cornwallis. They are shown weapons, old swords, shields and guns that gleam where they catch the dull light. They stand before Queen Victoria's proclamation etched in gold onto the marble walls. "We trust that our present accolade may tend to unite in bonds of yet closer affection ourselves and our subjects—"

"I have to go now," Anjali hears a voice say. She turns around and sees a young woman in a forest green sari. "A few more minutes, please," says the young man with her. Anjali turns back to the proclamation. "...that from the highest to the humblest all may feel that under our rule the great principles of liberty, equality and justice, are secured to them..."

Meera, Anjali's dearest friend, comes up to her and takes her by the hand. "Have you seen?" she says, with the laughter rising from her throat.

Among the pillars and domes, other couples stroll, looking fleetingly at portraits, throwing a passing glance at statues and weapons, holding hands. A restlessness passes through the schoolgirls.

They go out to the lawns and walk near the ponds, underneath the large trees and the wrought iron lamps which will soon be lit. Slowly, as the girls walk they realize that all the people around them are divided into couples. The Memorial is one place where they can be alone, away from the moralists, the voyeurs, the disapprovers. Desire forbidden outside is released at last under the watchful pouch lined eyes of Queen Victoria.

On every stone bench, under every tree on the grass, dipping their hands into the water in the ponds—the lovers. The women adjust their saris constantly from the restlessness of physical desire, a pleat here, a wrinkle there. Anjali and Meera cannot not turn their eyes away. Passing close by a couple on a bench they see the man's hand inside the woman's sari blouse, and the woman with her eyes closed, her lips open. Again, near the pond, on the grass, a woman's anchal thrown over the man's lap, her arm disappearing underneath the fabric. Under the falling light of the sun, the gardens float in the air, impelled by the breathing of a thousand lovers. As the girls look they see a thousand arms going around a thousand shoulders, heads resting against necks, breasts rising avidly to meet the lover's hand.

> *"Season of mists and mellow fruitfulness*
> *Close bosom-friend of the maturing sun*
> *Conspiring with him how to load and bless*
> *The vines that round the thatch eaves run..."*

The large, dark green French windows of the classroom are closed to ward off the burning fire of the sun. It is May, and the tar has begun melting on the streets. Outside, the palm trees sway when a gust of hot breeze passes over them. The crows cry out endlessly. In the dark coolness of the convent they are taught many things. The French Revolution, geometry and the laws of physics, how to read the topography of land and river, and about forms of government. But what overpowers Anjali most of all is this poetry. Miss Jones first only reciting the lines, introducing the sounds and the rhythms, and only later prying the words open for their craft and meaning. Inside, in this humid afternoon darkness Anjali lives a season of the imagination so different from the physical season which is burning her, darkening her already darkened skin. She lives in this land and a land far away side by side, in a time which reveals one thing here, another there and sometimes she falls into the deep, deep ravine created between.

They have to memorize all the poetry they learn.

"To bend with apples the mossed cottage-trees,
And fill all fruit with ripeness to the core..."

Miss Jones shows them photographs of the poets, the landscapes they write of, she speaks of their lives.

"To swell the gourd, and plump the hazel shells
With a sweet kernel; to set budding more..."

One evening as Anjali is reciting this poem, learning it carefully, the flower seller walks by, crying "Bel-phul, Bel-phul" on the street below. The fragrance of jasmine floats up and in.

"And still more later flowers for the bees,
Until they think warm days will never cease,
And summer has o'er-brimmed its clammy cells."

The flower seller's cry disturbs Anjali's concentration.

"Who hath not seen thee..."

The fragrance pulls her in another direction, back into her childhood, her past and beyond that into a past which is not only her own. "Who hath not seen thee..." Suddenly it seems to her that it is the man crying "bel-phul" that is the past, no, more than that, he is stasis, because he will walk down this road forever crying "bel-phul, bel-phul" without change, and this poetry that is the future. "Who hath not seen thee oft amid thy store?" There are clearly two realities. How can the past ever equal the future, the known equal the unknown? Odes, alexandrines, sonatas, this crisp, precise language, spring gentle spring when the snow melts, daffodils, churches and cathedrals reaching the pale skies. Oh so gentle sunlight. "Who hath not seen thee oft amid thy store? Sometimes whoever seeks abroad may find..." All of this so clear, so visible, so understandable. Very far away, rarely encountered, like ruins deep in the countryside, the *Upanishads* covered with boulders covered with deep moss; the *Gita Govinda* and *Meghdut* buried under pigeon droppings; the language of Sanskrit over which tiny plants and grasses have begun to grow; Raga Deepak darkened with soot perhaps from too much light; "...thee sitting careless on a granary floor, thy hair soft-lifted by the winnowing wind..."; the Sufi singing his song among abandoned graves; the weaver spinning an intricate cloth, while dust settles on his bent head and his hands and lodges deep in the core of a flower he is shaping or in the inward curve of a mango leaf; temples with a hundred pillars each singularly carved, between which large bats fly in the utter darkness; the craftsman forging an iron horse in a fire that will leave nothing but ashes; the fingers of a miniature painter gripping a squirrel hair brush from which he will create so much space and dwelling and silence that people will mistake it for nothing at all; the dancer dancing under the full moon before Krishna on the day of Holi whose anklets are heard by no one for all abandon in worship happens in the deepest ruins far from where anyone lives and the sound of the anklets scatters the dark brown rats in all directions. "Or on a half-reaped furrow sound asleep... "Bel-phul, Bel-phul," the cry fades as the man walks away, further and further, though the fragrance lingers on till she finishes;

"Hedge-crickets sing ; and now with treble soft,
The red-breast whistles from a garden-croft
and gathering swallows twitter in the skies."

"Sammukhe samare pari, bir churamani
birbaahu, chali jave gela jampure,
akale, kaho, he debi amritabhasini."

When the Bengali teacher walks in, a dark, thin woman with rough, dry hair, the class falls asleep. Her name is Miss Dutta and she teaches them the most ancient prose and poetry, from a Bengali that no one speaks anymore. Her body is filled with an incredible restlessness as she teaches, as if she herself is questioning its usefulness. When Miss Walters walks in to teach the history of Europe, everyone wakes up. The Hapsburg dynasty, the assassination of the Archduke, the storming of the Bastille. In contrast the opulent Mughals, and Gandhi in his loincloth all enter the realm of the here, the ordinary. Miss Walters is thin and very tall, and often wears a sari because she is going to marry an Indian man. They love watching her when she does, because she wears a sari in the way that Western women do, as if it were a dress, without knowing how to receive its drapes and flows onto their bodies, moving against it instead of with it. Miss Walters has studied at Oxford. She is confident. Once, when a student asks her not to make the history exam marks public, she tells them, in her clipped monotone, that she will put the marks up in red on the white marble of the Victoria Memorial if she wants to. The Bengali teacher is not confident. She occupies only the edge of the teacher's chair.

"Uthila rakshaspati prasad shikhare,
kanak udayachale dinamani jeno angshumali."

Is it gone, this language with the rounded script, the circular sounds, will it never again be the language of her imagination, or the language she speaks to her lovers in?

Lakshmi stands on an open lotus, dressed in a blood red sari with golden butis. Her mother and her aunts have spent all day arranging oil lamps, bowls of milk and ghee, sweets, fruits, the necessary types of grain, flowers, cloth, each arranged in a specific, meticulous way, in the exact numbers prescribed for this particular puja. Once a year the family purohit comes, after sundown, to do the Lakshmi Puja. He is a handsome middle aged man with a strong chest above his white dhoti, and he always stands absolutely straight. Anjali is a woman now and he looks at Anjali often, his eyes moving all over her body.

Anjali has spent the whole day painting the feet of Lakshmi. She has learnt to paint the feet in a few broad strokes, curving the shape in at the instep, as her mother and grandmother have taught her. This is one ritual she has always loved, perhaps because it is simple and produces something immediately visible before her. She makes the toes from small dots of rice paste and comes to her favourite part, the paddy, flowers and leaves that surround the feet. As she paints the feet, going from the threshold of one room to another, she remembers her grandmother.

On this day her grandmother thickened milk in a large copper kadahi for most of the day, and when the milk thickened to a paste she made sweets from it. As she stirred she kept telling Anjali tales of the gods. "When Lakshmi and Vishnu sat on the Garuda bird, and the Garuda bird spread its huge wings, the sky darkened…"

"Did they really exist?" Anjali asked her once.

Her grandmother smiled. She turned back to her stirring.

"After I die I will still exist," she said, "and I will still look after you."

The puja begins with the ringing of the small brass bell which the purohit holds in his left hand. Once again the shlokas, once again the rituals, the placing of the flowers, the pouring of Ganga water. Once again that particular smell of incense mixed with sliced fruit and flowers, a puja smell, a Hindu smell, that she will recognize anywhere for the rest of her life.

It is the smell of stasis.

At the end of the Lakshmi Puja the purohit gives them the Shanti jal. They all have to cover their feet and heads. Anjali loves this time because it is the only time people touch each other, a little. Anjali's male cousins, uncles, the children, all come close to borrow the end of a sari from the woman next to them to cover their feet or a bent head. They all sit huddled together in the room as the purohit takes a mango leaf, dips it in a copper bowl filled with Ganga water, and sprinkles the water on their heads, saying, "Shantih, Shantih, Shantih..." Anjali feels a light spray of water on her face. "Om Shantih, Om Shantih, Om Shantih, Om Shantih..." When she lifts her head a little she can see the mango leaf being pointed in different directions. "Shantih, Shantih, Shantih, Shantih, Shantih..."

"Shantih, Shantih, Shantih," the purohit says. He stands up and ushers everyone out of the room, shutting the door behind him. After a few minutes he opens the door. The room is filled with incense smoke curling towards the windows. He gives everyone some sliced fruit and a sweet in their open palms. The rest will be served later on plates. Then he gets up and stretches. When everyone else has left the room he tells Anjali's father, gesturing towards Anjali with a slight shift of the head, "You must be careful with this girl. She will bring you a lot of grief."

Her father, astonished, gathers Anjali close and takes her out of the room.

At the convent the large assembly hall is flooded with light. Beyond the tall French windows the girls stand in their pale, plain chiffons, Anjali in lavender, others in pale blues, peaches and pinks. Finally, they are allowed to dress as they wish. Under thin chiffons the skin glows, the blouse makes a circle well below the neck, arms are exposed, and the careful pleats begin after the navel. From wrists and throats rise the most subtle perfumes.

Sister Teresa is there and Sister Miriam, looking after things, taking care. Anjali will miss them, she has grown up watching the lines change on their faces. Sister Miriam now has deep furrows running over hers. They break into a million wrinkles when she smiles. They are the kindest people in the convent, the Sisters, much kinder than Miss Walters and the one Indian teacher who has studied at Oxford. They haven't seen their own lands in decades, these nuns, and their pale skins still redden a little from the heat of tropical afternoons.

This is farewell. Twelve school years have been lived here. The assembly hall is gleaming and smells of new polish on the wood floor. Everywhere, cleanliness and shine. On one side there are long tables covered with thick white tablecloths on which the food has been served. There are pale, soft cucumber sandwiches, Madeira cake, small pieces of grilled fish, and fruit. The food tastes warm and full on Anjali's tongue. She wipes her fingertips on a white linen napkin. Mother Superior is ready to deliver the farewell speech.

She walks up on stage, a pale, serene woman, her black and white habit made more stark by the stage lights.

"My dear girls. Today is a very special day indeed, for you and for St Mary's. Twelve years of hard work and preparation have made you into wonderful, capable, young women. St Mary's is proud of you. I hope you will remember what you have learnt here and carry that learning inside you for the rest of your life. We have taught you to excel in whatever you choose to do, whatever you become—doctor, lawyer, wife, mother, and a true citizen of this country. So go forth and succeed. May God bless you.

"We will now sing Hymn no. 42."

The pages in the little white prayer books rustle in everyone's hands. Anjali is standing next to the window and she feels a breeze lift the end of her sari. She knows the hymn well, she has sung it many times over the years, but this time, as she sings, her voice is filled with a new emotion of loss, of farewell. Here, no one predicts grief lying ahead, here there is hope and faith in the future.

"Lord make me a channel of your peace
here a language that can be understood and its poetry felt
Where there is hatred let me sow your love
here a method, a rigour, in knowledge
Where there is injury your pardon Lord
here the heart so attracted to that which is different
And where there's doubt true faith in you...
here a freedom not possible elsewhere

Lord grant that I may never seek
and here everything, even the freedom,
So much to be consoled as to console
infused with a power already proven

To be understood as to understand

To be loved as to love with all my soul."

When the hymn ends, no one speaks. The breeze still blows in from the gardens, carrying with it a smell of rajnigandha—the flower of weddings and deaths – and dark rain clouds. Mother Superior steps down from the stage.

Sister Miriam comes and puts an arm around Meera and Anjali. She smells of soap and the starch in her white habit.

"Don't you take your Trinity exams next month?" she asks Meera.

"I'm working hard," Meera says, "and then I'm off to England."

"Both of you, play us something," says Sister Miriam.

Anjali laughs. "I've hardly been practicing."

"Sister Mave will be very happy if you do."

Anjali remembers Sister Mave's fingers next to hers on the keyboard, their feet together on the pedals below. She sits at the old Bechstein piano, opens it and is silenced for a moment by the familiar smell of warm, aged wood. It is a strangely secure smell. Sister Mave comes and sits near her. She is slim, sharp featured, with a skin so pale it is almost colourless. She does not watch Anjali's hands as she used to, she just listens. Anjali plays a nocturne from Chopin, the Nocturne in G Minor, Op. 15, No. 3. At the end when she looks up she sees Sister Mave bringing a white handkerchief up to her eyes.

Then comes Meera with Beethoven's Sonata no. 8 in C Minor, the Pathetique. The music fills the large hall with its chandeliers, the curtained French windows, and then moves out through the wide open doors into the hot summer night to meet the monsoon thunder and the approaching rain.

At ten, precisely, the farewell evening comes to an end. The nuns embrace each of them. From the piano come some simple chords to which the senior class sing, stretching their throats,

"Hasta la vista till we meet again
Hasta la vista friends
Hasta la vista until then..."

It is a summer night, just before the rains. As Anjali leaves, the convent is alternately light and dark, under the moon, under the passing clouds. When the light comes, everything turns luminous. The stone figure of Mary in the grotto with her palms joined, the nuns' white habits as they raise their arms to wave goodbye, the steeple of the church against the dark Calcutta sky. The carefully tended flowers catch the light, the leaves are in darkness.

Has all of this been auspicious?

Yes and no.

Yes because she has been given a double gaze, forever, a gaze that cannot help but split everything into comparisons.

No because the comparisons will take a lifetime to resolve.

Yes because she has been given the gift of movement between landscapes, forever, though she will have to try hard not to squander it.

No because for a very long time she will be under the illusion that the sufferings of one civilization can be redeemed by another.

The third thing.

Anjali had fallen in love. She was nineteen. His name was Riaz.

"Anyone else," said her father. "Not a Muslim."

"Why?"

"You haven't lived through Partition."

"That's right, I haven't."

"Don't argue with me," he shouted.

"You were the one who taught me to think for myself, to reason, you—"

"Some things, you will one day learn, have nothing to do with reason." He was still shouting. "Anyone else Anjali, I would have accepted anyone else, do you understand? A Christian, who knows, a Parsi, a foreigner."

Anjali's body was spinning. The room revolved around and around, sometimes resting at her father's face, where severity had replaced love. It was her body's way of surviving, for if it stayed still who knows what may have happened. It was something the body would learn to do from now on, to protect itself. Her father's words came to her through this spinning, unclear and truncated.

"You've…always…everything," he said. "Tell me…but you are the most…" he said.

After the spinning stopped she heard him say, "You betrayed me."

Then he said, "If you had told me earlier it would have been easier for you. Now, when you give him up the pain will be hard for you to bear."

"Give him up?"

"Yes. Give him up. You'll have to give him up."

"Trust me," said Anjali. "I would never—"

"I did trust you," her father broke in, so loud and sudden that she took a step back. "I did trust you," he repeated, like a curse. The veins on his neck stood out clearly. "And look where we are now."

Anjali looked, and she saw the deepest darkness.

"Listen," he said, his voice softening. Anjali looked at him with hope. "My only child, my golden one. I want to give you everything you want. But this. This I cannot give you."

Anjali stood up slowly and went to her room. She sat on her bed.

Had she loved a father who didn't, in reality, exist? This man, who had brought her books, taught her to read, brought her her first records, educated her, and said at all times, "You will do whatever your heart desires, my little daughter, just as a man does. Never, ever, will you be helpless the way most women are." He taught her many things to make her strong. Economic theories, literature, how to sign cheques, how to buy a car, how to buy the sweetest fish by pressing the body for firmness and checking the colour of the gills. He took her to America and Europe, London, where he had studied, he showed her the Western world. When she excelled his happiness overflowed, and when she failed he smiled tenderly and held her, telling her this was only a small failure on the road to a large success. Her father, her life, the increaser of all her possibilities.

Hours passed.

Anjali had never really known any Muslims before Riaz. She went over the many things that Hindus said about Muslims, small things and large ones, like Partition. But inside herself there seemed to be a natural knowledge of human equality. She could not rid herself of this knowledge even if she tried.

She went to him again. He was lying on the narrow bed in his study. She entered the smell of tobacco and books. His eyes were closed. She went and sat next to him on the bed. He opened his eyes. He looked at her, opening his eyes completely, the same large eyes as hers, looked at her full for many, many moments. She would never forget that look. It was the look of someone about to die and seeing everything completely for the last time, not with love but with the greatest bitterness. She knew she had lost him.

She went back to her room. She broke down and cried, as she would break down on countless evenings, alone. Then she slept the sleep of a dead person, as she would sleep on countless nights, without a single dream.

In a borrowed room, at the edge of the city, with peeling grey walls and shut windows, Riaz and Anjali made love. Because she had never seen her parents or her aunts and uncles, or her married cousins touch each other, she didn't know what to expect. Because her mother had never told her anything she had no idea how it felt. Because her mother was so hard she had never absorbed those things, the things that women knew to do before the men they loved. All the lack of knowing had driven her towards truth, away from artifice. When he undressed her, she knew only how to be herself. And for that he loved her even more. As he loved her more and more, from everywhere else the love drained away.

Riaz was a tall, quiet, heavily built young man, capable, secure, strong. They were in college together. His teachers felt he would go on to be a brilliant physicist one day, except for the fact that he drank so much that some days went by only in the drinking. As Anjali and he came closer she noticed how he would come to college in the late afternoon after he had been drinking since morning. She never remarked on it. As they spent more time together he began drinking less and less. In a few months he stopped completely. In six months of their being together he asked her to marry him.

"I'm going to take poison and die," said Riaz's mother when she heard the news.

She took to her bed and remained in her room for a month. She spoke to no one. Her husband, a calm, very gentle person, tried to placate her. He was the only one they didn't have to face resistance from, but he couldn't bring about peace.

"She'll be all right, said Riaz, "she needs some time."

She heard from others that Riaz's mother had already chosen a girl for Riaz, that this girl was very beautiful, that Riaz's mother had called Anjali "that dark skinned woman." This accusation of being dark skinned made her want to laugh at the accuser, to scorn her, for being stopped by what was so on the surface, but it made her heart want to weep, for herself.

"You didn't tell me there was someone," Anjali asked Riaz.

"There isn't, it's all in my mother's mind. I've barely spoken to the woman myself."

"Is she beautiful Riaz?"

He was quiet. Then he said, "Not more beautiful to me than you."

Riaz was incapable of a lie, of anything even remotely underhanded. It had to do, she later understood, with his lack of fear.

"Is she beautiful Riaz?"

"Yes," he said.

"And fair?"

"And fair," he said.

Anjali sat on the heavy, old stone steps of the college. Behind her was the wide stairway climbing up to the next floor, and at the landing a large black iron bell hung from the ceiling. Everywhere there was a smell of time, dampness and moss. This was Calcutta's most important college, from here had emerged great thinkers, scholars, artists, scientists and politicians who had changed the nation's life.

Riaz and Anjali had been brought up to value the intellect, and the human achievement that came with it. But, thought Anjali, nothing they had learned or were about to learn could teach them how to live what they were living. They never thought of separating, of ending this unexpected suffering. It did not even enter their minds. It was not something they discussed, or had to convince each other about. How did this happen? As the suffering gathered force, they became more certain, wordlessly, about their love, and that it would find its own way. They were told they were too young, they had not yet seen life, that life's harshness breaks the greatest love. It had no effect on them. They did not think of faith, or hope or trust, or try to make sure their love would really be everlasting. The mind had no place here. What made them feel, what made them act, was something that could not be named, and which in its turn was incapable of naming. It existed in Riaz and Anjali, independently, outside learning, outside age and experience, and because of this it had the energy to withstand anything.

Now Anjali knew that the myths and legends of love were indeed true. But the ideas of courage and greatness were not those of the lovers, for they had no need of these things, they were ideas given to the tales by people who could not make sense of it any other way.

Calcutta had been beset by a new wretchedness. There were power cuts every day, lasting for up to fourteen hours. In the day people were charred by the sun and bathed in sweat at the same time, at night they could not dispel their exhaustion in the still, unmoving darkness. Babies cried all day and night, and at twilight there was no more room on the lawns of the Victoria Memorial. Riaz and

Anjali, because they could not go to either of their homes, spent hours outside in the gardens and parks, or in restaurants darkened by power cuts.

One evening she returned home from an afternoon of lovemaking, with the smell of Riaz's body on hers, to a house and a street plunged in darkness. Her father was waiting for her at the top of the stairs with a lantern in his hand. The tiny generator, after running for six hours, had run out of fuel.

"Come," he said. "I want to talk to you."

They went to the large living room that opened out on to a circular balcony filled with creepers and plants. Anjali sat on the marble floor because the sofa was too hot to even touch. Sweat was collecting underneath her sari blouse, and running down her legs under the pleats. Her father sat on the sofa because he never sat on the floor. The lantern had been left in the hallway and here it was almost complete darkness, except for the faint moonlight coming in from the outside and highlighting part of a bookshelf, the brass of a tall lampstand. She could not see her father's face, only the outlines of his body. And sometimes, when he moved, the glasses he wore caught the faintest light.

"You've been with him, haven't you?" he said.

"Yes."

"How is he?"

"Well."

"I've been thinking..."

Anjali's heart rose at his words. At the house across the street a young man was standing on the terrace and singing a song in the darkness. It was something he did often at these times. It made the power cut more bearable.

"Aye re aye, lagan baye jaye, megh gurgur kare chander shimanaya…"

"I forbid you to marry this man," her father said. "If you still wish to do what you want, you will have to leave this house. I cannot give you my blessings. I tried, I really tried, but I can't do it."

She saw the shape that was her father leaning back and putting both his hands on the armrest of the sofa. Her body began to spin and this time because it was so dark she could find no anchor. She steadied herself with both her hands on the marble floor. She said nothing.

"How hard can it be to give him up? Can it be more painful than your child dying, or losing a parent at a very early age?"

How could Anjali know? She had neither had a child nor had she lost a parent. To her these were only abstractions, imaginary things.

There was not a shred of breeze outside. The plants on the balcony remained completely still.

"Dhinak natin tina, ke bajale pran bina…" the boy sang, full throated.

"I did so much for you Anjali, I took you all over the world, I did everything I possibly could," he said, his voice suddenly breaking. It did not seem like he was looking at her, or trying to.

"I gave you my life," he said, and she saw the shape of his head bending downward.

"Should I give you mine then?" she said.

She saw the head jerk back up. "All I'm asking is that you give him up. It's for your own good."

"I can't," she said, very, very firmly, although her voice shook a little.

So the vastness of her father's love also had limits, she thought, and such hard, unbreakable ones. A barrier that neither her love nor reason could break. It was too early for her to know that almost everyone's love has limits, but some are fortunate enough never to be brought to them, while giving or receiving.

"All right then," her father said. "I forbid you to meet him from now on. The driver has been instructed to only take you to college and back. If you still wish to meet him, you will have to find yourself a new home."

The lights came on suddenly, harsh and yellow, and the neighbourhood cried out in joy. It meant life could continue again, food cooked, meals eaten, work done, bodies rested. The boy across the street cut off his song in the middle of a line and went inside. In the new light her father's face was hard and relentless, the lips pursed together, and every muscle that held a face up was pulled downward, towards the rest of his body, towards the floor, falling, towards the end of his world.

That night the main door was locked with a special key kept by her father. Anjali shut herself inside her room. When the phone rang and she picked it up, thinking it might be Riaz, she heard her father on the extension.

"Hello."

"Hello," said Riaz. "May I please speak to Anjali.?"

"No."

"Is she out?"

"No."

She heard her father put down the phone.

In her room she did not open the windows during the day, or raise the blinds. In the evening she did not turn on the lights. There was nothing she wanted to look at. The things she saw did not require a physical eye. She saw herself living a tale that had been lived and told thousands and thousands of times in this land. It had been lived in vast fields under open skies and by oil lamps, it had been lived through violent rivers that needed to be crossed without boats, in the harshest deserts, the coldest mountains, the most temperate, flower filled valleys where shepherds herded their cattle, and now it was being lived in cars, to the sound of airplanes, in restaurants and universities, without any change, in the nature of either the love or the terror, for no matter how much the world changes these things always remain the same, it had gone on and on for centuries and each time it passed through the one in love, like her, it came with the memory of these centuries and the twisted hearts of endless lovers to say that here youth did not matter because the past was always more important than the future, the old more important than the new, and love did not matter because it came from far inside the self, and that self was less important than keeping the family, the gotra, the caste, the clan, the tribe, intact.

"We're going away," her parents told her one morning, smiling and bright.

"Where?"

"To Rajasthan, for a holiday, to take your mind off things, to forget."

They all went to Rajasthan. They crossed a boat on a lake to get to the hotel, an ancient palace. But she didn't really look at the lake, or the sky above it, so clear in the winter light. She looked down from the boat at the quiet water, very close, below her. Her eyes saw only things very close, and so things only in pieces, never a whole, like a sky or a landscape, or even a whole palace. At the windows of this palace she came to know parts of arches and ledges very well, the pigeons that came to sit on them, and on a particular ledge a rectangle of sunlight that fell there just before sunset. Her body was pulled inwards and down, her head bowed, her eyes lowered to whatever was closest to her, very often her own hands or feet. Once when it was almost evening and she was all alone, she raised her head after a long time and looked at the darkening sky, open, spreading, expansive, and her heart twisted in pain. Courage, she thought, her friends always told her she had so much courage to be doing what she was. But the courage was in the feeling of everything to its very limits. Action was only a consequence. When her parents returned to the room they saw her crying.

"Don't you dare cry," said her father. "I know you're thinking of him."

The darkening sky stayed with her. She began turning her gaze upwards from hands and feet, outwards from ledges and arches. Through the ancient windows she looked far across, to the other bank of the large lake, with its white, white houses and dark green trees. At first she was waiting, for this endless time to end, for her lover, for a storm, for the day to turn into evening. But as she kept looking she began to see further than her love.

She emerged from the hotel room and wandered in the town, into forts and temples and palaces. There was a large mausoleum on top of a deserted brown hill. Dogs lay underneath the ancient sandstone arches, next to a few beggars sleeping in the shadows. A lean and hungry tour guide basked in the winter sunlight. Inside there was a very small, slim tomb, perhaps that of a child's. On top of it were a few withered marigolds. But all the carving and painting on the walls had disappeared, leaving only the sandstone beneath. Everything was bare and colourless. It was a plainness that was never meant to be, a plainness that would have broken its makers. Anjali looked all around the circular mausoleum, at the floor, at the walls. Nothing but bare stone anywhere, broken, discoloured. At the end she turned her head up to look at the high dome and in all the plainness of that deserted place, there was suddenly the most intricate dark and light blue pattern of flowers and leaves, protected somehow from time and still filled with life.

By the time she left for home there had begun a sight in excess of what was before her, and a strength in excess of her love.

They came back home after a month. When she sat in the car to go to college, her old driver, Osman Singh, who had seen her grow into a woman, looked into the rear view mirror and said, "Didi."

Osman Singh was a Sikh with a flowing grey black beard, strong, broad and tall. He was a very quiet man and always did as he was told, not in a servile way, but with the greatest dignity. He had the large, kind eyes Anjali had seen in so many Sikh men, eyes near which his turban passed upward.

"I can't see you like this."

Anjali, surprised, looked up and met his large eyes in the rear view mirror.

With his voice almost a whisper he said, "I will take you to him, and no one will know."

They met at the house of a friend. Three and a half months had passed since they last met. During this time there had only been messages sent through friends. Riaz was wearing a white shirt that gathered in all the sun that fell in through the windows. He took her in her arms. Anjali could not speak. Suddenly he raised his head and looked at her.

"How thin you've become," he said.

Anjali still said nothing. Riaz had brought her earrings made of the finest, lightest rubies. He kissed the palm of her hand. He had already brought her the thinnest, most delicate silver ring, carved with leaves, that she always wore. But every gift they gave each other, rings, pens, watches, everything got lost along the way. They had recognized each other. The force of that recognition swept away all that was not utterly necessary.

"How thin you've become," he said again, looking at her.

She nodded her head.

The friend's house was filled with family. They made love in the bathroom, very large and impeccably white, with fresh white towels hanging from the bars, the sunlight dim here through small windows. When he kissed her breasts, bit her nipples, desire and pain came together. When she touched him between the legs, pain and desire, their tongues in each other's mouths, pain so much pain, when he was inside her, pain and desire. For the first time they had made a love where desire, pleasure and pain could not be separated. In the end, standing in each other's arms, they each saw the other crying.

When they raised their faces up, they suddenly noticed a large pool of blood on the floor, a large spreading circle, breaking up into lines that were beginning to fill the cracks between the white tiles.

"What happened?" Riaz said. "Do you have your period?"

Anjali checked herself.

"No."

They looked at each other, astonished, they examined each other's bodies carefully, but they could not find the source of the blood. They used Riaz's large white handkerchief to clean it up. Then they washed out the handkerchief in the sink to keep it from dripping blood. Riaz put the wet handkerchief in his pocket and said, "We'll be together. We must believe that."

Anjali's father took her to a psychiatrist.

"Why?"

"To help you cope, calm you down."

The psychiatrist was a handsome Muslim man with grey hair. He sat behind a huge desk piled high with papers.

"So, you're in love."

Anjali looked at him.

"Can you describe the feeling?"

She had a sudden desire to explain, again, to talk about her love, but she knew that no one wanted explanations, no one wanted the opportunity to change their minds.

"I can but I don't want to."

"I had an arranged marriage myself, so unless you tell me what you're feeling in love, it'll be hard for us to talk about it."

"That's all right. I don't really need to talk about it."

"Your father said it was like being hit by a bullet when you told him."

"I wouldn't know."

"What are you planning to do now?"

"Wait and see." She had learned not to reveal things any longer.

"Good, and soon you'll see you've forgotten him. There's no point hurting your parents like this. I'm told you're a very intelligent young woman, you have everything ahead of you. Apparently the college has already given you a scholarship."

"What do these two things, my career and my falling in love have to do with one another?"

"It's like this. You continue your studies, properly, without any distractions. Take me, I did very well in school and college and when I became a psychiatrist my parents found me a girl. Love is a disruption."

Anjali smiled. The doctor looked surprised.

"Look, I'm going to give you some medication. It'll keep you calm and make you feel better. Two pills a day, one in the morning, one in the evening. He wrote on a piece of paper and gave it to her.

Her father bought the pills. He brought her a glass of water every morning and evening for the medication. After he left the room she drank the water and threw the pill out of the window. It fell at the foot of the tree where the queen of the night was blooming.

Otherwise, Anjali barely saw her father. When he was home he locked himself up in his study. When they met at mealtimes, or in the corridor, he would say, "Pass the bowl of fruit," or "There was no fish in the market today, it's rained too much," or "The lightbulb in the hallway needs to be changed." They were all statements of fact, never a question or a point of view which might give rise to communication.

Through these times, Anjali's mother became suddenly kind.

"It must be so painful for you," she said, and stroked Anjali's head.

Anjali realized with a daughter's precise intuition that the kindness came from not having been wounded, as her father had. It came from not caring at all. Without any anger, she took away her mother's hand.

It was the car that was a place of comfort for her now, a place, however constricted, where she could be herself. She could close her eyes, or weep, or put her feet up and rest her face against her hand, and when the pain became unbearable she could clasp the edge of the long seat as if it were the last thing in the world. Osman Singh took her wherever she wanted to go. Sometimes, she just wanted him to drive, past the lakes, past the wide tree lined roads near the Victoria Memorial. Once, driving by the riverfront in the afternoon, watching the barges and ships on the water, the smoking factories on the other shore, Osman Singh began to sing a song from the Punjab, where his family still were, his two daughters married, his son looking after their lands.

"*Rabb jhooth na kare*
Hove Ranjha
O.
Main chaur hoi
mainu patteya soo
God let it not be a lie
It seems like Ranjha
I lose control,
I become unanchored…"

Anjali looked towards him in surprise as he sang, without looking back at her even once. She had never heard him sing before and now she heard his voice for the first time, the voice of a strong man, a strong and melodic voice, but broken suddenly in unexpected places, and with the long, sustained cry of open lands in it, and the sound of a life lived, a life with everything in it, high peaks with clear air, and great troughs of darkness. She watched his back gather and release itself, over and over again as he sang.

"*Jogi hoya pinde nun khaaq malke*

– 64 –

Laah nang naamus nun satteya su.
Smearing ash all over his body, a jogi he's become
Nearly naked now he's thrown his fair name to the winds."

She knew he was singing a song of Heer Ranjha, the lovers from centuries ago, and the stretching of the syllables, the stresses, the rise and fall of the song was enough to communicate its meaning.

Osman Singh's voice rose, opened even more.

"Bukkal vich chori chori Heer rove
Hiding behind her veil Heer cries, silently"

The voice now fell very low.

"Ghada neer da chaye palatteya su
As if a pitcher of water were being overturned"

The voice rose once again.

"Rabb jhooth na kare
Hove Ranjha..."*

A younger aunt took her to an astrologer.

"If he approves of this marriage, I will personally convince your father," she said. "He's a great man, a great astrologer. Whatever he says, happens."

Anjali went with her heart rising, because in these times hope attached itself to the most unexpected things.

The astrologer lived in a large, but narrow house, three floors high. They climbed all the way up to the top. He was a thin, tall man, with a pencil moustache and sharp eyes. He seemed to know her aunt well. He motioned to Anjali to sit down on a sofa. Her aunt went to wait in another room.

"Name," he asked. "Date and place of birth. Father's name."

Then he asked her how long she had known Riaz, details of where they had met and how.

"Has he kissed you?"

"Yes."

"What kind of kissing, just with the lips or with the tongue."

In response to the look on Anjali's face he said, "I need to know all these things in detail to arrive at my conclusions."

"Both the lips and the tongue," said Anjali, trying not to look at him.

"All right. Now what about when he kisses your breasts. Is it kissing, or biting or licking?"

Anjali stood up from the sofa.

"Please sit down, be patient. Can I get you some tea? No? All right. I need to know, have you gone all the way?"

Anjali opened the door and walked down the stairs. She waited for her aunt in the car.

After ten minutes or so her aunt came down.

"He says this marriage won't work, it's best to break it right now."

Anjali didn't say anything.

"Everything he says, happens," said her aunt.

One day Riaz asked her to come to his house to meet his mother. She had emerged from her room, Riaz told her, and was speaking to everyone again. Riaz had held her in his arms, the son so much taller now than the mother, and she had wept there for a long time.

When Anjali went that evening to Riaz's house, his mother, dressed in a violet silk sari, was sitting in her living room. She stood up when Anjali walked in. A kalbaisakhi began almost immediately and before the servants could rush to close the windows the room was covered with a fine layer of dust.

"Remember to clean the carpets tomorrow morning," Riaz's mother told the servants.

Outside the shut windows, the storm beat down the trees and obscured the neighbouring houses in a constantly rising swirl of dust, dry leaves and scraps of paper.

"Come, come and sit near me," Riaz's mother said. Anjali sat next to her on a large divan.

"Let me look at you," she said, with a smile.

Anjali thought of what she had said about her dark skin and was silent.

"So much suffering," she said, touching Anjali's face lightly. "Riaz has told me everything."

Anjali surprised even herself by beginning to cry, silently. She was amazed at how things changed in a day, anger released, love expressed, gestures that had been ripening underneath bursting forth to blossom and fruit. Somewhere the kalbaisakhi banged a window shut.

Riaz's mother sat quietly, letting Anjali cry. When Anjali finally looked up, she asked, "Do you have the strength?"

"It isn't a question of choice."

"There is always the possibility of choice, no matter when, no matter how late."

"Not for me."

"All right then." Riaz's mother sat silently again, looking at Anjali without curiosity or question, her body and face completely at rest. Anjali envied the calm, the security, the composure.

"I'll be back in a moment," Riaz's mother said. She got up and went into the kitchen.

The walls here in the living room were almost bare. Only, on the wall directly opposite Anjali there was a miniature painting of a Sufi, an old man, reading a book. Behind him was a vast sunset sky. She went close to the painting. The Sufi had a long white beard, he was wearing white, and he was absorbed in his text. The grass on which he sat was soft and glowing green, the sky infused with a faint golden light. It could have been sunset, it could have been dawn. There seemed to be so much space here, so much serenity, that Anjali could not look at the Sufi and the sky above him for very long.

Riaz's mother returned with a bowl of kheer.

"I'm not hungry," Anjali said. "I can't eat anything."

"Just one small spoon. From where will that strength come?"

Anjali smiled and ate a spoonful. The kheer left a very delicate taste of saffron and milk on her tongue.

As she was leaving, Riaz's mother covered her own head with the end of her sari, took an old, dark blue copy of the Koran and held it over Anjali's head. She asked Anjali to walk backwards out of the house. Anjali took steps in reverse, carefully, Riaz's mother moving in front of her, both of them in a paired walk, one forwards, one backwards, close but not touching one another, the Koran held steady above Anjali's head.

At the threshold, she touched Anjali on the shoulder.

"Now turn around and go, and don't look back."

Anjali turned around.

"Khuda Hafiz," Riaz's mother said.

How could you do this to your father? Your father. Your father. And where will you go? Go. Have you thought of that, where will you go? This man, he probably doesn't even love you. What will you do? Love. Bel-phul. Bel-phul. At this age the body becomes infected with a disease. That is all this is, a disease. You're risking everything.

Bukkam vich chori chori Heer roye. When I fell in love, my father showed me his gun. He had a gun. And he told me he would… A face avid, eager for disaster. Eyes lit by the desire to hurt. A face turned away in pleasure at having inflicted a blow. You won't inherit. Any of your father's property, both the houses will be given away to someone else. Kada neer da chahe ulataya su. You'll be alone then. Absolutely alone. Be absolutely. Your father could fall ill, very ill. Moner katha balibar. He could have a heart attack. I had fallen in love too once…A heart attack, a stroke. You will most certainly have to leave this house if you want to do as you wish. I'm so glad I didn't marry the man I fell in love with…Nayan mele dheko Radha, nadi bhara pani, nadi bhara. Money, money. You'll have no money at all. A foul disease. Bel-phul. Bel-phul. Bel-phul. Bel-phul. Bel-phul.

She always put her finger down her throat and brought it all up so that none of it remained inside her.

Anjali knew she was absolutely alone. Had there been one kind aunt, an understanding cousin, had she had her own flesh and blood, a brother or sister to whom her pain could be communicated, perhaps even without words, had there been any of this she would not have become so depleted, the breathing shallow, the limbs exhausted, the blood barely able to flow. Had there been any of this, the ground she had stood on would not have given way so completely, till she had nowhere to rest her feet. But Anjali did not know then that had there been someone, perhaps that other ground would not have been prepared, that ground hard and firm and unbreakable, on which she would walk the rest of her life.

The days, and especially the nights, prospered from her grief and grew relentless and outside her window the queen of the night bloomed, smelling of sweetened blood. Even then, not a single doubt ever entered Anjali's mind. She did not yet know what it meant not to doubt. She did not know that to those who do not doubt, the universe offers itself.

Many months passed. In Anjali's home nothing changed. Once in a while, for an hour or two Osman Singh drove her to Riaz. They had decided to leave the country, to put into motion a plan they had always had, like so many others of their age and privilege, to go and study in America. Forms had been filled, applications made, cheques sent, all in secret. Riaz received his scholarship first. He said, "I'll postpone it till next semester Anjali, we'll go together. I don't want to leave you here."

"No, go now," she said. "I'll come soon. I know it."

The day Riaz was leaving she went to his house. When Anjali walked in his mother said, "What happened to you? You're as thin as a stick. And your face," she said and touched her lightly on the cheek with one hand. "Like you haven't eaten for months. Sit down."

Riaz began to finish packing his things into the suitcases that his mother had already half packed. A servant brought in lunch on a large tray. Riaz's mother put the food on a plate, prepared a mouthful of dal and a piece of kabab, and said, "Riaz come and eat." He came, bent down his tall frame, and his mother put the food in his mouth.

"Come Anjali, eat something," she said. Anjali got up to take a plate.

"No," his mother said. "Come here."

When Anjali came and sat near her, she began to feed Anjali, a mouthful for her, a mouthful for Riaz. They ate in silence. Anjali hadn't been fed like this since she was a child. Looking up at Riaz's mother's face Anjali saw that her eyes were filled with tears.

"He's my only child," she said to Anjali. "I've raised him well. He'll never let you down."

Who was there to chronicle the times when history did not take its usual worn out path?

Anjali could not go to the airport because she could not be away from home for so long. Riaz came with her in the car, halfway to her home. When the time came for them to part, it was Riaz who was crying.

"You know what to do if there's any trouble, don't you? Just call my parents and they'll put you on an airplane to me. Can you pull through Anjali, can you?"

He was holding her so tight she could not answer him.

Finally, when he looked at her, she said, "I'll come before you know it."

Riaz got out of the car and said to Osman Singh, "You will look after her won't you?"

Osman Singh, tall and straight with his white turban and long white beard, his eyes brimming, brought his right hand to his heart and bent his head.

The car started again, but a few minutes later Osman Singh pulled up to the side of the road.

"What happened?" said Anjali.

"I can't see anything," he said, his voice shaking and Anjali realized he was crying.

She put a hand on his broad, strong shoulder.

"Don't cry," she said. "It's all right. Let's go home."

One night, long after everyone was asleep, Anjali locked her door and began to pack. She opened the heavy wooden cupboard, intricately carved, from the time of her parent's wedding. It gave out a smell of heartrending security. She began taking out a few saris, jeans, blouses. She did it slowly, without hurry. She packed in the darkness, by the sound of the night dogs and the light from the street was enough for her to recognize the things she needed. She looked at the bottles of perfume which threw out a dull light in the darkness. Chanel, Joy, Dior, the perfumes her father had brought her, so many that most of the bottles were still full. She stopped before the bottles and sat down, in front of the cupboard, on the floor.

The dogs barked incessantly. The cats began to cry, the sound so much like a baby weeping. There was in this land, Anjali realized, an inability to act, an inability to act except to restrict, to oppress, to crush. No action was ever taken to set someone free. Her father had always been the opposite of this, but now he had become part of the lineage of disinheritors, disowners, oppressors, no longer an individual. It was she who had to be an individual now, truly alone.

Anjali stood up again and chose one bottle of perfume. She put it into her bag. She took a few books lying on her desk, books she had already chosen last evening. When she had finished, she closed the bag and pushed it far under her bed. A crow let out its sharp cry in the darkness.

In the morning, as soon as she opened her door, she saw her father sitting next to the large wooden desk where her grandmother had always sat till she died. He was looking down at his hands.

"Don't leave," he said.

More morning sunlight than she could possibly bear fell into the room.

Her mother came and held her.

"How will I, without you?" she said.

"Stay, and we'll talk," said her father.

"About what?" Anjali said.

Her father did not reply. He kept opening and closing a large pair of scissors he had found on the desk, opening and closing them very close to the skin of his arms.

"You've already told me whatever you had to," Anjali said.

"That's true."

"Then?"

"Please," he said.

That was the only moment when Anjali saw her father's pain, sharp and clear, even though she did not understand it. She saw that two people, however bonded, cannot save each other once they have been sundered. Her father would have to follow the course of his suffering to the end, as she would have to follow hers, like a river to its sea. Anjali dragged her bag out from underneath the bed and walked towards the large front door. She would never see her father, alive, again.

"Have you taken the perfumes?" he asked. "They were only for you. Who else will use them now?"

On the way out, though she passed by the puja room, she forgot to look at the photograph of the family guru as she had been taught to do. It was the only face in the puja room she was drawn to. She had never seen him because he had died before she was born. He was a slim man with one piece of cloth wound around him and his hair was in a knot on top of his head. They say that rishis have no need to look at distances. This man's eyes had pupils which seemed to have moved that minute distance towards each other, inward. She walked down the stairs without remembering them.

What ritual can a time of upheaval possibly contain?

Was all of this auspicious?

This was the most difficult one of all. She didn't know, she didn't know. So much loss, so much gain.

But perhaps in the end it was. For one reason, above all the others.

It showed her that sometimes there was no way to separate a gift from a curse.

She began to walk. She had to cover long distances. She was going not only towards the man she loved, waiting on another continent, she was going towards herself. Everyone at birth is given a mark that is their other face. Anjali's mark was that of vastness.

As she walked, people asked her, "Where are you going all alone? Be careful." They would say, "Go back home, little mother, it is not for a woman to wander so far."

The sunlight ebbed and evening came, she travelled far away from the landscape filled with rivers, ponds and trees. As the water and green fell away she found herself in a city which had once been a desert. There were only a few trees and the sandiest of soils. She came to a large field of sparse grass and soil that she knew she had to cross. At the entrance to the field were some decrepit huts, large piles of dying garbage, and urine running in trickles, wetting the dry soil, joining green streams of water with more garbage floating in it. She walked through all of it and began crossing. As she walked she saw a large building on the other side. It had very old clothes being dried on an upper balcony, patches of old colour on its walls, blue and green, and portions of bare concrete.

As she reached the end of the field, she could see people in rags sitting outside the building, silently. A goat was tied to a lamppost. Next to it was a cart filled with large pieces of goat meat freshly cut, over which flies hovered in a cloud. The goat turned its head from time to time to look at the meat, then turned away. There was a huge pit filled with dead flowers, roses, marigold, hibiscus. Anjali walked on.

She entered the building. There were beggars sitting in a row on the floor, their legs stretched out in front of them, some holding out dented, blackened aluminium bowls, some only their palms. She walked further in, through rooms and corridors, and sudden turnings around which cripples stood, with a stump for an arm or a leg, hunchbacks bent to the floor. Everywhere, people deserted by hope. Anjali walked on. Under her bare feet was dust, mud, and unbearable heat. In the heart of this building, in a vast courtyard, she stopped at a towering black stone wall. The wall was shining in the light. The wall was breathing. A strong, vast breath like the waves of an ocean rising and falling. She stood still before it. There was a man kneeling at the foot of the wall, facing it. The upper part of his body was shaking violently. Anjali realized he was weeping. She saw another man to her right, standing there looking at the wall, while all the time caressing his hands, one with the other. She sat down.

Over the hours, as she sat, the wall took away the shallowness of her breathing, it filled her with its own breath.

It was not a personal breath.

Not the breath of one being only.

The crow slept in a large cave at Ellora. It was black, crow black, without the usual grey on the head and the chest. It slept as the rain fell outside. On one side of the cave there were steps leading down to a large pond, now overflowing with the rain. On the other end, a giant Shiva, a corpulent Shiva, carved into the high wall. Beyond Shiva the cave extended into a long courtyard, a place without a roof, through which the light came, birds flew in, and through which the rain now entered to form a small pool. The crow slept near this. It had been sleeping for many years.

What woke him was time.

Not the time which was confident of what it had achieved, not the time which regretted that all things were gone and over, but the time not sure, vacillating between fullness and emptiness, all or nothing, between what to keep and what to let go.

The crow awoke, with sleep still in his eyes, and a little cold. He flew once around the cave, stretching his wings, inhaling the humid air. There was some grain collected on one corner, he ate. From the pool under the skylight, he drank. Then he listened, carefully, his head turned to the left, to what the cave was telling him. He was told to go on a very long journey, told that he would find his way as he went, that he would know his destination when it had been reached. And although the journey may be difficult, he was not to be afraid.

The crow looked once around the cave where he had slept. Two pigeons sat on Shiva's shoulder, gazing at him silently. Large field rats ran up and down Shiva's legs. On the floor all across, the droppings of different birds, giant chameleons in and out of their hollows, and in the air, a wild animal smell.

He flew up through the skylight on the side of the cave, straight into the late monsoon rain. It was hard to see, and his feathers began to get soaked. He discerned the outlines of the low, undulating hills in the distance, a small white temple, and beyond it, the empty town of mosques and dargahs, and trees greened in the rain. He began to fly higher and higher, parting the rain with his wings, beating against it and going forward. The rain was in his eyes. As he flew, the raindrops became larger and began to fall too heavily on his body, hurting him, wounding his outstretched wings. His chest ached from the beating of the drops and his wings could barely rise and fall.

He had flown for several hours and as he was wondering how long the rain would fall so hard, he began to recognize the faint gold of sunshine far away. The rain became gentler and eventually gave way to a weak sun. The crow felt his feathers drying, the warmth spreading inside him, the ache in his body flowing away. Now he could see clearly everything he passed down below. He saw rivers which always moved and could never stay still, hills that could hold still forever but not move, and then he reached the edge of the country, he reached the ocean, and was surprised to see that it could move but could not flow.

Flying over the ocean, he realized he was leaving the country behind. The ocean below was vast and continuous. He saw this was an ocean without islands, and with a damp wind in which he tasted the flavour of salt. The rain had become lighter and the sun was beginning to set before him. The western sky was a sunset orange and then red, a very, very deep red such as the crow had never seen before. He came closer and closer to it and as he flew through the redness he closed his eyes. When he emerged the sky was much darker. His wings began to merge with the colour of the sky, and as he lifted his left wing to rise higher, he saw that it was stained by a very large drop of blood.

When night thickened so much that he could barely see his own wings, he flew down and reached the land. There was a city below, with very tall buildings and many windows. He rested on a window sill, very silently, moving only once. A woman slept inside the room with the window and, waking up suddenly, saw night open its wings. She went to the window to look, but there was nothing there, only whatever it had opened inside her.

The crow had left the window before sunrise, when he could sense the approaching light behind the darkness. He flew onwards crossing a small sea, sensing the sun rising behind it. The sun in its first hour, with its light of the most brilliant gold, surrounded the crow. It felt warm as the gold penetrated him, through the beak down to the feet, and out through the outspread wings. As he flew over different landscapes, deserts, valleys, forests, towards the last ocean he would have to cross, evening came again. As it grew dark, the crow noticed a circle of light in his beak, perfect and golden. This time he could see his own wings clearly and separate from the night as he flew, for the circle of light, though small, was brilliant. But he chose to rest, he was getting tired and once again there was a city, by the ocean he would have to cross the next day. He rested in a tree, near some buildings. A man in a house nearby saw a small circle of light coming down from the sky, into the tree, and disappear among the leaves. It left the man with an inexplicable longing.

The crow crossed the last ocean. It was day and he could see ships crossing the waves as if without movement, fishing boats near the edges. But this time he could also feel what he could not actually see. He sensed the fish swimming beneath the surface, the smaller fish and swaying weeds that stayed close to the edge, the whales deeper inside, and the fish near the darkness of the ocean floor, those which created their own light. He began to understand that the ocean was dark, and vast and necessary.

He marvelled at the way that knowledge came, unbidden. This thought was so clear and simple that he decided to protect it forever under the beam of his left wing.

The crow flew in to the continent of his destination. It was very cold on this new continent and the sky changed constantly between clouds, sunlight, snow and rain. He now became aware that all the time he had been flying westward and north, he wondered how long he had flown.

It began to snow as he flew further and further into the land, and he prepared himself for the bitter cold. He descended a little lower to get more warmth. But here the lands were absolutely flat, there were no hills and very few trees to bar the wind. The wind flew here in all its fury, flinging the crow up and down, making him lose his sense of direction. It was much harder than flying through the rain, something he had never known before, and he grew afraid. This northern wind was hard, sharp and unpredictable. It began to pry off some of his feathers as he flew. The crow was flung down till it fell into a high tree, the branches and thorns scraping his body. He was shaking. He decided to stay there awhile, even though the tree swaying violently. From here the crow saw that he was in the middle of wheat fields to which there seemed to be no end. Scattered on the edges, a few farmhouses. The light above them thin and fragile. He stayed in the tree for at least a day. At night, the light in his beak helped him to see, and he ate of the small fruit on the tree's branches. The fruit was sour and pungent. When the wind seemed a little less intense, the crow left again for the sky, hesitantly.

At last, when he saw below him the town with small houses, snow on the fields and ice on the streets, he went down slowly. He flew around the town, till he found the house, his journey's end. The house had red brown gables, a tall chimney, bay windows, a porch with a swing that creaked, and maple trees in the garden.

Autumn had just begun when Anjali reached the eastern coast of this vast country. She walked into falling leaves, and an air that was thin and golden and kind. The dense, thick air of the tropics had been left behind, and would only emerge unexpectedly when she opened her suitcases, or even later when she first unfolded a dress she had brought along.

She began her life in this country at a college in a city in the east. The college had carefully preserved eighteenth century buildings and green lawns, but the town was an old mill town, with more than its share of unemployed people, abandoned warehouses and factories. Decrepit middle aged men in sad brown clothes walked the streets near campus, drinking beer from bottles covered in light brown paper. Their eyes were small and red and moist. She was told that if she was late on campus, at the library, the campus police would have to escort her home. She was told not to wear jewellery, or carry much cash. This was a place negotiating the consequences of its own history, thought Anjali, but because it was not hers it did not weigh her down.

She spoke to Riaz the day she arrived. He sounded so close, almost touchable, but in reality he was one thousand miles away. She was overjoyed that both of them were here, away from all the pain, but there was the seed of something else, of something not so joyous, something unfulfilled, growing inside her. Riaz had begun classes, he was very happy with the department of physics, he had made some friends. His voice always sounded full and warm.

She was sharing an apartment with a woman called Susan. After two or three days Susan asked her, "Is that your boyfriend you talk to for so long?"

"We're going to get married."

"Oh." There was surprise on Susan's face, and then a sudden sadness which passed quickly, like a moving shadow. "Isn't it early?"

"Early for what?"

"To decide you want to get married. I mean, you're still so young."

"No, not at all." Anjali's sureness made Susan smile.

Susan had light brown hair, full of curls, cut short, just below the ears. A very pale skin. She wore a peach coloured shirt and jeans. Around her neck was the thinnest gold chain, with a tiny star hanging from it. Anjali noticed the muted colours, the lightness of the jewellery, everything toned down. Slowly her eyes would get used to this, clothes always in solid colours of lemon, sky blue, or beige, hardly ever any but the tiniest of prints.

"Hey," Susan said. "I like you."

One day, sitting in the library before a large, clear window, looking out onto the green lawn with yellow leaves falling on it, the small seed of unhappiness that had been growing in her split open and revealed its meaning. After so much, Anjali felt, she was still so far from Riaz, now the only person she had in the world. A thousand miles still, after everything. She wanted to go to him without delay, right now, to close this distance and begin her life with him. She picked up her books and walked out of the library.

Anjali went home and sat in her room alone. The room, hardly lived in yet, looked abandoned and empty. She lost her composure, her strength, her energy. She broke down. She called Riaz.

"You'll be all right Anjali," he said. "Maybe it's just a new place. You're getting used to things."

"I don't think it's that, Riaz, I don't know what it is." She couldn't stop weeping, she couldn't put down the phone.

What had happened to her? Could she not live without Riaz? Had there been too much lovelessness in what she had been through? Had she left an essential part of herself behind, or had it been irreparably damaged? In the end, was this proof of what she never wanted to be, a weak, helpless woman?

For the first time her body gave up. She could barely move. She spent two days not leaving her room, in complete immobility. Susan took care of her, brought her food, but she found it impossible to eat. After these two days she called Riaz again.

The phone at home did not seem to be working. She went to the apartment below, rented by two young Greek men. They seemed pleased to see her, in a shy way, and she called Riaz. She wept as she spoke, and explained as best as she could what she was feeling.

"All right, Anjali. It's all right," Riaz said from the other end. "Come here if that's what you want. But what about college? You'll have to apply all over again here. It may mean a break for you, because the semester has already begun and I don't know if they'll admit you and fund you at this time."

"It doesn't matter to me Riaz, I've thought about it. I'll start from next term if that's the only way."

"Take a day or two and think about it. I'm here and the minute you decide, you can come."

"All right," she said, trying not to weep even more.

The two Greek men, Bill and John, watched her as she spoke. They had not left the room. When she finished Bill said, "Thees ees love."

"Yes, yes," said John.

"Oh, to be een love like thees," said Bill.

Anjali smiled through her tears. She sat down.

The living room had dull yellow and brown sofas, a brown carpet, and white curtains. There did not seem to be anything personal in the room, anything that reflected them or where they came from. Did they carry all that was personal only deep inside them?

"What's your name?" she asked Bill.

"Bill," he said.

"No, you're real name."

"Vangelis," he said. "You come down whenever you need to use the phone."

"Thank you so much," Anjali said.

She had made up her mind. Riaz may have asked her to think about it, but she was already packing her bags.

"I'm leaving," she told Susan. "I'm going to be with Riaz."

"You're sure?"

"Of course."

"And are you sure Riaz wants you to come?"

"Of course, Susan. What do you mean?"

"I'm just asking Anjali, making sure." She came forward and embraced Anjali. "Be happy," she said.

Anjali looked at Susan, and a tenderness passed between them.

That night Anjali lay in bed, her bags almost completely packed. Light from the street fell into her room and onto the bed, the chest of drawers and the wooden floor she was soon to leave. It was Anjali's need to leave, to go to Riaz. He was comfortable, confident where he was, knowing they would spend their lives together. Perhaps that comfort, that confidence, was more easily given to a man. And she was leaving what most students would never give up, a fellowship, a tuition waiver. But inside her it did not seem like she was giving anything up, for something else. She was following through the one action that seemed to her deeply necessary.

She closed her eyes and fell into a light sleep. She was woken a little later by a woman screaming on the street below. She sat up. "Anjali, Anjali." There was a pause. "Help me, please help me, Bill...Bill..."It was Susan. Anjali rushed to the window and saw Susan struggling with two men. She opened her door and ran downstairs to find Bill and John already there. Seeing all of them, the two men jumped into their car and drove away. Susan was sitting on the ground. There were bruises on her left eye and on her upper arm where the men had hurt her.

John carried her up the stairs to her bed. Anjali brought the first aid kit. They cleaned her bruises, put ice packs on her eye.

"Hey Susan, what happened?" John asked.

It was a story that had probably taken place many times in this town. She was walking back home when she noticed a large blue car driving slowly next to her. There were two men inside, very drunk.

"Need a ride?" one of them said.

She was almost home so felt she would be all right. But the car stopped and before she could begin to run the men had grabbed her, and tried to pull her towards the car. They were so drunk and uncoordinated that they took time to do this and while she screamed she hoped someone would hear her, and thank god, thank god they had.

"You're going to the doctor first thing in the morning," Anjali said.

"I'll take her," Bill said. "And then to the police."

When Bill and John had left, Anjali turned off the light and sat on a chair near the bed.

"I'll be here all night Susan, so try and sleep."

"Thank you," Susan said. After a while, as Anjali was trying to get back her own calm, and wondering what Susan must be feeling like, Susan said, "Anjali come in here with me."

Anjali went and lay next to Susan. When she touched her Anjali saw that Susan was trembling. She held her close.

"Those men put their hands underneath my skirt and between my legs...Their fingers...They hurt me on my breasts," she whispered. She unbuttoned her shirt. Anjali saw on her right breast, on the pale skin, a large purple swelling. She got the ice pack and the ointments again. As she began to put these on the wound, she saw Susan was crying.

"I was walking straight into a rape," she said.

Anjali did not know what to say. She remained silent, holding Susan close. Neither of them fell asleep till dawn.

Anjali stayed an extra day to be with Susan. That day she went to meet the Chairman of the English department, a bald, old man. When he heard what she had to say, he told her, "Look, why don't you go and meet our resident psychoanalyst, Dan Jennings, or Lucy Harrison, the counsellor."

"There's nothing wrong with me, Dr Fields."

"If you wish not to acknowledge it that's another matter," he said, with a calm, cool superiority. "You are also setting a very bad precedent for students from your country. We'll think twice before admitting an Indian again."

A sudden anger flashed through Anjali.

"I'm not here as a representative for my country," she said, and left the room.

As the large grey bus pulls out of Worcester, Anjali takes off her shoes and sits cross-legged on the seat, making herself ready for this journey of one thousand miles. The bus travels silently through the astonishing brown, dark red, and yellow ochre landscape of the East in autumn. She has been in this city for only a month, among people she will probably never see again. A few facts about the city begin suddenly to pass through her mind. That it was situated on a river called the Blackstone, that it was the second largest city in the state, that corduroy was first produced in the mills of this town. She lets these details go because she does not need to hold onto them, and as they go she feels a lightness pass through her. What you barely know is so easy to describe, easy to look at, she thinks. What you know, so difficult, because its existence is inseparable from your own.

This one month has not been a new beginning. It has been a month of residues, of pain left over, remainders of confusion.

They cross the Massachusetts border, into upstate New York, then on to Pennsylvania. When night falls, Anjali falls asleep in the darkened silence. She wakes when it is already bright and opens her eyes to a landscape slowly losing the deep colours of the East and its hills and valleys. There are milder undulations now and the green is becoming a new green, lighter, as if in one layer only. The residues begin slowly their falling away from inside her, and she rises out of sleep, out of the weight of what is already past.

The bus stops at a station in Pittsburgh for breakfast, a station that looks exactly like the one they stopped at before, and like the one they will stop at after, with its brightly coloured chairs, vending machines, and cafeterias with dark walls. She drinks her coffee. She notices that many of the people here are Afro-American or Hispanic, that almost everyone, without exception, looks restless, anxious, and without the capacity for hope or dream.

Next to her on the connected row of orange seats is an old woman, maybe about sixty-five, in a bright purple coat with very large lapels. On the right lapel there is an artificial diamond brooch. Below the coat, her thick white legs are ravaged by a network of swollen blue veins from the knees to the feet.

"Where are you from?" she asks Anjali, without a smile.

"India."

"Oh. I read some books about India once. Beautiful country it's supposed to be. Where you going?"

"To be with my fiancée."

A smile crosses her face, with its watery eyes, large, thick nose and swollen cheeks.

"That's very exciting," she says, and a sudden, hidden, almost lost youthfulness enters the smile.

After a pause she says, "I've been married twice myself. My first husband was a bastard, he left me. For another woman. Then I married him." She points to an old man sitting next to her in a black coat, hunched up, and looking steadily at the floor.

"I just married him for some company, nothing more. At least he doesn't tell me what to do, order me around, like the last one. It's not great. But it'll do."

Anjali tries to look at the old man, to see his face, but he doesn't raise it.

There are still three more states to cross—Ohio, Indiana, Illinois.

There are many smaller towns now. Often these towns have a high water tower near the highway with their name painted on it. "Rapids City," or "Greenwood." Between the towns there are often large wooded parks in which picnic benches and tables stand abandoned after the summer, along with large pits for barbecues. When she has already been on this bus for twenty seven hours and they are well into Illinois, the last state before Anjali's destination, the land flattens almost completely. The vegetation is very sparse, not many trees or bushes, but there is land in all its immensity, stretching, in every direction, endlessly, till the sight, unrestricted, meets the immense sky. It is a kind of landscape she has never encountered before. The wind blows through the tall grass, in waves. Sometimes the tall grass turns into cornfields, shining in the sun, for many, many miles, and sometimes into fields of wheat. Now, everything that has held her back falls away completely. The space heals her with its unimaginable immensity. Only now the time that had always been fractured becomes whole. The past becomes past, the future lies ahead, and the present is where she is at this moment.

It is not chance that has brought her here. She looks out and sees a house in the fields, but there is no one outside. Further on some cattle grazing. But these things, animals and houses, even when present, are not capable of disturbing the vastness, of diminishing it. It is not chance that has brought her here. At this very first sight she is drawn to this landscape, its bare endless austerity. This is a place where she will be able to consider things, to hold them up to this compassionately pervasive mid-continental light. Here is her refuge. She is unaware as yet that there are others she will meet, from vastly different lives, who also regard this as a place to rest, to heal. But she knows that here she will find the strength to accept things, or be allowed to forget them for as long as she needs to, and learn the things she must know in order to go on. She does not yet know that one person's refuge can be the place from where another has been forced to flee, that the name Iowa belongs to a North American Indian tribe who were driven from these immense lands into reservations. Years later she will see a picture in a museum of an Iowa chief, decorated carefully, elaborately, with feathers and bone, whose name was White Cloud.

The end of a journey can never be imagined, it is found.

Anjali began her life with Riaz, this man she loved so much, clear and true like sunlight, without, she felt, a shred of darkness in him. This was a University town, cut in half by the Iowa River. They moved into an apartment south of this river, on a street called Linn, on the top floor of a house. Apple trees crowded in at the windows. In the early morning when they woke, there were birds. They drank their coffee in silence, in the bed still warm from their bodies, waking slowly to this new place, this new closeness. It would always be like this, even many years later. The morning would be the true source of their day, when touching each other, knowing the other there, they would then slowly move out into the world. In the evening they ate dinner at a tiny table for two, with two chairs facing each other. At night the undisturbed sky above them was filled with stars.

At last, Anjali felt she could look around, see where life had led her. She wrote a letter home, telling her father where she was. There was no reply.

Anjali would have to wait till next semester to begin classes. She took a job at the University banquet hall, where there were dinners for a hundred people at a time. Anjali's job was to be part of the team which served these sit-down dinners. The very first day she was asked to pick up a huge tray with twenty large plates and some glasses on it. She picked it up and dropped it immediately. She was astonished to see that nothing had broken. When she looked at the others who had also joined with her she saw they were managing perfectly. None of them were nervous, their bodies were straight, without a trace of bending or gathering in that betrayed hesitancy.

Anjali's second job, in the late afternoon, was at the University laundry where she had to fold clothes which had just been washed and dried. They came in huge canvas tubs, one between two people, and her job was to fold the green pyjamas and shirts, hospital green, and white towels, both small and large. There was a Bangladeshi man at the table next to hers and they began to talk. It was a relief, while folding the same things, incessantly. After they had folded pyjamas for three hours, even a tub full of towels was a change. She watched the Bangladeshi man who said he had been here for a year. His body had the same tentative ways as hers. He spoke to her about the small town from which he had come, the river that flowed near it shaded by large trees, the brother that had drowned in its waters, the sweetness of the hilsa that he missed, especially when it was cooked in the most pungent mustard paste. He said he liked it here. He told her that he wanted to get married, and could she help him find someone? After two days, they were separated. The supervisor, a huge man in grey clothes, came up and said, "Listen here, this place is not for talking but working."

"But it's not interrupting our work," said Anjali.

"Supervisor says, no talking," he repeated, in the same monotone.

It was for her, like so many others of her kind, a vast new country. But they came here already filled with a kind of knowledge about it. They knew the capitals of states, the names of cities, they were comfortable in the jazz bars of Chicago, they knew the music, sang the songs, wore the clothes, knew the language. It took the rough edges away from being a foreigner, smoothened them into an illusion of ease.

In the first months, when she had not yet returned to her studies, the time and space she had led her to a concentrated watching. She watched women walking on the streets, arching their backs and stretching their thighs. She saw the way bodies occupied their space in classrooms, restaurants, park benches, always with a great assurance and certainty. Once while she was buying a doughnut in a cafeteria, an older man behind her had asked, "You from India?" "Yes," she had smiled. "You know what your problem is down there?" he said with a smile back. "You have too many people, that's what." There was complete assurance in that statement. Often people she met would ask her, "India! What's it like?" Even in the question, a great certainty.

Walking by the river one day, she remembered the Victoria Memorial. The Lords in their portraits and statues had a certain set of the jaw, a firm line that Miss Walters had called "dignity of expression." The rajas had faces whose outlines merged with the dark backdrop and soft eyes unsure of their royalty. She remembered the tall statue of Lord Curzon at the north entrance. The eyes were focused as if on a single point, the jaw set, the lips tightly closed, and he stood with his right foot forward, in a stone cape tied with stone tassels, his left hand on the hilt of a large sword that hung from his waist.

There were so many of them in the Victoria Memorial, Lord Hastings and Clive, Cornwallis and Wellesley. She began to look through their writings and speeches, to enter their thoughts. Among the first she read was Macaulay, that very important Lord, because he had put so many significant things into motion.

"What is power worth if it is founded on vice, and on ignorance, and on misery; if we can hold it only by violating the most sacred duties which as governors we owe to the governed, and which, as a people blessed with far more than an ordinary measure of political liberty and of intellectual light, we owe to a race debased by three thousand years of despotism and priest craft? We are free, we are civilized, to little purpose, if we grudge to any portion of the human race an equal measure of freedom and civilization."

These words burst forth from the little book in Anjali's hands, bringing with them a vast hall under a large dome perhaps not unlike the one in the Victoria Memorial, the sound of the words resonating far and long. "To have found a great people sunk in the lowest depths of slavery and superstition, to have so ruled them as to have made them desirous and capable of all the privileges of citizens…" How would Lord Macaulay have stood as he said these words? With the shoulders thrown back, of course, the body absolutely straight. "Our plain clothing commands far more reverence than all the jewels which the most tawdry zamindar wears; and our plain language carries with it far more weight than the florid diction of the most ingenious Persian scribe. *He would have stood like a rock that can resist anything, even the greatest beauty, in a grey stone cape with stone tassels, the veins running hard under his pale, almost transparent skin.* The plain language and the plain clothing are inseparably associated in the minds of our subjects with superior knowledge, with superior energy, with superior veracity, with all the high and commanding qualities which erected, and which still uphold, our empire.

"The sceptre may pass away from us...Victory may be inconstant to our arms. But there are triumphs which are followed by no reverse. *The eyes were focused as if on a single point.* There is an empire exempt from all natural causes of decay *the jaw set.* Those triumphs are the pacific triumphs of reason over barbarism; *he stood with his right foot forward, displacing not space but all matter that would stand in his way,* that empire is the imperishable empire of our arts and our morals, our literature and our laws." *His hand on the hilt of a large sword that hung from the waist.*

In the unimaginably cold Iowa winter Anjali joined the English department with an assistantship. There was light snow, bright sunshine and sub-zero temperatures with raging winds. The winds rolled across the plains of Iowa and Illinois sometimes at a hundred miles per hour. People changed, became more quiet and withdrawn, looking down as they walked, keeping to themselves. Some days there was black ice on the streets. Cars spun around in circles, and walking to campus everyone slipped and fell. Sometimes Riaz and Anjali drove out into the countryside. It was brown and white with snow and the bare branches of trees. Miles and miles of this under the immense sky, and every few miles a grain silo on a farm. And always the sunlight falling over everything, illuminating the endless distances. A fragile light this, looking as if it could vanish any time, but in fact, extremely worthy of trust.

In class, Anjali did not speak very much. She noticed how much everyone else spoke, asked questions, and articulated their opinions. She listened very closely to everyone. She read the texts with care, sometimes discussing them with Riaz. When it was her turn to present a paper she worked hard. After the reading of the paper, there was a long silence in the class. Finally, the teacher, John Greenwood, said, "Anjali, that was an amazing paper! I didn't know there was so much behind your quietness."

The class burst into a discussion. Anjali replied, answered, argued, analysed. It broke the silence between her and the class, she began to make friends.

The love between Riaz and Anjali was seamless. From the morning when sometimes Riaz would gather her out of bed in his arms and take her to the windows to look at the crisp, golden light. Till the night, when they would walk back from somewhere, very often later than midnight, under the sky of stars in the perfect winter silence. The miracle of Anjali and Riaz's life was this, it seemed they had found a love that was unbroken. It was the love that everyone dreamt of and people would try to look in the corners and unlit spaces of their lives to find its secret.

There wasn't one.

Spring came. The icicles on the roof melted and came down in fat drops at the ledge of the window. People smiled and said "Good morning" to each other on the streets. "Nice day isn't it?" they said. They looked up and ahead into the new light.

The warm, humid Iowa summer arrived. On their drives out into the country the fields were golden with ripening corn. Outside the farmhouses, the row of trees, planted to bar the wind, were full and tall. They could go boating on Lake McBride. In the summer Anjali and Riaz drove to Utah in a large van that belonged to Leonard, a student of philosophy, whom they had met some time ago. They were going to meet Riaz's family there, and then to get married, at the home of Riaz's aunt. Anjali had written a letter home to her parents, giving them the date of her wedding, the first of June. There was no reply.

The road to Utah went through the vast lands of Nebraska, and then through Colorado, through the Rocky Mountains. They drove through the night. It was three in the morning and they were travelling through the craggy peaks, underneath the clearest sky Anjali had ever seen, with a moon as luminous as the sun. Leonard was driving and she stayed awake with him, talking, listening to music on the radio. Riaz was stretched out at the back, sleeping. She was thinking of her father. Most days in this country she avoided the thought of him, held it at bay. But on this, her first long journey since she had been here, pushed away thoughts began to emerge from their hidden places. In the new time and space they began to unravel themselves. The pain of separation from her father came and held itself inside her for a long time.

Leonard switched off the radio and asked, "Are you sleepy?"

"No," she said. "Are you tired?"

"A little. Maybe we'll stop for some coffee. But I think it'll be a while before something comes up."

Leonard was a tall, slim man with a soft voice and a very serious face. Anjali liked him. He seemed to have in him large, unknown spaces.

They drove on in the absolute silence, the moon travelling straight ahead of them.

"You're the most incredible woman I've ever met," said Leonard, without taking his eyes off the road.

Anjali, surprised, felt a sudden shyness.

"I, I don't deserve that," she said.

Leonard's eyes were still on the road ahead, with its sudden curves and turnings.

"No, it's true," he said.

Anjali liked the directness of men, how they said what they had to say and did what they wanted to do. This was not the last time she would hear words similar to these, and they would always be said simply, directly, only with a difference in pitch and tone, but so clear that she could touch the edges and contours of the words. But because this was the first time, she became quiet. How could you know what you seemed to someone else?

"A few hours more till we're out of the mountains and into the valley," Leonard said, and smiled.

At Riaz's aunt's place, a large brown and white house with a garden at the back, his parents had already arrived. They wept to see him and they embraced her, with nothing held back. It moved Anjali. Leonard walked in, taller than everyone. He was given breakfast and he took a shower. Anjali had bathed, washed her hair and was sitting outside in the summer sunlight, in the garden where she could see the hills that surrounded the city. Leonard came and stood at the steps leading to the garden. He stood there for a while, looking out at the hills.

"I'll get going," he said. He was going on to California, to his parents.

Anjali walked up to where he stood. His face had a smile, a very gently spreading smile. He looked at her. He reached out and touched her wet hair with the back of his hand. Anjali noticed how the back of a hand was always used for a tentative touch, the palm for a touch more assured.

"Have a good wedding," he said.

In the kitchen there were kebabs being made and biryani, wedding food for the next day. Anjali and Riaz did not feel the wedding was a significant thing in their lives, they had already come together, and no ritual could invest it with greater meaning.

As night approached Anjali left Riaz with his family and went for a walk on the quiet streets with large houses on them. Below these streets the rest of the valley sparkled with lights. She remembered weddings at home, the ones she had seen all her life and whose rituals had passed into her blood. She remembered the sound of the shehnai, the anticipation everywhere for the groom to arrive, everyone leaning from balconies and windows looking for the groom's car covered with flowers, the married women welcoming the groom with oil lamps, flowers, and sweets, the bride sitting on a flat wooden piri and being carried around the wedding fire by the men of her family. She remembered the way the bride's arms went around the necks and shoulders of her brothers and uncles and cousins who carried her, the shlokas of the pandit around the fire, the marriage bed under a canopy of flowers. Anjali was outside this tradition now, though she would never forget even its tiniest details, she was outside this, with a different life. She did not regret anything, but today, for the first time, there was a feeling of loss, of having left something behind. She did not know then that just as she had left ritual behind, ritual had left her, and that beginning with her wedding, nothing in her life would follow the patterns of a ritual. She would not need it.

As she walked back towards the house she saw Riaz walking towards her.

"I was getting worried," he said. "Anjali, can you go through with it?"

She went into his arms and put her head on his chest. Here she was protected, secure, and free. A sudden pain came and assaulted her, and the night, the valley falling away, the silent, large houses, increased it and made it sharper. She wept, for herself, for her father, for the world's unfathomable ways. When she stopped weeping, her body still in the aftermath of tears, Riaz took her face and held it in his large, long hands.

"Look at me," he said.

She looked up at him. His eyes were clear and shining.

They were married in the house by a registrar. Anjali wore a red and gold Banaras sari, brought her by Riaz's mother. She wore a ring of sapphire that had been in their family for generations along with a broad sapphire necklace set in gold and pearls. It was given always, they explained, to the daughter-in-law. When the wedding certificate had been signed and the registrar pronounced them man and wife, everyone in Riaz's family began to weep. They embraced Riaz and her, each one of them, every embrace long and almost unbreakable, while weeping and wiping their eyes. Later, the wedding photographs, for some reason underexposed and dark, would show a groom and his family with overflowing eyes, sitting with a bride in a red sari who looked straight and clear into the camera.

Three years passed.

In this time, questions came and fell away, were answered, or turned into new ones. Anjali saw that comparisons had a life of their own and that life was without end. She read late into the night, she read Fanon, Cesaire, Gandhi, she read the history of India. The same learning that had not helped her in her earlier life would help to transform her in this one. Perhaps it is experience that breaks down certain protective walls, and learning other ones. She was turning, around a very unexpected bend. It was slow this turning, so slow it seemed almost without movement, and later when Anjali looked back it would be impossible to trace its beginning.

In this country, town after town seemed essentially the same to her, the houses, the shops, the way people moved, the language. Only nature was diverse, as it was everywhere, knowing no limitation. Was it this sameness that was the source of people's assurance, what led them to walk straight and tall, and with the utmost sureness?

At school the nuns always told them to be confident. When they went up on stage to recite something, for a debate, for a play, even to sing a song. It was an attitude of speech and manner they were talking of, an attitude for the outside. She realized now that they were talking always of the consequence, for the source of real confidence could only be in conviction, which formed on the inside, and how could that ever be taught? How many young people had she seen, even in her schooldays, trying to be confident, but with their concave insides of doubt falling out of them despite themselves?

She remembered the balcony of her father's house where she had spent much of her childhood. Even from here, which was not yet fully the outside, she could see, looking down, the land's diversity passing below. Hawkers and beggars, madmen and mystics, people with everything to lose or nothing. And the family on the balcony, placed precariously in between, linked to the people on the street by a reciprocal necessity. Where the other is so close, it is not easy to be assured. The more the self has to stretch, the more tenuous it becomes, less sure of itself.

While reading in the library one day Anjali comes across a large book of paintings from the *Akbar Namah*, the official chronicle of Akbar's reign. It is a manuscript of miniatures rendered by people who seemed to have perfected their skill over generations. She marvels at the paintings. As she looks closer she begins to notice the expressions on the face of this emperor. It is very different from the Lords in the Victoria Memorial, much closer to the Rajas. She sees him in many different situations. He sits beneath an orange canopy in his court watching dancers from Mandu, with the imperial army he crosses a dark blue Ganga astride a large elephant, he is on a pilgrimage to Ajmer on foot over the greenest grass. His gaze is never focused, always looking beyond what is before him, his body active and firm but always bending, flowing, turning as much inwards as out, the jawline light, barely distinguishable. Always like that, while supervising the building of Fatehpur Sikri, even while entering Surat in victory, or receiving in his court the prisoners of war.

It is not wealth or power that gives the body its language, it is a person's relationship with these things.

Do you open the world or does the world open you?

But it had been three years and one day Anjali, trying on a skirt in a shop, was looking at herself in the mirror. It was a long, black skirt, made of very light wool, cut straight down to the ground, with a single slit at the back. She looked at herself and found she was someone else, not the woman who had arrived here three years ago. Her body had changed. Unknown to her and what she thought or desired, the confidence that she observed with such fascination had seeped into her and filled her body, her eyes, with an assurance that would never, ever leave her.

Anjali was with her friend Ann, who was trying on the same skirt. Ann was slim, almost bony. Anjali watched Ann watching herself in the mirror. As Ann turned and looked at herself, from the front, then sideways, then turning her back to the mirror and looking over the shoulder, there was the same complete assurance as a person merged with a woman's endless doubt.

"What is it?" asked Ann, catching Anjali's eyes in the mirror.

"Nothing...I...I wouldn't be able to put it into words."

"Try me," Ann said, and smiled.

As they left the shop Anjali had a strange sense of the future. She would be one of those people who would always be assured, at home in the most flung apart of geographies, in the most new of situations, at anyone's table, in anyone's home. It was an assurance that bridged all differences, but lightly, without foundation. If she was not careful and aware, she would reach that most dangerous of places where the source of assurance was in the education, in the knowledge of multiplicity as fact, not feeling, nor experience.

She and Ann had been friends ever since Anjali arrived here. In the last month they had moved even closer to each other. One early morning Ann had called Anjali, "Can you come over please?" She could barely speak.

"Are you all right?"

"Please could you come?"

Ann was sitting in her living room, her face so pale it was almost white. It was clear she had been crying. She hadn't raised the blinds, or turned on any lights. She was sitting on the wooden floorboards in her nightclothes. In the half darkness Ann said Mark had left her. Then she began to weep again, quietly. Anjali knew this was the man Ann had been with for two years now and that she loved him very much. She sat in front of Ann and began to stroke her head with its light, thin brown hair, like one strokes the head of a child. Directly opposite Anjali, on the wall behind Ann there were two large maps, one of India where Ann had never been and one of France, where she had spent a year. Above these two hung a Peter's map of the world.

"There's nothing to say," Ann said. "There is absolutely nothing to say. There is, suddenly, someone else."

"But—"

"I know, we were beginning to talk about marriage." The dark wooden floor around them was strewn with white tissues. "My therapist is out of town…"

"I'm here Ann," Anjali said, almost severely.

"It's not enough," Ann said, with equal severity.

Anjali got up and opened the living room windows. The spring light fell over everything.

"I'm sorry," Ann said.

"You look pale Ann, very pale. Have you eaten anything?"

"Not since yesterday. But maybe I look so pale to you because you've never seen me without my makeup."

"What?"

"Yes. I never, ever step out without my make up."

"I never even noticed."

"Because I do it skilfully. I think I need to go and lie down, but will you stay? If you don't have a busy day. It would mean a lot to me."

"Of course I'll stay."

Ann pressed her hand and went into the bedroom.

Later in the day came their other friends, Rowena and Leonard.

"So," Rowena said. "Have you been to your therapist?"

"He's on vacation," said Ann.

"That's hard," Leonard said.

Anjali was quiet but Ann turned towards her.

"When you went through all that with your father, were you…by yourself?"

"I had Riaz, I had friends."

"But, not…"

"No."

After a silence, Anjali said, "Suffering is natural isn't it, not an aberration. To think that there can be a life without suffering, I can't understand it. I've been through mine."

"And how do you know we haven't?" Rowena said.

"You don't allow yourselves to suffer."

"Don't judge us Anjali." Rowena got up from her chair and pushed back her thick, dark brown hair, she adjusted her glasses. "The ancient civilization that always knows better, has discovered all the fundamental truths. India, the land where Hinduism, Jainism, and Buddhism was born and where perhaps even Jesus went, to learn. Don't judge us."

"Am I?" Anjali asked.

Rowena looked at her. "It's in your voice," she said.

Everyone became quiet.

"If we talked," said Anjali, "if we could talk with each other…"

There was silence again, but this time there was movement underneath it.

Anjali waited for a very long time.

"We never talk about love," Rowena said. There was a long silence again.

"What's out there," said Ann, "what's out there affects us too."

What was out there? The clear spring light, the wide roads, the future, great achievements, men on the furthest planets. But she knew Rowena meant the other things, those not so buoyant, not so easy, and not at all understood. When they left Ann's apartment in the evening, what was out there was only a spring breeze that ruffled their hair as soon as they stepped onto the porch and which brought with it the smell of flowers blooming.

Was it the things she was beginning to see that made her want to write?

Not necessarily. Anjali had always felt drawn to the way language opened a world, a life. This was why she had moved towards the study of literature. Now she began, hesitantly, to write stories, and she liked very much the act of arranging the words, of making connections, of expressing a thought or feeling that till then did not have a form.

She wrote a story about an old man who had been part of the struggle for Independence and who was being given an award for this towards the end of his life. It was a man she had never known in reality, but whom she saw clearly when she closed her eyes. She discovered the magic of an imagination anchored somewhere in life. The story was called "The Journey". It began:

"In Manik Sen's dream, the monsoons had begun. Thick drops of water fell tumultuously through the dark and the wind swung around in circles, from land to river to land. At first, in his dream, Manik was a child out in the rain, trying to gather the falling drops in his small palms. He let the rain pour into him, layer by layer, through his clothes, his sweating skin, and into his child's heart. There was only water, night and fulfilment. Then, slowly, the dream began to change. It was an older Manik who stood in the rain, in the centre of a violent thunderstorm. The river rose, finally bursting through the levees. There were roofs flying away and houses collapsing, his mother crying for help in a back room and his father running. After that, an even older Manik, sitting with his parents and sisters among the storm's wreckage. No more rain, only the soft drip of water, from leaves and trees and rooftops."

Anjali was only beginning to perceive what it meant to write. She changed to the writing department. It was a hesitant, groping time but also a time of great ease, of having found her place of labour.

After a writing class one evening, they had all gone to a bar. They sat at a very long wooden table next to the equally long window. She would never forget this image. Everyone talking in that bar filled with people, the table wet with rings of water and drink, the snow falling steadily outside. Anjali was talking to someone sitting in front of her, and during a pause in the conversation she saw a man sitting two chairs down on the opposite side, looking at her. He leaned over a little, stretched out his long arm with sleeves buttoned to the wrist, held out his hand and said, "We haven't met. I'm Richard Coleman."

"Anjali," she said.

He was an Afro-American man, with a slim but strong body, and an old world manner about him. When the student she was talking to left, he came and sat opposite her. He told her he had started here only last semester, that he was working on a novel. When everyone was ready to leave he said, "Will you have coffee with me tomorrow?" He had a very shy smile.

"Sure," she said.

As she walked back home, through the plaza, past the new Indian restaurant, the bookstore, then past Van Allen Hall, she thought about him. He was quiet and had barely spoken to anyone else.

The next day at coffee, three hours passed. He said he was from New York, and asked her questions about India. They were very informed questions, much more so than what she was used to. When she told him that, he said, "I read."

He asked her about her writing. After they had spoken for quite some time, he said, "You know one very big reason I'm here with you?"

"What?"

"You're not a white woman," he said. There was a directness in his face that was completely unpremeditated, a directness without defences.

It was the first time Anjali had been confronted with such a hard racial separation. She felt disturbed by it.

"Do you like them?" he asked.

"Who?"

"White people?"

Anjali smiled. "Really Richard…"

"You're under an illusion," he said. "There isn't one among them capable of leaving their whiteness behind, or of being a real friend."

"That's not true. "

"For me, that's one of the few things that are beyond doubt," he said.

As he spoke Anjali looked at his face. It was different from yesterday, in the formality of a first meeting. Today she noticed the eyes, large and shining, a little moist, a face where the emotions revealed themselves quickly, without self consciousness, and beneath all this something also immovable, a gravity which never left it.

They became friends. For the first time, as Anjali walked through campus, and in the town, she noticed how few Afro-Americans there were, a fraction even of the Indians on campus. During the day she wrote and so did Richard, and very often they met in the evenings. As they talked she noticed the way his body moved. It was always nervous, anxious, on edge, perpetually alert, as if anticipating something unexpected all the time. At times it contradicted the quiet, open quality of his face.

Richard had read more than anyone else she knew in her generation. He had a prodigious memory and could quote from books he'd read in high school and what someone had said in class months ago, word for word. His knowledge of India was vast.

"Why India?" Anjali asked.

"Oh, I don't know really, Gandhi perhaps." He was smiling.

Then, with that sudden change of emotion she was still getting used to in him, he said, in a very quiet but definite voice, "It's important to read." He looked out of the window. "I grew up in the slums of New York." He was quiet again.

"It's important to read," he said, "even though it increases the rage."

Anjali wanted to read something Richard had written.

"When I'm ready," he said.

"You've already shown it in class," she said.

"When I'm ready to show it to *you*," he replied.

Anjali's own writing was beginning to change. She was looking for new forms. The older narrative ways would not hold the things that were now rising inside her. She realized that it was not only what she saw that made her write, it was also the writing that made her see new things. It was hard to understand how the act of saying brought so much sight.

She wrote a story called "As If It Were My Native Land." The title came from a poem by the Bengali poet Michael Madhusudan Dutt:

"And oh I sigh for Albion's strand
As if it were my native land..."

In it she merged essay and fiction.

"In the first reading of a story the eye travels along the words in a linear way, sometimes going back, sometimes leaping forward. But the true reading is like a gyre, a circling deeper and deeper into the tale to reach the point from which everything emerges. The centre of a story is beyond writing, but not beyond communication."

She spoke of the colonial history of India. She spoke of the constantly increasing desire of people to leave the land not for new shores, but for a specific new shore, a specific life. For the first time she found it difficult to express certain things in the English language. She wrote:

"A writer would have to bring into this script so straight and erect, a sense of the curve and roundness of Bengali, or Tamil or Gujarati. The English language is not meant to express certain sorrows."

For the first time she used a few Bengali words, and one or two Sanskrit ones.

It was only after Anjali had written the story that she sat in the library with a Sanskrit dictionary, trying to find the meaning of certain words. She opened the dictionary towards the beginning. Before she could look for the meaning of the words she needed, her eyes began to move from one word, in "a", down to the next.

Aakasha	sky, ether, atmosphere
Abhavasunyata	not-being

Abhimana	self conceit
Adbhuta	marvellous
Advaita	the undivided, the not two
Agastya	a sage
Ahamkara	egoism
Ahimsa	not to wound; non-violence towards living beings
Aksara	imperishable
Alaknanda	a river that rises in the Himalayas and flows into the Ganga
Amba	mother
Amrta	immortal; the liquid of eternal life
Ananda	joy, bliss
Ananta	infinite
Anirukta	inexpressible
Antahkarana	the seat of thought and feeling; the heart, mind, soul
Apana	out-breath
Aparimita	boundless
Aranya	forest
Asana	sitting down; a special posture of devotion or Yoga
Asrama	hermitage
Asva horse	
Asvattha	the sacred fig tree
Atirikta	overflowing
Atma	self; soul
Avadhuta	one who has shaken off worldly feeling and obligations
Avalokiteshvara	a Bodhisattva
Avatar	an incarnation of a divine being
Avidya	ignorance
Avykta	unapparent, imperceptible

These words could not be said quickly and forgotten. They had the most elongated of syllables and saying them had to be slow, the sound drawn out till it disappeared into the silence that ended it.

Chris Davidson, a student in the graduating class and a very good writer, was throwing a large party before he left. He called up Anjali and made her promise she would come. She liked Chris, a quiet, serious man from Florida. A while after she spoke to him, Richard called and said, "Hey, did Chris invite you to his party?"

"Yes. Why?"

"He didn't invite me, the bastard, he didn't invite me." Richard was brimming with nervousness and anxiety.

"He just called me, he'll probably call you any minute."

"See what I keep telling you about white people. I mean Chris is supposed to be my friend!"

Eventually Richard was invited. He picked her up in his old brown Chevrolet. He came around to open the door for her as she sat and again when she got out. When she smiled at him, he said, "That's the way I am, I guess. My parents came up from the South to New York. From hopelessness to despair." He gave Anjali a broad smile.

The party was crowded. It was spring and people were out in the garden, under the budding leaves. John Coltrane was playing "My Favourite Things."

Anjali had worn a kurta and churidar, with a dark red bindi, which all the women found beautiful. Two women who had just joined here looked at her bindi and said, "What is that, what does it mean?"

Rajan, another Indian and a friend of Anjali's said in a deeply serious voice, "It's menstrual blood. Basically it's an offering to the great sun god. And you freshen it every month, on the first day of your cycle."

Fascination and disgust moved across the women's faces at the same time. Anjali tried to keep a straight face. But opposite her she saw Richard breaking into a grin and then slowly doubling up in laughter.

Among the conversations in the party she saw people looking at Richard, discussing him.

"He's from reform school," someone said. "Used to be a juvenile delinquent. But man can he write! The guy's brilliant."

Richard was talking to Chris Davidson. She saw Chris put an arm around Richard's shoulders. She saw Richard flash him a very warm smile.

Before dinner was served Richard came up to her suddenly and said, "I'm leaving. Do you want a ride home?" There was an immense rage building up behind the familiar gravity of his face.

"Why're you leaving?"

"Do you want a ride home or no?" he said, the rage beginning to express itself.

"All right, I don't need a ride home, but I'll come with you."

In the car, which he drove at breakneck speed, Richard did not say a word. She didn't ask him anything, either about what happened or about what she had heard. When they had almost reached her house, he said, "They always change. You just never know when. They turn. And sometimes when your defences are down." There was sweat on his forehead, even in the coolness of the spring night.

Anjali was quiet. Again, he came around and opened her door. As she turned to walk up her lawn, he said, "I've never known a woman like you before." He said it as nervously and anxiously as he had said everything else on the drive back.

"Bye," she said and walked across the moist grass.

In August of that year Riaz and Anjali moved to a new house. The house had red brown gables, a tall chimney, bay windows, a porch with a swing that creaked, and maple trees in the garden. Above it, a very large sky.

In August, to celebrate Indian Independence Day, there was a dinner and film screenings. Anjali was there, and she had brought her friends, Rowena, Ann, and Leonard. One of the films screened was of Indian writers at an international writer's conference in Bonn earlier that year. After a series of interviews with some of the writers, with the most routine of questions, there suddenly began a ten minute long sequence at the cafeteria. The writers were serving themselves the food and eating. The camera stayed very close to faces and bodies and it caught the way the food was being chewed, sometimes very fast and gulped down, sometimes slow with staring eyes while moving the food from one side of the mouth to another, very often with the mouth slightly open, the fork handled awkwardly, the knife kept to one side. Often, morsels of food remained on someone's lips, or while putting the food into the mouth on a fork, some spilt out at the lips, and back onto the plate. As Anjali watched, she felt enraged. She knew these faces. There was a woman from Bengal whose novels were about tribal life in the interiors of her area, a man from a small town in Madhya Pradesh, a man originally from a village in the South, people from traditional lives, people who were also in the process of questioning those lives, people who were more used to eating their food off bell metal plates, and then sitting at their tables talking for hours while the food stains dried on their hands. They were writers from a generation where longing and suffering were different things, and a generation where suffering was not limited to the self.

In the still dark auditorium Anjali got up and left.

Summer was coming to a close when Richard gave Anjali his novel to read.

"It's ninety seven pages," he said. "I'm working on the next part."

That night Anjali stayed up and began to read. The novel opened with a family who lived in a tenement next to the train track, and a little boy who would watch the trains come and go. The prose was of a kind she had never encountered before, with its own rhythm, its own violence, and its own tenderness. She did not put the manuscript down till she reached the end of the ninety seven pages. There was no doubt that this was the beginning of a very special work. The next morning she called Richard as soon as she awoke. There was no answer.

For the next week Anjali called him, went to his apartment, to his class, but Richard was nowhere. Finally, at the end of that week, she saw him walking down the opposite side of the street.

"Richard," she called out.

He turned around, looked at her, then turned the corner and went on.

Two more days passed. On the third day he called.

"I'm sorry," he said.

"You're forgiven. As always," Anjali said. "I read it Richard. I don't know what to say. I think it's going to be a great work."

"You think so," he said, quietly. There was a silence. Then suddenly he became angry.

"You're too careful with me Anjali. Too kind. What do you think, I can't take it? I'll crumble, because I'm black?" He put down the phone.

The next day Anjali was sitting and reading under the maple tree in her front garden in the afternoon, and she saw Richard driving up the street. He got out of the car and walked up the grass, in a white shirt, his skin shining in the sunlight.

"Thought you might want to go for a ride in my Cadillac," he smiled.

"I'm very tired Richard, I don't know what to make—"

"Please." He kept on standing there, looking at her.

Anjali stood up and closed her book.

They drove out to the autumn countryside, past small lakes and farms storing their grain for the winter.

"So much space," Richard said. "Too much. It drives me crazy. If you go into one of these farmhouses we're passing by, and look at the faces of the people who live there, I'm sure you'll find them helpless, bewildered. Space pressing in upon them from every direction…"

Anjali noticed his body was quieter today, his face calm.

They stopped at a stretch of wheat fields, a sharp wind blowing through them, a wind with winter in its heart. They leant against the car and watched, drawing in and buttoning their jackets against the wind.

"What's been keeping you away?" Anjali asks.

Richard continues to look out across the fields. The wind keeps on. A long time passes.

"Hopelessness," he says.

Anjali looks at him. A long time passes again.

"I give you my novel, you read it, you're moved. I know it's good work—everyone knows in the end how worthwhile their work is or isn't—a part of me is so happy, so full, because I couldn't even read properly till I was in high school, but then what?"

He stops. He looks at her.

"Almost everyone in that class, trying to be writers, dying to be writers. The longing in all those people, it chokes me, I can't breathe." He holds his throat with his hands.

"I've written to save my life. And now I see. It can't save me."

They drive back as the sun throws its falling light only on the crowns of the red cedar trees, the single evergreen in these parts, and the rounded tops of the silos filled with grain.

They drive to Richard's apartment on the upper floor of a bright, white house. Inside, Anjali notices the light fall over Richard's writing desk, and his neatly gathered papers. As she is looking at it, Richard gathers her in his arms, he touches her hair with the back of his hand. They make love in the utter silence of the room, with all the windows closed. They meet more as man and woman than ever before, yet for the first time they are also much more than man and woman, much more than even the closest of friends, much more than two people with vastly different lives.

As they make love she is amazed at how much her body has changed, how much more it has become the body of a woman, knowing what to do. Richard's body is at least two shades darker than hers and she sees how in certain places the darkness gathers, at the crook of the arm, the inside of the thighs, and below the stomach where the hair begins, gathers and becomes almost black. As they make love Richard loses his nervousness, his hard edge, his anxiety.

It is only later that she notices the cuts on his chest, a deep line across his stomach, the nicks on his upper arms.

"What are these?" she asks.

"They're what happened to me as I was growing up," he says, the nervousness returning again.

"So many?"

"It's rough out there. I told you that."

"Richard…"she begins, but he interrupts her, "Okay. I grew up in the slums of New York, I grew up fighting and thieving in the street gangs. I was arrested as a juvenile and put into reform school. It was only there that I began to read and study and write. I went on to Rochester for college. There I met a teacher, who became my mentor, and it was he who urged me to write. That's how I came here."

He tells her all this as fact, without any emotion at all, and as if he has said it this way several times before.

"Is that good enough for you?" he asks.

When they are getting ready to leave, and Richard is putting on his shoes, she sees him pick up a small knife, and put it into his sock on the right foot.

"What is that?"

"A knife. You've never seen a knife before?"

"Richard why are you carrying a knife?"

"Never know when you need it," he says and laughs.

"It's not very funny."

"I carry it all the time. It's just a habit Anjali."

"You're in a university town, in *Iowa*."

"Don't you have habits Anjali?" he asks, raising his voice, the edginess and nervousness now settled completely back into his body. "Something from the past which never leaves you?"

But as he drops her home in the car, he quietens again, and when she leaves the car he kisses her hand.

As she went to sleep that night one thing came to her with certainty. There are many lives that can be lived by a person, not just one. She did not know that the old life was waiting, holding its breath.

The next morning, Anjali woke to the harsh cry of a long familiar bird. She opened her eyes and on the maple tree in the garden she saw the most familiar bird of her life, a crow. She went closer and saw the crow looking at her, steadily. A crow in the middle of this northern land where winter was approaching? From where? She looked at it carefully again and it stirred, it moved its crow black wings. The first thought that came to her was that it had come to tell her something.

It was the most ordinary of Indian birds, seen every day, everywhere. Yet it was also the bird of death. It was the bird that came and tasted first of the food cooked on the thirteenth day after a person had died. It was the bird she had seen her grandfather feed on the large balcony, because, as he said, they carry the souls of our dead ancestors. It was also the bird that mourns its own dead, elaborately and with ceremony. She had seen about fifty of them flying up and down in large circles and shrieking around a dead crow below. They flew and shrieked for hours.

The second thought that came to her was this. The bird had come to tell her that her father was dying.

She turned back towards the bedroom and looked at Riaz sleeping. Nothing lost yet for him, no one.

Two things came back to her:

When she was still a child, she remembered her grandfather

going for his walk, every evening and every morning. One evening he took a long time to return. Anjali's aunt, who lived ten minutes away, called in tears. Was her father at home? She said an old man had been hit by a car and killed near her house. He had been taken away in an ambulance, but people were saying he was tall and slim, like her father. Was he back? Another aunt who was with them burst into tears, her father left in his car to look for him and find out about the accident, the servants stood with terrified faces.

Anjali remembered her grandmother, sitting on her chair near the large wooden desk, one arm resting on the green felt that covered the writing surface. She did not speak, her body completely silent as she looked ahead of her, through the window at the evening sky. After about an hour, her aunt called from the balcony, "I see him, I see him, he's coming." She rushed inside and down the stairs. Her father also returned at the same time. In all the relief and happiness no one noticed her grandmother. But Anjali saw her, sitting as silently after her husband had been seen on the street down below. Only, a single tear dropped from her left eye, rolled all the way down her cheeks, and over her chin.

Her grandfather, always calm, always vast, came back, put his cane next to the door, and said, "It would only have been death, nothing more."

The second thing she remembered was this.

Her grandmother, who Anjali believed was the woman that she had descended from, not her mother, was in hospital, very ill. One afternoon as they all waited, her father, her aunts, two cousins, to go to the hospital at four, the telephone rang. Her father answered it.

"Yes?" he said. "Yes. All right."

He came into the room and said, "She's taken a turn for the worse. Let's go."

Anjali started to weep, as her father held her. In the car they all wept at different times, sparked off by who knows what specific memories, what specific loss. Only her father was silent.

At the hospital, no one wanted to wait for the large elevator. They all began walking up, running up the stairs. Anjali, fifteen, ran up as fast as she could, her long hair flying behind her. Suddenly she realized her father was nowhere near. She waited. Then she saw her father walking, very, very slowly, putting one leg ahead, then another, almost as if it needed determination. The stairs were dark and grey and steep, and at every landing he paused for breath. Each landing had a large window, and as he paused, his face and body were flooded with sunlight.

"We have to hurry, come on," Anjali said to him, taking his arm. But he only told her very softly, "I'm coming, you go ahead."

Whenever Anjali turned back to look at him, she saw him with his slow stride, going into the darkness, out to the radiant light and back again. When she reached her grandmother's room, she heard the sound of weeping inside. When she entered she saw her grandmother lying on the bed, as if in sleep, with her mouth open, dead.

It was years later she understood that her father had known all along. But he, from the long habit of patriarchy, of being the eldest child, a son, the elder brother, the father, had suspended his own grief to protect the rest of them.

Anjali remembered these two images, but she could not possibly learn what they could teach her. Perhaps the containing of death in these ways needed a time, a life, where everything had not been shaken—geography, the most essential bonds, what constitutes the deepest self.

When she entered her office that morning the secretary said, hesitantly, and with an unusually kind face, "You just had a call from India, from your home. They want you to call back, it's an emergency."

When she called home, she heard her mother's voice after four years. It sounded exactly the same. She told Anjali her father was dying, he was in intensive care, he had cancer.

In five minutes Anjali was at the travel agent. When she said why she wanted the earliest ticket out, the woman at the desk took some papers and made some calls. In ten minutes she had her ticket. As she was taking out her credit card, the manager came and said, "You're a student here. If there's any problem with you're paying for this now, please feel free to pay us when you come back."

"Thanks," said Anjali. "I have my card."

"Don't forget to get your I-20 to leave and re-enter the country."

She had forgotten. Her next stop was at the International Student's Centre. She was wary because she knew this would take time, normally a few days. But the head of the Centre walked out when he heard, and he held her hand.

"Give us twenty minutes," he said.

Anjali went home and called Riaz. She waited for him on the steps outside the front door. He came and said, "Listen, I'm coming with you. If something happens..."

Anjali looked at him.

"If something happens, he should know how we are together."

They leave, from Cedar Rapids, through Chicago, Frankfurt, then New Delhi. It takes twenty-eight hours. In New Delhi there is a long, long line at the immigration counter. Anjali goes up to the man checking passports and says, "Could you do mine out of turn please? My father is dying, I have to take the flight to Calcutta."

He is a small man, with a big moustache. He begins to laugh, showing his sharp teeth.

"They all say that."

"But I'm telling you the truth," Anjali says.

"They say that too," he grins.

Anjali misses the connecting flight to Calcutta. They take the next one, five hours later.

At the airport there is no one from Anjali's family. Riaz's mother and his sister are waiting, with darkened, uncomfortable faces. She embraces them. As she turns away she hears the words "passed away", she hears, "two hours ago." She sees Riaz turning towards her. She sees him extending his arms to hold her, very, very slowly. He takes her close and says, "He's gone."

Anjali rips and tears out of Riaz's embrace. She feels an actual fist of great weight and power, plunging into her stomach.

Who is it, the air, life, death?

Who is it?

She doubles up, and the huge, brightly lit hall of the airport swings around her, and she screams and screams and screams.

They have to carry her to the car, and she sees nothing on the way, till they reach the bridge before her house, when suddenly the bridge and the buildings and streets come alive, the police station on the left, the petrol pump after it, the Chinese restaurant on the corner, the bank, and then the turn that brings her to the street her house is on. The house is overflowing with people and slowly she realizes some of them are coming towards her, holding her, cousins, aunts, uncles. The rest stare at her, in her blue sweater and jeans and winter boots, till she walks through the large rooms and reaches her parents' bedroom where her father has not slept for years. She sees him lying on that bed of pain, with a body half its original broad size, a face of severity and lips pressed together in an expression she knows–being his daughter–means great grief and bitterness.

Later Anjali would know that it was only from now on that forgiveness would become possible, on either side. Only now she would learn the things her father could not teach her when he was alive, just as she could now show him what she thought he needed to know. Now, they would begin again, hesitantly, like strangers, to nourish each other.

The family, in this moment of loss, in the days after the death, begins to welcome Riaz. They bring him clothes appropriate for a son-in-law of the house, a starched kurta with gold buttons, a churidar, a shawl with a paisley border. They put their arms around him, the cousins coming towards him as friends and the elders touching his head in blessing, including her mother. It is a change she has not expected, but how could she forget that this was a land which always overturned expectations? Just as their oppression was unreasonable, so was their full hearted acceptance. Anjali does not know how to question it.

In a crisp new sari, white with a deep red border, she sits once again in a room with a purohit, the flowers, the incense, the cut fruit. She is older now, she has reflected long on these rituals, on these forms of worship, and found them unworthy. But because this is not worship or celebration, she becomes uncertain again. In the new pain of death, it is difficult to be discriminating. If this is another way to touch the contours of her father's death, then she does not want to give it up.

She sits among many things not familiar to her from her childhood. This is a death and not a puja. There is a small bed, plates of cooked food that her father had loved, ilish in mustard paste, prawns in coconut milk. There is of course a photograph of her father, smiling, and she remembers that in it he is smiling at her, on a cruise on the Aegean Sea. There is a dhoti, a chadar, as well as a black umbrella. The purohit, not the one from her childhood but a much older, kinder man, sits next to her and asks her to repeat the shlokas after him. She does so. He asks her at regular intervals to put certain flowers near the photograph, or on the bed, to sprinkle the Ganga water over everything. Anjali remembers her father, performing the shraddha of his father, and asking the purohit the meaning of every single gesture, every single shloka. On the middle finger of each of her hands the purohit has tied a thick bunch of grass. She has to keep them there through the shraddha.

But sitting there, not even really looking at her father's photograph, Anjali feels nothing. The rituals, inexplicable, have no meaning for her. All these objects, the bed, the dhoti, that umbrella, the grass on her fingers, the flowers, seem inescapably lonely, cut from their roots, wherever they are, and they can no longer speak the things that need to be spoken in death, or comfort, or explain, or console.

Anjali asks the purohit only one question.

"Why is the family 'ashaucha' when someone has died?"

The purohit looks at her and smiles, as if pleased that she has asked this question.

"Because the grief of death has taken you away from the Self. After the mourning is over you return to the Self again."

"Why did no one ever tell me this?"

"Perhaps because they did not know."

"But this changes everything for me."

"Good," says the old purohit and smiles again.

On the day of the shraddha, Riaz's mother brings Anjali a loha and puts it on her. Watching it, the women in Anjali's family have tears in their eyes.

"Please come," they say to Riaz's mother, bending their bodies in welcome, and she enters the room and watches Anjali perform the rituals, bending her own body and her sari covered head in the end to receive the Ganga water.

In the temple at Puttur, in Karnataka, among the palm and areca nut trees, the black bodied granite Shiva is deep inside. Two small but long rooms lead to Shiva, two dark, narrow rooms lit by oil lamps hanging on the walls blackened with soot. Because the body must stay where it is, the eye travels inside in one long rush, taking in the trembling lamps along the way, to the innermost chamber. In the day it is relentlessly bright outside and the eye sees the form of Shiva, is that a smile on his face, but not very clearly, in the shaded darkness inside. Evening comes, the oil lamps balance light and darkness, the balance changing all the time as the flames shake, fall, rise. Sometimes a leaping flame lights up more of the dark face, makes fully visible an arm, makes the chest shine. It is again not possible to see clearly the face and form of Shiva. Carvers of stone and wood, makers of temples in the image of the body, lighters of oil lamps, builders of steps and squares of doorway, chisellers of the eyes of Shiva, all knew this. What is necessary is sight, not the reality of complete illumination. What is necessary is the privilege of shadows.

Outside, above the large temple courtyard, there shines the full moon.

So far above the earth, the darkness seemed complete. But when Anjali looked carefully, throwing out her sight as far as it would go, she saw the first star, eye to eye. As her sight opened further she saw behind this first one, numberless stars of different intensities. No less the mystery here, even though things were closer, no more the ability to understand what passes outside. Riaz was asleep next to her, his head on her shoulder.

Many hours later the darkness began to clear, but so slowly, that it took hours to turn into light. When it came, the sunlight was pure and clear and golden. It fell on the rows of people inside the airplane in long, wide, diagonal shafts, setting afire a touch of golden hair, a resting arm, an infant's face in the hollow of his mother's neck.

They were over Chicago, where there had been a great snowstorm, the heaviest one in thirteen years. The airplane circled over the city, waiting to land. Beside her Riaz was waking.

"There's been a snowstorm, we're over O'Hare. The pilot says we have to be in the air for two hours or so. They have to clear the runways."

As an answer he took her hand and kissed it. All these days he had been with her in the greatest quietness, always standing close behind, never too close or too far, with the most precise understanding of distances. A shaft of sunlight fell over their bodies starting at the neck, leaving their faces in the soft, grey light of the shade.

"You're my personal saint," she said.

He shook his head and held her close.

More than two hours went by as the airplane continued its circling.

"Riaz, I want to tell you. About Richard."

"What?"

"That I—"

"I know."

She looked at him.

"It's all right," he said. On his face there was a great tenderness and a shadow of pain together, creating a third thing that brought to his face a look she had never seen before.

"It's not from a lack in our love, not from anything that is less. But if you feel—"

"No. I know what you're saying."

"But if you feel in any way..."

"I don't," he smiled. "I really don't. The only thing I wouldn't want is to lose you."

"That's not even a possibility."

She looked at him, trying to smile, but she could not.

"Who are you?" she said.

He looked at her. There was the touch of a smile on his face.

For a few days, Anjali sat in her house, looking at things. The curve of two quilts on the unmade bed, the angle at which the snow fell, her hands, the fading of daylight. It was a new looking, without any thought, conclusion, or significance, a simple looking that contained nothing beyond itself. Among all these things, one day there was Richard's face.

He came and sat near her on the sofa. There was a great distance between them. This happened to her with Riaz too, if they were seeing each other after a month, or even two weeks. The distance contained the cities one of them had visited, the streets they had driven on, the kinds of trees they had passed. They never came close to each other immediately, it was always slow, hesitant, as if they were in some way beginning anew.

In the fading light Richard sat for some time. Then he reached out and touched her fingertips with his. Not the palms or the fingers, just the fingertips. His hands were much larger than hers and they remained suspended, only the tips of his fingers rested against hers. She looked at the joined fingertips of both their hands like one more thing, without thought.

"I'll get over it," she said.

"You'll never get over it," he said. "You'll never get over it as long as you live."

Fear entered Anjali. Richard watched her. She thought now, for the first time, that she had not felt any unbearable pain after that time at the airport when the fist of death had hit her. It had been easy, this mourning. Then she began to see that the mourning had not yet begun, it was still lying in wait. Outside the light had faded almost into evening. The two of them were shape, curve and fold. She looked up at Richard's face. His eyes had filled.

"You're wiser than your years," she said.

"I've used up my life," he said.

Anjali began everything again, classes, writing, and the everyday work of living. She knew now the mourning was not yet over but she let it be. There was for now, Richard, there was Riaz, and therefore, an amplitude of love.

Although, she never thought of Richard as someone she loved. The word love was only for Riaz. In the myths of love that she had read, that she had heard told, nowhere did they talk of another, a third, even a third who you may not love, but feel close to in spirit, who you may want. Anjali had never thought of this possibility, that there could be another. How could you be prepared for something like this, she thought, when not only these tales but everything else only spoke of what was bordered, definable. You had to grow much older to learn how much of life was lived between the boundaries of two things. She met this new experience with the same quietness and resolve with which she had met other things in her life for which she had been equally unprepared. But there was something in this less clear, of many more dimensions.

You are at a friend's parents' house. She has taken you there to show you where she grew up. It is almost evening and the windows which go all the way up from the floor to the ceiling are the only thing which separate the huge living room from the tall trees outside, turning red and yellow with the fall. The friend has invited you, an Afro-American, another Indian and a Puerto Rican to dinner here. You have all come to honour her wish because you all have a great affection for her honesty and genuineness.

The friend is spinning the lettuce in a lettuce dryer in preparation for the salad.

"What is that?" the Indian man asks.

"It's a lettuce dryer," says the friend.

"Why can't you just wipe the lettuce dry?" he asks.

They both begin to laugh as she keeps on spinning the pale green plastic bowl.

At dinner they all sit at the long dining table, next to a set of the large windows, beyond which the trees grow dark in the fading light. The friend's father, mother and an aunt join them. The father is a tall, large boned man in a shirt and tie.

"Good evening, everyone," he smiles, stressing the word "good."

He sits at the table and says grace. The mother has laid out the food, a salad, roasted Cornish hen, parsley potatoes and bread.

"So, where are you all from?" the father asks, picking up his knife and fork, looking at each of them, in turn.

The friend answers for them. It almost looks arranged, these guests, this dinner, but it is not.

"All here to do college," he says, while slicing up his Cornish hen with a skill that the two Indians and even the Puerto Rican admire.

"Well, my daughter tells me you're all artists, writers, filmmakers, painters. I have to tell you, as I keep telling her, I don't know anything about the arts. I'm a doctor, and it seems to take all my time." He smiles at them over his half-rimmed glasses.

"Now, now, now," his wife says.

"Well, did she take you for a walk around these parts?" he asks. "It's beautiful here you know, in upstate New York."

"Yeah, we did walk around a bit, " the friend says.

"So, how's things down in India? The economy wasn't doing too well last I read about it," the father says.

"Yes..." says the aunt, hesitantly. "There isn't enough food for everybody down there."

You do not wish to say anything. Outside, there is the most beautiful kind of twilight.

"And Puerto Rico, young man. I went down there a couple of years ago, and I must say, I didn't like what I saw. So much poverty."

"Sir," replies the Puerto Rican friend.

There is now only the sound of knives and forks. Everyone eats quietly. The food is passed around, across. You glance at your friend and you see that her pale skin is beginning to be touched with red.

"Do you want to go back home?" the aunt asks you. Her bright pink lipstick matches her dress. Perhaps she addresses only you because you are the only woman amongst the guests.

"Of course," you say.

"Why?" she asks you, putting a slice of bread into her mouth carefully.

"Well…" you begin, putting down your knife and fork, and straightening up. The knife suddenly slides out of the hand of the Puerto Rican friend sitting next to you and drops to the floor.

The friend's mother immediately gets up to bring him another knife. You notice that not much food has been eaten by the guests. You also notice that not a single question has been addressed to the Afro-American man.

"Well, I suppose everyone loves their home," says the father, genially, "no matter what it's like." There seem to be a few murmurs of agreement. You let it go.

Everyone falls silent after that. This is the consequence, you think, of coming to another civilization with empty hands. The friend stops eating, having left most of the food on her plate, and waits for the others to finish. You remember what the friend has told you about her childhood here, about the ivy league schools that are a tradition for both men and women in this family, about her closet stuffed with clothes, about losing herself in the huge woods behind the large house, to find herself.

After dinner, the friends move to the porch, into the largeness of the evening, from where they can reach out and touch the tall trees. They stretch, they talk and laugh. But the friend, who is leaning against the wooden ledge in her delicate, slim boned way, is silent. They let her be and continue their own conversations.

"Listen," she suddenly says, loudly. You all look at her.

"I'm so sorry," she says, her voice dropping as suddenly, and they see her wet eyes.

"There's nothing to be sorry about," someone says. "It's all right."

"Teach me," she says, "how to be so gracious, so generous as you were at that table. I have never seen anything like it."

About a month before the next Christmas, Richard moved into a new apartment. It was on the upper floor of large house owned by an old couple called the Englerts. From the roof of the house flew the American flag. Anjali helped Richard move in, and met the Englerts for the first time. The woman was short and round, with tiny round eyes and a kind face. The man, with a beard and glasses, was tall and handsome. He looked well travelled and sophisticated, although in fact he had rarely stepped out of this town.

At the foot of the stairs in the hallway there was already a huge Christmas tree. There was also a collection of hats, put on the heads of wheat coloured, sharp featured mannequin faces. Hats in different sizes, shapes and colours.

"Are they hats from all over?" Anjali asked.

"Yes, from all over this area," she smiled. "We have more upstairs."

She turned on more lights so that Anjali could see properly. With the lights on she saw something on one side of the tree and went closer to look. It was an almost life sized Santa Claus, sleeping, on a rocking chair.

"He snores," said Mrs. Englert.

"What?"

She went over to Santa and pressed a button. The chair began to rock and Santa began to snore softly.

"My little granddaughter loves him," she said.

After Anjali and Richard had finished moving most of the things upstairs, Mrs. Englert invited them to come and have a cup of coffee. While the coffee brewed, fresh and strong, and Mr Englert talked to Richard, Mrs. Englert showed her two other collections, in the living room and near the large dining table. There were geese made from porcelain, rubber, glass, wood, and always in pairs.

"This region used to be called 'Goosetown', so we decided to collect these," she said.

Near the dining table, on a sideboard, there was her third collection, of tea strainers. Again, in different materials, silver, steel, porcelain, pewter. For this Mrs Englert gave no explanation, and Anjali didn't ask why.

The house was large, seemed lived in for years, and had a warm energy.

They had coffee together and Richard, talking to Mr Englert, seemed unusually without nervousness. When they got up to go upstairs, Mr Englert said to Richard, "Good talking to you and meeting your girlfriend."

"Thank you," said Richard with a smile.

In his apartment, Richard sat in a deep, comfortable armchair. He looked around the room.

"So. Are you my girlfriend?"

The question made Anjali uncomfortable. She didn't like the question.

Richard laughed. "Good folks though, aren't they?"

"Anywhere else," said Anjali, "all those collections would be ugly, impossible to even look at. Here…"

"They're more than just things."

"Even the Santa," she laughed.

"Even the Santa," he said.

"Well, here I am in my new apartment. Hope I can do some writing here."

Richard had put his desk against a window. The window overlooked a large, empty parking lot.

"This place really is a refuge," he said.

"Yes. It's a place where people transform and move on," she said.

"For me it's a question of where to move on," he said.

"I finished reading your new story," he said. "It's excellent. I learned a lot. You need to go back don't you, quite soon, when you've completed your readiness."

"Completed your readiness. What a precise way to put it. You understood," she said.

"Of course. My sight, it goes very far. But I can't always give it form, and that's hard."

"But the work…"

"My insides are not quiet like yours are. No matter what you go through you're quiet somewhere at the centre." He went and sat at the desk, and looked out at the parking lot. There was a sheaf of papers neatly arranged, a holder with sharpened pencils and pens. "And the writing is one more thing where no one can help me. I'm alone, and it must be called up from the depths, like everything else I've learned and come to understand. Who knows whether I'll be able to keep writing."

Anjali was silent.

He turned to her suddenly and smiled.

"You didn't say, oh my god, no you have to, you're so gifted, how can you say that…"

She did not smile in response, she shook her head.

He came over to her sitting on the bed and put his arms around her. He kissed her very gently because he knew she was still thinking about what he had said. When he made love to her it was with the greatest tenderness that she had ever known in him, the way he took her nipples in his mouth, the way he kissed her stomach, the insides of her thighs, the soles of her feet. Her heart twisted, it turned. He stroked her hair, he kissed her eyes. When the evening had turned into night, lying with his head on her shoulder, he said, "My options are everything, or nothing."

It was with Richard, when he read her work, that Anjali learnt the place of the written word, for herself. The things Richard read were things she could never express in speech to anyone, because they would never take the form of speech. She had seen that speech was close to thought, that more often than not you spoke what you knew, but that writing was close to consciousness, vast and in constant movement.

"It's a gift from life," Richard would say. "Keep it safely."

"So should you," she would say.

Richard saw and heard many things in her writing that she could never speak of to him. And she in his. They saw into each other from the most unexpected angles.

She wrote from, not about. She attempted to create a space, a vast space where many things could dwell at the same time, and where each thing could become more than itself. For Richard too, writing was many of these things, but it was not, as for Anjali, a place where everything came and rested, it seemed only a place to stop along the way.

Inside a self there are things far older than memory.

The boatman rowed in absolute silence, passing sometimes banks of the deepest green forest and sometimes nothing but a horizon far away. The only sound you could hear was of the broad, flat, oars parting the waters and the waters closing up again behind them. It passed through sun and shadow, the boat, the burning sun and deep shadows of these parts. The water was colourless, completely clear. You could see the fish swimming beneath the surface, river fish, without the weight of the sea, without the heaviness of salt. There were pale green and light yellow weeds that the fish fed on. Occasionally the boatman rowed past nets in which a crowd of fish were caught, forever.

There were only two places the boatman stopped, at the shore, where he moored his boat, or in the middle of the vast river where he looked at something very far away. When he sat like this he put one hand, usually his left, into the clear water. It was dark brown, and rough from rowing, the fingers pointing in different directions, and it hung so quietly that the fish brushed past it on their way, thinking it was a weed, a softened rock, or some other thing that the river had thrown up to the surface.

When the boatman moored his boat on the shore, he sat there in silence. But when he sat in the middle of the flowing river, he sometimes broke into song. The song had no words, only syllables, long and trailing, sustained for as long as the boatman had his breath. When he sang like this, there seemed to be more fish passing by beneath. The fish were silver, white, greywhite, bluewhite, black, very light browns merged with faint pink. Their shapes were as varied as their colours. At the time of the boatman's song the fish gathered near and passed more carefully by in the water than they otherwise did, their fins and tails moving slower and more attentively in the clear water.

You have never seen a boatman from your ancestral Bengal, ever. Yet this image comes whole, unbidden, to take you, not back, but to the sources of things, and therefore, forward. Only when these images appear are you brought to certain decisions.

"India, what is it like?" is no longer a question which enrages you, with its assurance of every other culture far away, at the edges of the world, and therefore easily summed up. It makes you silent. Since you are yourself moving towards the sources of things, you notice the artifacts of this age, Japanese tea bowls, brass lamps from India, a shawl from the Sioux tribes, sweaters woven on the hills of Peru, sometimes even the food on restaurant tables, food from far away lands placed in careful bowls, under a careful light through which a far away music passes, all these things have been left loose, to fend for themselves, made incapable of commitment, lonely.

"India, what is it like?" You are not old enough to yet be nostalgic, and as for memories, they have not yet acquired a life of their own. When you hear the komal rishabh curving, falling, in Bhairav, a whole sub-continent suddenly opens up, because in your hands and in your ears these things lose their loneliness, they become understood.

All of this happens slowly, after the boatman comes, and you know these are your last months on this continent where you have lived so many years, and learned, and been part of the long lineage of trying to understand a particular kind of bifurcation. *"India, what is it like?"* You know now that you are doomed to comparison, yet privileged, to be able to compare.

In all this there is no sentiment, no romance. You know, because the strength of what you feel has no place in romance and sentiment. Perhaps sentiment is where it begins, but very soon you cross the line of sentiment into real feeling, because it is reality that is your concern.

Anjali needed a new pair of winter boots. Richard came with her to buy them. They looked around together inside the shop. The salesman, a small man with sand coloured hair and a sparse, sand coloured beard, came to help.

"What size?" he asked.

"Definitely the smallest you have," laughed Richard.

The salesman looked at her feet and smiled. "Sure is."

Anjali tried on a black pair, ankle high, lace ups. She walked up and down to make sure they were comfortable.

"Those feet are so small they'd look pretty in anything," the salesman said. He had watery, shining eyes.

"What do you think," Anjali asked Richard.

"I think they're good. But are you comfortable, and are they sturdy enough? You know how you slip easily."

The salesman looked at Richard. "Your wife Sir—"

Richard looked at him.

The salesman repeated very gently, with an almost indulgent smile, "Is she your wife?"

On Richard's face there passed a great tenderness shot through with an even greater vulnerability, and both of these were joined by an oncoming pain. It was the same look she had seen on Riaz's face on the airplane, in reverse.

The look was an answer.

The salesman said, "Oh, your girlfriend then. Your girlfriend–"

Anjali had her left foot in the salesman's hands, and Richard was looking at the boots.

"Your girlfriend," said the salesman, "has such small feet that not many of my sturdier ones will come in her size. But let me go take a look."

He returned after a while to find them sitting very quietly. There was little conversation after that. He didn't have anything else she liked, so she chose the black ones.

"I'll pay for them," said Richard, without meeting the salesman's eyes.

The indulgent, gentle look returned on the salesman's face. He smiled at Richard as he took the money and gave him the bill but Richard was looking away, to the far side of the room.

The past returns in unexpected ways.

You remember a story your grandfather has told you. It is a story about a man from a hundred years ago.

Nabeen Kumar Mukhopadhyay was a man of fifty five. He lived in a small town in Bengal, not very far from Calcutta. Zamindari went back a few generations in his family and even in his own life Nabeenbabu did not have to do much work. Every day, after lunch Nabeenbabu prepared for his daily trip into the town centre. Normally, at this time everyone was asleep, and his wife begged him to lie down and rest. Even though he did this every day of his life his wife thought perhaps one day he would change his mind.

Nabeenbabu was a serious man, and not a man of many words. His wife called the servant. The master was brought his fresh white kurta and dhoti. The kurta was starched and stiff, the dhoti soft and comfortable with a lighter starch. As was the style of those days for any self respecting zamindar, the transparent sleeves of the kurta had been carefully pleated and then released, leaving behind a delicate pattern like the pleats of a Japanese fan. His dhoti too had been pleated in front, the loose end held casually in the left hand. In deep seriousness Nabeenbabu put on his clothes. Shined leather shoes were eased on to his spotless feet, gold buttons in the kurta buttonholes, and he was ready. The last thing was a watch and chain, the watch in the left pocket of his kurta, next to his chest. His wife hands him a shining shell comb. Nabeenbabu combs his hair carefully, then his beard and moustache. His wife looks at him, making sure everything is in place.

Outside the sun is ablaze, and only in the two or three months of mild winter is it a true pleasure to go out at this time. But the story remembers him more in the burning sun when no one else is about. Outside his horse carriage awaits him, the coachman standing attentively, even though he is as drowsy as the flies that hum in the heat. Nabeenbabu climbs in with the help of the coachman and with the pull of the two horses, well groomed, and the rolling of the wheels, they set off. At first the carriage is slow but soon they move faster and faster, the coachman whipping the horses to run, because he knows his master is in a hurry, though he says nothing.

From the outskirts of the town they move towards the centre. The sound of the horse's hooves become clearer as they pass from dirt roads onto paved, cobblestoned streets. They pass by markets where no one is to be seen at this time, and the huge vegetable baskets under the shop awnings are covered with different coloured cloths. Deeper inside the fishsellers are asleep among the blood and fish scales. They pass by the Muslim neighbourhood with its great white mosque in the centre. The horses run faster and faster, Nabeenbabu becoming impatient now, leaning out from under the shadow of the canopy to see how far they have come. Finally they reach the absolute centre of the town, at the foot of the tall stone clocktower, with its elaborate carvings at the top, and a spire, like a church.

Nabeenbabu comes out of his horse carriage and looks up at the huge clock with its deep black hands and beneath it, encased in glass, a large brass pendulum. It is seven minutes to three. He takes out his pocket watch, gold with a gold chain, and waits. After those seven minutes have passed the great pendulum on the tower swings from side to side and rings out three times over the sleeping afternoon town. Each gong is definite and long and merges into the next one. Nabeenbabu matches the time on his watch. It is about a minute slower than the clock on the tower. He adjusts the minute hand and for the first time since he has left home, he smiles. He listens, raising his left ear towards the tower, to the loud, resonant ringing of the bell.

At the ringing of the bell a woman emerges from behind the clocktower. She wears a faded sari that is dirty and torn, her hair is thick and ropelike from not being combed, and her eyes have the look of someone who does not live in a physical reality. She carries a cloth bundle, holding it with both arms against the stomach. She is the madwoman of this town. She lives beneath the tower and when it is very hot or very wet she takes shelter under its one arched alcove. Always, on the hour, she emerges at the sound of the bell and looks up at the great clock. Nabeenbabu never looks at her.

With the smile still on his face, Nabeenbabu gets back into his carriage and rides home. On the entire way back he can be seen smiling to himself and thinking, leaning back against the seats as if without a care in the world. The coachman too, relieved now, is carefree and whips the horses only once or twice, without much force.

The story could have so many meanings, but your grandfather did not specify one over the other. You do not remember why he told you this story. You remember him as a very untroubled man.

Rowena pushed back her large, dark hair and said, "Well, people are talking."

They were sitting at a restaurant, having coffee.

"About what?"

"What do you think? He's great looking too you know."

Anjali is quiet.

"And you are married...."

"You know I don't care about what people say."

"It might begin to get uncomfortable. For you and Riaz."

"Whatever."

"Whatever."

Rowena smiled. "I was only—"

"I know," Anjali reached out and took her hand.

"So, I have a new boyfriend. He's a student of mine."

Anjali smiled.

"You're laughing at me."

"No. It's just that I've lost count."

"Well! I can't help it! The last one was awful, I never even once had an orgasm. What was I supposed to do?"

She took a sip of coffee and shook her beautiful hair.

"Anyway, this guy, he's incredible."

Anjali saw Richard enter the restaurant and look for them. She raised her arm. He came over to them and smiled. He never touched her in front of other people. They got up to go to Rowena's apartment for a drink.

It wasn't quite dark yet. The three of them walked a few blocks till they reached the street that Rowena lived on. As they turned the corner they saw two young men coming from the opposite direction, quite far away. Something in the way they moved and swaggered alerted Anjali and, she could tell, Richard. They were masters of context, of the way bodies moved, theirs and other people's. As the men came closer, Anjali felt anxious. When they were very close Richard suddenly put his arm around her. One of the men bumped violently into Anjali, so hard that she fell onto the ground. They continued walking. After a few steps they stopped and yelled, "Hey, why don't you go back to where you came from, both of you!"

Rowena began to walk towards them.

"What did you say? What the fuck did you say?" she screamed, and ran towards them.

"Rowena, come back," Richard yelled. "There's no point."

The men began to run and soon disappeared down the road. Their large footprints remained on the freshly fallen snow. Anjali was helped up from the ground and though her left arm and shoulder ached where she took the weight of the fall, she seemed to be all right.

In Rowena's living room, evening came, but no one turned on the lights for a long time. The darkness turned into something raw.

Richard became very still. He kept looking at one particular spot on the grey carpet. Rowena was restless. She kept walking up and down the room, past tall, full bookshelves that seemed suddenly without any use or function.

"I've never seen anything like that happen in this town before," Rowena finally said.

"This is America isn't it Rowena, a town in the United States of America? It's going to happen sometime, in some way, on some street exactly like this one," Richard said.

"I guess you're right."

"I should go away," he said. "I should go away to a place where I know when and how to expect this. Where there are no surprises. Where I'm always alert."

Rowena went to Richard, bent down and gathered his head in her arms.

"What's the matter," he said, "you think I'm being cynical?"

He put his arms around Rowena.

"Sometimes," he said with his face in her thick hair, "I don't even feel like a human being."

On the way home, Richard held Anjali close, very close. She felt he was trying to protect not her, but himself, he knew he was the one who needed it more. Before they turned onto her road, he reached down, took the knife out of his socks and flung it away on the snow. At the door he started to say something, then stopped.

"Thank you for your silence," he said.

"This question of who you are, you can come at it from the inside or the outside, depending on which side pushes you far enough," Anjali said.

On the table between Richard and her, a candle was burning with a steady flame.

"I drove in the very remote rural areas of Orissa once," said Anjali. "Through the paddy fields, through hills and valleys, waterfalls, large ponds crowded with lotuses—"

"Lotuses?"

"Yes, why?"

"I've never seen any."

"Driving through these places, we would get down and drink from the waterfalls, bathe in the rivers. We passed by small tribal villages…It began to make me think what it must have been like for people to have been so completely unprotected, to have had very little but nature to rely on. They *needed* to have faith then, and so much surrender. Perhaps only in those circumstances could anyone have made the leap from so much self-interest, from food and shelter and the hope of rain, to something that did not look out but inward. An immense leap, the leap from the Vedas they say, to the *Upanishads*…from ritualism to the Buddha…"

Richard was quiet, looking at Anjali.

"I've never been to a place like the one you just described. The most outside a city I've been is here," he said. "You've seen a lot of beauty in your life. That's important. It's important to have known beauty."

As they talked Anjali noticed a new twitch that had appeared on Richard's face. His lips moved at regular intervals sharply to the left and back again, pushing up even further his high cheekbone, violating the face. It was something he was completely unaware of. Anjali tried to get used to it but it disturbed her, it stayed suspended in the middle of the conversation. They were at a restaurant, for dinner, and suddenly Anjali felt everyone would notice the twitch on Richard's face.

"Are you trying to tell me something?" Richard said.

Anjali closed her eyes. She could still see the flame, burning. "Richard....I'm trying to understand something, first of all for myself."

"I have no distance from my suffering, I'm locked inside it. Is that self interest? I don't know, perhaps it is." said Richard.

He looked around the restaurant as if he needed space, needed to move physically away from the emotions rising inside him.

"Look at them," he said, pointing to a middle aged white couple. "They look so utterly lonely."

Anjali looked at the man and woman, dressed perfectly, eating. Light from the candles on the table fell on the woman's face and the carefully exposed upper part of her breasts, which she held up at a very precise angle. The man was muscular and strong. They did not look at each other even once, or exchange a single word. All their movements were smooth and graceful, the way they raised the food to their mouth, the way they drank their wine from the tall glasses and replaced them on the exact spot from where they had been taken.

"White people are the loneliest people in the world," Richard said, "even when they are together." He raised a candle and held it near Anjali's face, looking at her. "That is *their* suffering."

Anjali could feel the warmth of the candle flame in her eyes. He raised the candle up and around her face. He looked at her. "I love the small, unexpected spots on your skin, this slight darkness under your eyes. Oh, and here's a brown mark near your right ear that I hadn't noticed before. I like these things, imperfections if you like. They let me move closer to you."

He put the candle down.

"Our anguish, mine and of my people, is cried out, cursed, laughed, sung, played, danced. That sets us free. And because we know the contours of our pain it makes us strong, spacious. You need to know the bumps and hills and rivers of your grief. But theirs is so deep inside them that they cannot even reach it, and even deeper inside them are bits of *our* suffering. In such pain there is no strength or sight, only destruction."

"Can I bring you some more wine?" the waiter asked with a smile. He looked at Richard, who examined his wine glass, and when he turned back the waiter kept looking at his face, at the sudden twitch.

"Why not?" Richard said.

"You will one day write a novel with great spaces," Richard said, picking up his nearly empty glass of wine. "Writers can always see far ahead," he smiled, before the twitch overtook him again. "Haven't you noticed how you write something before you understand it, or before it happens? That's much more than foresight. It is sight, only a sight unable to recognize itself immediately."

"Maybe," Anjali said hesitantly.

"And when you write it Anjali, I'll feel I too have written it, because in it you will say things I would have said myself, in a different way. All those unspoken things that must be spoken, but lightly, carefully, like a knot in the air."

"How do you—"

"Know this? It's the sight of a dying man, my love."

At the next table, there was an elderly man, with a young woman. As the waitress stood there taking the orders, the man said to the woman, "I'll treat ya, so eat up, okay, whatever you want."

The woman smiled, and the waitress, with shining white teeth, shining white skin and shining golden hair, said, "Oooooh! Aren't you lucky!" and spun around on her toes and went to get their drinks.

When they went home to Richard's, Anjali noticed that the twitch had stopped. As the days went by she would see it happen only when he was outside his apartment, in restaurants, on the street, in bookstores, talking to people.

Wherever she was during the day and in the evening, at night Anjali returned home to Riaz, her love. Riaz held steady during all this time, immersed in his research, never once questioning her actions. Never even asking, "Where did you go today with Richard?" or "What was it you talked about?" He let Anjali tell him what she had been doing, where she had gone. The few times that the three of them met together, had dinner, Anjali was moved by the way Richard and Riaz behaved with each other, with quietness, respect and dignity.

"It's not possible," her friends would say.

Anjali herself moved between her love for Riaz and her being so drawn to Richard. Riaz was her home, her other self, the man whom she would love all her life. Richard was the world, with its movement. Looking out of the bay windows, she knew that what she felt for Richard did not make anything less true between her and Riaz. But what it showed her was something she had never expected to be shown, the desire in every being to love eternally, to love just one, and its opposite, to want another. Sometimes she wondered, what if her love for Riaz ebbed, what if she were to want to be with Richard more? There was nothing in living that was not possible, because nothing was changeless, and even eternal love needed the presence of its negation.

Were things necessarily clearer because one had lived?

Anjali remembered two self portraits of Rembrandt her father had taken her to see at the National Museum in London. In the younger of the two, Rembrandt was thirty four. He was richly dressed, in a dark velvet frock coat, with fur and gold rising at the collar. His right arm rested confidently on the table next to him, a large velvet frill rising from it. The arm and the shoulders were thrust slightly forward and the posture already began to suggest what the face then confirmed, a clear self assurance, a silent pride. There was a large, soft velvet hat on his head. The hat came down over his left ear, and flared out over the right side of his head, flamboyant in its attitude.

The other portrait was of Rembrandt at sixty three, the year of his death, from almost the same angle. Here he was far more simply dressed in what looked like a deep rust coloured coat or jacket, with plain sleeves and a round, simple neck. He had on a cap fitted very close to the head, without any flourishes. The shoulders were rounded and sloping slightly downward. The arms were not resting on anything here but were close to the body. The hands were clasped together in front. In the body so much had changed. But one was still unprepared for the face. Here, from the cheeks, the broad forehead and the eyes, there rose a great question, the question of existence.

Both she, only eighteen, and her father, fifty-seven, found it equally impossible, even after a long time, to turn away.

Exactly at the time when Anjali beginning to believe this was the way it would always be, though she knew it could not, that she would have Richard, she would have Riaz, and she would have her.

life, joyous, that is, exactly when she tried to turn her back on time, on change, they turned towards her.

Richard and she had been in Richards's apartment, talking, making love. It was late evening, almost night, and Richard said he wanted to go for a drive. It was December and snowing, but Anjali did not say no.

In the car, as his twitch began, Richard said, "Listen, I think I'll be going away for a while."

"Where to?" Anjali asked calmly, although a turmoil began inside.

"I don't know, I guess back to New York."

"For how long?"

"Maybe a few months."

"Why?"

In answer Richard sped up the car suddenly and she lurched forward, hitting her forehead against the window. He drove at great speed down the snow covered streets which had not yet been cleared, and the wheels kept slipping on the road. He kept looking straight ahead.

"Why?" he said, raising his voice above the engine and the screeching wheels. "Have you ever thought about what this is doing to me? How much you're hurting me?"

"I could not hurt you Richard, I could never hurt you."

Richard took the sharpest turn possible. His lips had moved violently up and to the left.

"Do you think it will go on this way forever? That I will continue to love a woman who is someone else's wife?"

"I didn't ever say—"

"I know, you didn't ever say you would leave Riaz, and I would never ask you to. But do you know how hard that is for me? Have you ever thought about that?"

"Can we stop driving, can we just stop here for a moment?"

"No, because I don't want to stop." Anjali knew the car would collide with something very soon, and terror rose inside her.

"So, tell me, what do you think I should do?" he asked.

She was quiet.

"Tell me," he said again, raising his voice higher.

He kept on driving, in his rage, through what seemed like half the streets of this town, the car lurching forward, slipping, sliding, sometimes turning half a circle. Anjali's body began to hurt from the tensed muscles, the anticipation of a terrible accident.

"I want you to stop and let me out," she screamed.

"I don't want to let you out," he said quietly. "I want to drive."

The car was at the beginning of a slope going downwards. It began going down, spun around once, stopped for a moment, slowed down a little and began to rush down again. At the bottom of the slope there were buildings on the right and to the left the river with an iron fencing along it. There was not a single person on the streets on this cold December night, and there was no sound except the harsh, aggressive sound of the car and the running wheels. They came down the slope, veered left, and collided with the fencing by the frozen river.

Anjali opened her door to get out. Richard held her tightly by the arm.

"You're not going anywhere," he shouted.

She somehow broke free of his hand and tried to climb out. He gripped her shoulders with such force that it hurt and dragged her back in. He shut the door and locked it.

"You haven't answered me."

"Richard you knew when—"

"Does knowing always make things easier? Now I just need to go away, and forget about everything, and it'll be all right?"

"I don't know…"

"And what if it's you that I love? Do you see Anjali, how you can hurt someone even when you think you're not, even when you don't mean to, do you see how things are not as neat and perfect in their conclusion as you may want them to be?"

"I never–" she says. It's the first time Richard had ever used the word love.

"Do you?" he shouted.

"I do," she said, looking down at her trembling hands.

She climbed out of the car. The night wind was so cold and sharp that it whipped her hair back and brought tears to her eyes. Her entire body, so taut and tense inside the speeding car, relaxed just a little. She began slowly to walk through the mounting snow, back up the slope.

There was not a single sound. The river was frozen, the streets and sidewalks covered in deep snow, the streetlamps making the snow golden in places. As she walked, her arms and shoulders began to hurt where Richard had pulled her. She left the main avenue and walked down side streets, past houses, some of which had already begun to put up their Christmas lights. Did she always think that once the cause of suffering had been understood one could travel towards a solution? It had been that way when she wanted to marry Riaz, she knew what was right, what she wanted, and she went towards it. But this time?

She walked for a long time. Then she went towards Richard's apartment. Outside she saw the old Chevrolet, beaten up on its left side. He was back. Upstairs, she found the door open. He was sitting at his desk, looking out of the window. He turned around when he heard her. His shirt was crumpled, unbuttoned. There was sweat on his forehead. She sat on the edge of the bed. In the soundless room, on the soundless street, there was complete silence because they did not speak.

After a very long time had passed he came and stood close to her.

"Do you still love me?" he asked.

The second time he had used that word. Anjali was surprised, and had to think for a moment.

"Yes," she said.

"Then everything is all right, isn't it?"

"You're still going away?"

"Yes."

"What about the work?"

"I'm not able to work, you know that."

"But it might be worse if you go away."

"I doubt that."

"Well…are you giving up this place? It'll be hard to find something else as nice when you're back."

"We'll see about that when I'm back. Are you trying to make me stay?"

"No Richard. No," she lied to him for the first time. She couldn't help trying to make him stay.

She stood up and put her head on the bare skin of his chest.

"You trusted me," he said, "you trusted me."

It is a time of transformations.

You are standing on the balcony of your father's house. Across the street in the house that belongs to the neighbours, you see your grandmother framed in one of the windows. Just behind the white wrought iron grill work of the open window she is sitting with her back to the outside. You have not seen her for many years, but you instantly recognize her posture. She sits with her face resting against her right hand, her elbow propped up on a table, and her whole body leans towards the right. She is wearing a white sari with a deep red border, the sari covering the back of her head, but leaving her right arm bare, so that her golden bangles catch the sun. You are surprised to see her, and unbearably happy, this grandmother that you can never think of in English. Your love leaps across the sun filled street. You call out to her and she turns around.

She smiles, a large smile, and her rounded face and plump body lean against the grillwork.

"Why are you there?" you ask her. "Come here, come home."

"Why don't you come here my golden one?" she asks.

"But this is our home, this is where you belong," you tell her.

"All right," she smiles and gets up.

You turn back towards your house and await her. Almost instantly you see her at the other end of the long balcony. But as she comes near you see that she has changed. The person coming towards you is a thin, grey haired, sophisticated woman in a silk sari, with a cardigan on. She walks with great elegance, not moving unevenly from side to side on unsteady feet like your grandmother. You are afraid of this woman, and as she comes closer you begin to despise her. She looks at you sternly, nowhere that incredible, utter indulgence of your grandmother. Her back is straight, her body held in and stiff, nothing like your grandmother's soft, plump amplitude. She goes into the house.

The loss you now feel takes away your breath. It seems like a loss that can never be replenished again, ever. You wish you had gone across the street instead and maybe your grandmother would have been there for you, as she always was till she died. But you did not.

You are out walking in the adult snow now, in the landscape of your maturity, putting one leg surely before the other. When you reach an open white field, you walk through it, winding your way through the tall, dark brown trunks of leafless trees. You marvel at the great, vast beauty of this large skied landscape. There is a great tenderness you also feel towards it, because it has helped you to claim your own images, claim all that emerges from them. A refuge is a space that allows you to look and see. And you have looked, and seen.

What did you think when you arrived here, on this continent? Did you think of staying here forever? No, you did not think so specifically of the future. Only two things were important, the leaving of an oppression that left you free to love, and the education, that object of desire and possibility which has yet to be clearly understood. You, like most others of your kind had come to another civilization with empty hands, from nothing to everything. This change was supposed to make everything possible, but what if your understanding of the possible began to turn, what if the nothing began to fill, and the everything to empty itself?

Things seemed to change not only their form, but also their essence. You learned to honour every landscape. As a result you could no longer believe in that which was "cosmopolitan," in the random assemblage of incredibly separate things, of everyone knowing everything, tasting everything, wearing everything, hearing everything, seeing everything.

You had understood. You had seen the vast divide between the large gestures of freedom in the myths and in the art of your land, and the frequent smallness of real lives. You had understood something about repetition and recurrence and the complicated task of differentiating between the two. You had understood that possibility overtakes reality, you had felt a praise beyond reason. You now knew that only praise could be educated.

You walk in curves on this snow covered field, the way a river travels over a plain. As you walk the sky moves above you, as you walk you wonder where the squirrels go in the winter. You are free now to love this landscape and to leave it.

Richard leaves one early morning before Christmas. She goes with him on the forty-five minute ride to the airport. The sun is beginning to rise. As long as the light is still gentle, things inside Anjali remain contained. As the light grows stronger it opens up every closed space. There are feelings spreading, falling, brimming all over. Some are so small that they get left behind in the fields they pass, perhaps getting buried in the deep snow. Some are so vast and unknown that they will remain with her forever.

Richard holds her hand as they pass white fields and farms, as the tall, slim old man who drives the taxi asks them, "So, you two going away for Christmas?"

"Just me," Richard says. "Going home, to New York. Are you from around here?"

"Yep. Born and raised here."

Here is the deep blue skies they drive under, the vast, vast white fields that they pass, with one or two houses, once in a while, far away. Already distances are entering the space that Richard and Anjali occupy, the distance that he will travel now, the distance that will leave her behind.

He takes her hand close to him and says, "Anjali?

"Yes."

He is quiet.

Then he says, "You know, Riaz may protect you, but he's not your protector."

She looks away from the white fields, towards him. She does not know what he means.

"No one is," he says.

Her arm is stretched as he holds her hand close, and she lets it be that way.

"I don't have an address for you Richard, or even a phone number."

"You won't need it. I'll be back."

"There's where I grew up," says the driver, pointing at the fields on the right. "On that farm right there." They see a farmhouse with a brown roof sitting in the middle of the white fields.

"There was no highway here when I was a child. We used to come right up here and build snowmen on the road," he laughs.

They all look at the house till it passes out of view. Richard looks at her and they know the same thoughts are crossing their minds. How simple, this farmhouse, these deep blue skies, this life here. Without the conflicts of culture, past and present, unnamable relationships, the complicated pain of race, violence, great distances. A cliché, this comparison, but inevitable, born of their helplessness.

"Does your family still live there?" Richard asks.

"My brother does," the driver says.

At the airport the moment she fears draws closer and closer.

Richard stands in the queue.

The fat man in front of him has five heavy bags and takes fifteen minutes to check in.

Finally it is Richard's turn.

He shows his ticket to the young woman at the counter. She looks at him once, then again with desire. Anjali cannot see how he looks at her.

The woman writes something on his ticket.

He checks in his bags.

He turns around and walks towards her.

They are calling the flight.

He holds her very close. Are there no other ways to express except through this gesture, except through the same used up words? When she looks up he is smiling. He kisses her on the forehead, turns around and walks away.

Anjali stands on a strip of her heart. She does not know whether to push the pain back with both hands, or let it enter her completely.

On the way back, she sits up in front, next to the old man who drives the taxi.

"Where you from?" he asks her.

"India."

"Is that somewhere near China? I'm sorry, I've only done high school."

"Quite close," she says.

"I bet you miss home."

Anjali does not reply.

"There's your farm," she says as they pass by it again.

"You remembered it." He smiles. "It's not mine anymore. It belongs to my brother. There was litigation. I lost."

"Oh."

This man has very long, beautiful hands, with blue veins running through them. The hands are perfectly at rest on the wheel.

"It's gonna be a cold Christmas," he says, looking at the road he must have driven on more than half his life. He must know all its bends and turns.

She will wait to see Richard again, when he comes back. Of course, he will never return, but she does not know that. To see into the future you have to be one with life's movement, like a river bed with its river. She doesn't yet have that ability. There are things she sees and things she doesn't.

There are people in your family, old aunts, grandmothers, who believe your skin begins to lighten if you live in the West long enough. Perhaps it is true. You stand on the deck of the boat and look down at your arms, your legs and hands, you find that the loam brown has lost its richness, the earth colour beginning to fade.

From the boat on Lake Michigan, you look at Chicago in the mid afternoon light. All the city's elegant old buildings are hidden by towers of glass and concrete. You are on a tourist boat alone. The wind from the clear blue lake blows your hair back, and narrows your eyes. As the boat leaves the harbour you look out, surrounded by plump women with children, old couples and a few high school students dressed in bright candy colours. The waves splash violently against the boat as the locks open and you glide on to the surface of the lake, a lake as vast as a sea. Standing there, in the bright summer sun, you are a bend, a curve, in history's flow.

You remember that in 1832 Raja Rammohun Roy petitions to allow the unrestricted settlement of Europeans in India. His petition is divided into two sections, "advantages" and "disadvantages". You remember some of the things he says in "advantages".

"— By a free and extensive communication with the various classes of the native inhabitants the European settlers would gradually deliver their minds from the superstitions and prejudices which have subjected the great body of the Indian people to social and domestic inconvenience, and disqualified them from useful exertions.

— The presence, countenance and support of the European settlers would not only afford to the natives protection against the imposition and oppression of their landlords and other superiors, but also against any abuse of power on the part of those in authority.

— The European settlers, from motives of benevolence, public spirit and fellow feeling towards their native neighbours, would establish schools and other seminaries of education for the cultivation of the English language throughout the country, and for the diffusion of a knowledge of European arts and sciences... "

And some of the things in the "disadvantages."

"— The European settlers being a distinctive race, belonging to the class of the rulers of the country, may be apt to assume an ascendancy over the original inhabitants, and aim at enjoying exclusive rights and privileges, to the depression of

the larger but less favoured class; and the former being also of another religion, may be disposed to wound the feelings of the natives, and subject them to humiliations on account of their being a different creed, colour and habits.

— The second probable disadvantage is as follows: the European possesses an undue advantage over the natives, from having readier access to persons in authority, these being their own countrymen, as proved by long experience in numerous instances; therefore a large increase of such a privileged population must subject the natives to many sacrifices from this very circumstance."

Rammohun cautions again allowing the disadvantages to overtake. He suggests some remedies, a chief one among them being that European settlers, for the first twenty years at least, should be from among educated persons of character and capital, since such persons are very seldom, if ever, found guilty of intruding upon the religious or national prejudices of persons of uncultivated minds...

He concludes the petition by saying:

"On mature consideration, therefore, I think I may safely recommend that educated persons of character and capital should now be permitted and encouraged to settle in India, without any restriction of locality or any liability to banishment..."

You admire his attempt at balancing advantages and disadvantages, you understand what he truly wanted to do. You have studied at the college that he helped to establish, writing to Lord Amherst, in the same spirit, in 1823, "...the Sanskrit system of education would be best calculated to keep this country in darkness...But as the *improvement of the native population is the object of the government, it will consequently promote a more liberal and enlightened system of instruction, embracing mathematics and natural philosophy, chemistry and anatomy with other useful sciences which may be accomplished with the sum proposed by employing a few gentleman of talents and learning educated in Europe...In representing this subject to your Lordship I conceive myself discharging a solemn duty which I owe to my countrymen..."*

So, you admire Rammohun, understand his desire for balance, realize the complexity of what he was trying to attempt.

"There is the Water Tower Plaza," says a tour guide through a huge microphone. "It's the tallest residential building in the world." Everyone on the boat looks up at the grey-black building with its head in the sky. "And there, the Prudential Building, the largest insurance building in the world." The sun is the bright sun of an American June and its rays hit the towers of glass and jump right back into the eyes of the people on the boat. From here the city looks uninhabited, inhuman. You turn your back to the skyline and sees boats that are strokes of pure white in the distance.

In 1835, three years after Rammohun Roy's petition, Lord Macaulay is already saying, *"There are triumphs which are followed by no reverse. There is an Empire exempt from all natural causes of decay..."* The desire for balance is countered by sharp turns, reversals and collapses, and astounding leaps of power.

"Ladies and gentleman, there is the McDonalds where I have my hamburger for a dollar," the tour guide says, and everyone laughs. Those who are tourists look up and ahead as the guide speaks and those who are there because it is summer hold out their faces to the sun and breeze. You watch them stand there with the light hearted confidence of people who would always know their place in the world.

In 1842, Michael Madhusudan Dutt writes, *"It is the glorious mission of the Anglo Saxon to renovate, to regenerate, or–in one word, to Christianize the Hindu."* He also writes, *"I say, give me the language–the beautiful language of the Anglo-Saxon!"* In 1865 he writes from France to a friend, *"If there be anyone among us anxious to leave a name behind him, and not pass away into oblivion like a brute, let him devote himself to his mother tongue. That is his legitimate sphere, his proper element. European scholarship is good in as much as it renders us masters of the intellectual resources of the most civilized quarters of the globe; but when we speak to the world, let us speak in our own language...I should scorn the pretensions of that man to be called 'educated' who is not master of his own language."*

In 1940, Rabindranath Tagore, at the age of eighty, writes an essay in Bengali called "Sabhyatar Sankat," or "The Crisis of Civilization." He says, *"I had at one time believed that the springs of civilization would issue out of the heart of Europe. But today, when I am about to leave the world, that faith has gone bankrupt altogether ."*

On this lake, in a light white dress, in a lighter skin, the mystery of the city returns, like it was when you first saw it. It returns because you now know you are leaving these parts of the world. "There, a little to your left is the Standard Oil Building, the tallest oil building in the world..."

The crow stirs with the spring, with the melting of the snow that he can feel and the new blades of grass that he can see pushing through the damp soil. He stretches his wings. All these months in the bitter cold his body has been cramped, curled against the winter. Now, he can fluff up his feathers again, spread his wings. He has barely been out of his nest, except in the afternoons, when it is warmest, to look for food.

In the nest, with nothing else to do, he has been thinking, for months.

When he flies, the thoughts emerge from within him, out into the open sky, to test themselves.

It is late afternoon, the sunlight falling fast. The crow sits on the rim of his nest and stretches his wings, up and backward. He sees down the road the woman who lives in this house returning and in her swiftly moving body too is the new warmth of spring. This woman he knows has an immense capacity for joy, and an equal capacity for pain. He has been sent to protect her and he knows the bends and turns of her life, but he is not always sure what protection means. He knows it does not mean shielding her from pain. He knows he must watch and see, but never come too close. What it does not mean he seems to know, but what it does mean?

The crow spreads his wings and soars out of his small nest. How warm the air is! He comes out of the maple tree, over the woman's house, and is in the clear blue sky above the town. Down below, there are children running, young men and women in large groups walking on newly greened lawns, lovers sitting close. The only kind of people he does not see are old people, only rarely one or two standing at the porches of houses. This is the land of perpetual future, thinks the crow, of that whose consequence is yet to come. He flies over rooftops and trees and cars, over the river, in which bits of ice still float, the drop of blood on his left wing, and the gold in his beak both gleaming in the setting sun. He cries out many times, if only to hear the sound of his own voice which has remained silent for so long.

The sky, the sky once again, the sky his other home. A wind today behind him, pushing at his tail. Every day the wind different, in texture and speed, every day the sky different in its quantity of light, its variety of clouds. He flies higher and higher till the river is a band of brightness, and the trees and grass are only colours. All these months he has thought of distances, dreamed of skies. In the nest, the tree is a canopy above; it is the three large maple leaves hanging on one branch just outside his nest. From here, there is no single tree, there are not even trees, there are only different kinds of green. From a distance things change not only their form but also their essence. He was born with a sense of the near together with a sense of the far, and they have grown in him all his life.

He cries out loudly again, and sees afar other birds circling, some even higher, stretching their large wings. There far away is an eagle golden in the sun. The crow flies and flies, the sun disappears, evening turns into night. The sky is filled with stars and half a moon and their luminousness. Are there birds that can fly that high, that far, to the stars? Down below there is only the faintest of human lights. What does he know of human pain? Not very much, but he is learning, and he has begun to understand. He begins to fly down, leaving the brilliant stars, going towards the gable roofed homes placed neatly on tidy roads, feeling drawn towards all those people below, stirred like him by the coming of spring.

He nears a grove of trees and suddenly hears the most beautiful song. He goes closer and tries to locate where exactly it is coming from, but finds it difficult to tell. He dives into the trees, going from branch to branch, tree to tree, the light in his beak guiding him. He has to find the source of this song, so moving, so enchanting, and he keeps searching. Finally, at almost the other end from where he began, deep in the new leaves, on one of the centremost branches, he sees a nightingale, with its golden brown body, singing its song. The crow is astonished. He has never heard such song before and he listens without stirring. The song emerges from the tiny throat and beak and fills the entire tree and all the trees near it and then the fields and sky beyond. From where does this song come? Before he knows it a great cry of praise emerges from him, his harsh cry, and the little nightingale breaks off its song. It is quiet for a few moments, but then it starts again almost exactly where it had stopped. In the body of the crow is created a new space, for this wondrous song and for the praise it brings along. After a long time the nightingale stops abruptly and looks at him, through the leaves. Perhaps the light in the crow's beak gives him away. The nightingale flies away in one swift upward movement. The crow thinks of his own harsh voice, he thinks of the nightingale's gift, and sees how the gift of another is not easy to accept. As he flies back towards his own maple tree, he looks at the pain that the song has brought him along with the praise, and he is bewildered. He flies over bars and restaurants out of which fall pools of light and from where there is the sound of music and laughter.

It is late at night as the maple tree comes into sight, next to the house with the bay windows and the swing on the porch. He can see the future of this woman, but so what? Things must, for the most part, be lived through, without avoidance. But he wonders, on this starry night after the nightingale's song, if he is protecting this woman, who is it that takes care of him? He does not know.

Although sometimes, when he wakes from sleep, he feels a hand stroking his head. He does not know whether it is a human hand.

He falls asleep as the light from the windows of the house still partly reach his nest. He dreams of the cave, that ancient place, from where he has come. In the dream there are people approaching the cave, coming in, their faces dark because the sunlight is behind them. Inside, they look at the Shiva carved in the wall, touching its corpulent arms, its rounded belly. They walk around, looking even at the bare stone walls, holding their faces up to the sun in the sudden courtyard. Their movements become gradually slower. They stop talking to each other and become quiet. One or two sit on the stone floor, near a puddle, looking down. When they leave, they are putting one foot very slowly ahead of the other, and they go out into the sunlight again with the darkness of the cave on their backs.

Then the animals emerge again, the animals that had hidden in crevices or in puddles, or in the dark corners of the open courtyard. A bat flaps its large black wings and lands near the feet of Shiva, the pigeons flutter up and down looking for food, chameleons dart across the floor, and a rat sits quietly in a corner, looking around. A pale green caterpillar crawls on Shiva's right arm.

The crow sees the people that have left the cave going on to the other caves nearby, caves that have been carved into this hillside hundreds of years ago. There are maybe seven or eight of them, men and women, a very young girl, and a little boy. In one cave they see pillars carved with lovers in different postures. They marvel at the carvings so near the alcove for the deity although the alcove is empty now. At another they see a skeleton Shiva, with a begging bowl, his entire rib cage hard and protruding. In yet another they come upon a whole lake behind, brilliant in the sun. The crow can no longer hear them speak for they have fallen completely silent, but from time to time, he can hear half a syllable escape from one of them, or a short intake of breath, as if speech had been broken down to its smallest elements.

Something moves them to climb up to the ridge above the caves and on to the top of the hills. It is a steep climb, and as the sun sets they discover, up on the ridge, large pools, and small waterfalls fed by the monsoons. Past the pools and waterfalls the rocks give way to a cover of fresh monsoon green, and a surprised shepherd tells them the way to the other side. The sheep, untroubled, continue to graze in the fading light. These are city people, the crow can tell. They are not really walkers, yet they all walk on without a single shred of tiredness. Even the children walk on and the little one walks holding his father's hand. Sometimes they stop but it is not out of tiredness, the crow can tell. He can hear their steady, rhythmic breath. It is out of the need to look around them. He can see everything that passes over their faces, wonder, surprise, wistfulness, history, joy. It brings into his heart an unbearable hope.

When they have crossed the hill and reached the other side, they pass by a little town of mosques and dargahs, where no people are to be seen. The mosques and dargahs are made in brown and black stone, the grass around them springing a lush green and climbing up the ancient walls of these buildings as moss. They sit down here, amidst these silent monuments, leaning against one another, under the monsoon sky of endless movement.

When the crow wakes, he knows he will return soon, to the land from where he has come.

As Anjali began to pack, bringing everything in their apartment out and into packing boxes, a letter arrived from Richard. Inside, on a white sheet of paper, he had written in pencil, "There were three reasons for my leaving. One, because I no longer wanted to hide. No refuge is for ever. Second, I knew I was never going to write again. And third, I realized I was capable of love."

That was all. There was no "Dear so-and-so" or a "love, Richard."

On the top of the envelope there was a return address. She wrote back a reply.

Dear Richard,

I'm going back to India soon. When I'm there I'll send you my address. Will you come visit?

Love, A

A few days later came another letter from Richard. This time inside was a white sheet with only one line on it. "Will I be a nigger there too?"

Anjali sent back a reply.

Dear Richard,
Perhaps.
Love, A

Riaz had not yet finished the research he had recently begun, so it was decided that he would stay on for a few months. When it came time for Anjali to leave, the sharpness of her desire to return wiped away any sense of loss at leaving. It was as if this place had given her whatever it had promised, and so had completed its usefulness. She was also not afraid of the loss that leaving brought about, she had already lost so much more than a place. Anjali, surrounded by friends before she left, took no photographs. It was her friends who kept taking them, anxious to preserve something.

This is how she came to have a picture of herself from those days, taken by her friend, Tomas. It was a black and white photograph, and she was sitting, at home, in the middle of the sofa, with the bay windows directly behind her. The light outside was so strong that nothing could be seen except a large area of brightness. Inside, against this light, Anjali sat on the sofa in a white cotton shirt and a long, cotton skirt, her legs folded underneath her. It must have been summer. She had one arm up on the back of the sofa, the other against her right cheek. She was smiling at the camera and the sunlight outside threw in long, narrow rectangles of light which fell on the dark sofa, and curved up the bottom of her skirt. Next to her was a large black notebook, she couldn't ever remember later whether the pages had been ruled or blank. The notebook's texture had emerged very clearly in the photograph, and both the hard black cover and the white edges of the pages evoked a desire to touch. When she looked at this photograph years later she enjoyed it, thought it well taken, but that was all. She could never, through it, enter either the person she was then, or the time and things she was living through, or a place, a geography. It was only photographs of strangers, of people and places one had never seen that allowed entry, released the imagination, freed the emotions. That picture of three little German girls nearly fifty years ago, all in white dresses, standing in a photographer's studio with white mountains rising in a painted landscape behind them, looking straight into the camera; a dark skinned man with a butterfly net among thick trees, his back to the camera, only the face turned around in surprise; a woman in a burkha holding a child with a defiant expression on her face, behind her endless rocks and above her a wide sunny sky; all from years ago, why did they move the watcher so?

Years later she would be back here to visit and the friends who would come with her would go methodically to every place they remembered and see how things had changed. They went to disappeared restaurants, renovated buildings, the emptied mall in the centre of town, the houses they had lived in. Walking in the knee deep snow of a future Christmas, Anjali would not take a single picture. She would walk around more lightly than her companions, less anxious, less disturbed, because her memories were to her more real than these streets so many years later. The buildings and parks and restaurants meant very little to her. What the visit taught her was how memory has no need of a physical reality. The things that live inside cannot be nourished or destroyed by the reality outside, because these things have no correspondence with the external world, they cannot be compared, they are not related, this inside and outside.

On the flight back Anjali is weightless, her entire being turned forward with hope, with the keenest kind of expectation. Landing, late in the evening, the lights below are dim, much less bright than the cities she has come from, dim like she remembers it, the darkness thick. When she finally arrives at the house she gets out of the car and looks at it. There it is, long, with its long balconies below and above, the windows of every room along them placed at regular intervals. From the upper balcony aunts and uncles can be seen leaning out, having heard the car arrive, exactly like they used to, and Anjali smiles. She walks up the stairs at the head of which her mother is waiting along with everyone else. She looks widowed and thin. The house is filled with uncles, aunts, cousins, and everyone talks at the same time, sentences are left incomplete, there is laughter and mock anger and screams of surprise. For dinner there is Anjali's favourite food. The servants bring in bowls and trays, serving her with special care. The food is perfectly made, as she remembers it, but before she can say so, her mother asks, trying to sound casual, "Is the food all right, do you like it?"

"It's excellent," Anjali smiles.

After everyone has left her mother says, "How I've waited for you."

She is still astonishingly beautiful in her widowhood and in her growing grief, which seems to be taking on always newer and newer dimensions. The statement is made out of this grief and a new accusation. Before Anjali can respond she gets up and disappears inside the house. Anjali finds her and sees her finishing the day's rituals. Of course, she thinks, how could she have forgotten. Her mother never stops the rituals for anything, joy or catastrophe, and certainly not for a daughter's homecoming.

Change comes here only when the outside forces it, through death, illness, a new born baby, natural disasters. It appears never to come from the insides of those who live in her father's house, either her mother or the servants. She goes up to the terrace and looks out onto the roofs of endless houses whose insides are very much like this one. At the ledge of the terrace she startles two crows sitting quietly and they fly away to the mango tree next to the house and disappear among the leaves. As she continues to look at the quiet roofs and buildings she knows that coming back is only the beginning of a long, difficult work, of reconstructing, of going beyond, behind and before what shows itself in front of her. This house, where she has grown up is no longer her home. When she thinks of home now, she thinks of a larger geography, perhaps stretching till the edges of this land on all sides, and an even larger time, going far beyond and back from her own life, both in a sense more abstract, but to her completely real and filled with life. That is the home to which she has returned.

Anjali goes to sleep in her father's study, on the single bed that is still there.

"The study," says her mother, "is slowly being eaten up by termites. Only that room, perhaps because I hardly open it. I'm having the room treated. Why do you want to sleep there?" she asks.

The room smells of chemicals, moth balls, and of the old books and papers that have never been cleared out. On the walls there are thin lines of brown, where the chemicals have been carelessly applied to kill the endless termites. The books and papers are covered with dust. Inside the wooden cupboard which does not seem to close properly, her father's shirts and jackets still hang, the upper parts dusty and grey. They could have been better preserved or given away, but her mother is incapable of doing either.

Anjali lies down on the bed and closes her eyes. It is late now and she is tired. Through the windows that she has opened comes a smell of smoke and chapatis being made. It mixes with the pungent smell of queen of the night. Further away she can hear an old Hindi film song. Its particular tone of melancholy desire and a centre of terrible emptiness does not seem to have changed over the years into any genuine grief. Someone is having a conversation across balconies or between balcony and street. Anjali lies there, held in a cradle of sounds and smells that are deeply familiar. These will now be her life and at the same time instruments of her sight. She feels taken care of by them, indulged, and not even her mother can disturb the joy that she now feels at beginning anew from the old. She falls asleep very soon, in the middle of that texturous familiarity.

In the middle of the night Anjali is woken up by the barking of street dogs. She gets up and sees under the streetlamp many dogs fighting and barking at each other. She counts the dogs, there are seven. She turns away from the window and sits on the bed quietly. The dogs continue fighting. Anjali opens her door and walks out of the room. Right next to the study is the puja room, closed at this time, where her mother now prays, but where her grandmother used to sit and do her puja, morning and evening. Anjali remembers her with closed eyes, praying, and sometimes falling asleep as she did so. She remembers her sometimes cleaning all the little statues of the gods and some photographs, carefully with a damp cloth. Anjali used to sit at the threshold sometimes and her grandmother would give her a round, sweet batasa to eat, her grandmother of love.

Walking on in the middle of the night Anjali comes upon the semi-circular balcony, the wide ledge of which is filled with plants rising from a bed of soil and next to it the streetlamp, so close it can be touched. The plants are thick and lush, the air warm and damp, and she can see the sky is overcast with clouds. She walks down the long, inside corridor and comes to the large living room whose glass doors are locked at night. Anjali presses her face against the glass, and can see very little but the shapes of the old furniture and bits of the brass and silver shining a little in the darkness. At the far end of the house her mother sleeps in her bedroom, her lips tightly shut, and part of the anchal of her crumpled sari held tightly in her left hand. Anjali goes back to the study.

There, turning on the single lamp, she begins looking through her father's books and papers. There are yellowed newspapers, magazines, files of bills and accounts, travel brochures, mainly for the Far East. Her fingers full of dust, she comes across a long, slim diary, its colour a dark red brown, filled with tiny holes, the edges of it crumbling. When she opens it she sees her father's small, scrupulous handwriting, in which he had been doing his accounts. There is page after page of calculations and billing. After looking through many such pages Anjali is about to close the diary when suddenly on one page she sees what looks like a poem. When she looks more closely she sees what the lines say:

> *"Do not go gentle into that good night,*
> *Old age should burn and rave at close of day;*
> *Rage, rage against the dying of the light.*
>
> *Though wise men at their end know dark is right,*
> *Because their words had forked no lightning they*
> *Do not go gentle into that good night."*

The rest of the page is blank. On the next page, he had written one line,

> *"Another ten years. Only. If."*

Anjali turns off the single lamp. She sits on the bed, and for the first time since his death, she weeps.

She weeps without hope, without reasoning, without avoidance, without even the possibility of consolation, without turning away even a single feeling, with the knowledge of such complete loss as she has never known before, and perhaps will never know again.

Only when the weeping has completely emptied her does she

slowly begin to fall asleep. Before sleep comes to her fully she sees that returning home is as much an unknown as going away, because you cannot possibly know what lies in wait, even though streets and buildings and seasons remain the same.

The crow wakes to a warm summer dawn. Amazing, the ability of each morning to renew, to start everything afresh. He spreads his feathers, warms them in the new sunlight. When sleep has left his eyes he gazes as far as he can see. He stretches his wings, tests his muscles, becomes sure of himself. Then, without too much waiting, he leaves the nest which has been his home for so long and flies up into the clear summer sky. Over the houses in which people are still to awaken, over the winding river and the evergreen cedar trees, the crow flies up and up.

This time, on his journey in reverse, the crow is not afraid. He lets his thoughts wander, lets them come and go and disappear. Already he has seen the woman's life after she returns. He has seen her love, her insight, he has also seen an aloneness filled with blood and broken things. The task is to help her emerge, on the other side. The crow wonders how it is that he can see her life so clearly and not his own. He is amazed by the ability of every being to give another what it does not itself possess.

This time the much warmer winds caress his body and fill it with joy. From time to time he passes a large city, with tall towers and lights below. Otherwise, there are the fields of green and the trees of summer, and bodies of water with memories of ice. When he begins to fly over the first ocean he smiles. What was once a surprise and a wonder is now a companion. The waves, the ships, the fish, all seem correct. The damp winds of the ocean nourish his feathers. Day turns into night. For the first time the crow notices night's timelessness. In the dark there is no sense of time passing, everything is even, everything is one.

The air is becoming even warmer now, almost hot, the air of the tropics, an air he knows so well. Time returns to the sky slowly, returns with the coming of light which can always be identified, sourced, mapped. The light reveals a rugged landscape, trees of mango, and peepul and gulmohur, it reveals the hundreds of caves with dark, cool insides. The crow descends now, slowly, but not directly, he descends circling the caves and the trees, feeling the hot sun on his feathers, his alert eyes absorbing the old light, the old colours, the old shapes but experiencing them as new. Knowledge, the crow sees, is an abstraction, what you distil, something taken from life's movement. This is why it is good only for the moment, and the moment not very long. He does not know why, but this seeing brings him a sense of great lightness, although a lightness born from great loss. He goes further down, till he can see the curled edges of the mango leaves, the gulmohur petals fallen on the ground, the dark brown tamarind fruits hanging from the tamarind tree. He continues to fly at this height, where he can see everything clearly but touch nothing. When you go far, the crow thinks, you understand many things, when you come close you understand other ones. For a little while longer he will remain like this, suspended, not yet part of the landscape.

TWO

She stands with a veena in her arms. Three deer, two on one side, one on the other, look up at her face.

Beyond her is a pale, green landscape, very pale, with a few small bushes and even smaller undulations. There are no trees, no flowers, and the grass is sparse. Above all this is a pale sky, perhaps of first light.

Her lahenga is the same pale green as the landscape behind her. But on her lahenga there are flowers, diminutive flowers, not too many, not too few. The eye moves from the flowers to the landscape, wishing to bring some to the bareness outside. From the landscape, the eye moves back to the lahenga, wishing to bring the land's vastness to the flowers.

The landscape and the flowers, they desire each other. This desire keeps them in movement, going towards, coming back. The point of meeting, of that who can speak? Each time the possibilities change.

What can be whole only within itself?

Everything is broken somewhere, deeply, violently, and through this place of brokenness it leaves itself.

It lets itself be entered.

"It's not so easy to sit at the loom when you're pregnant," Gauri says. "My back hurts terribly," she smiles.

"Take a small break," Anjali says.

"I'm already behind, I should have finished much more by now. He'll come for all the saris by the end of the month."

In a small village in Bengal, Gauri weaves tangail saris. Anjali has found her on her travels through these parts.

The sari she is weaving is red and white, the same red as the coral bangles she wears on her arms, the same red as the sindoor in the parting of her hair. On both sides of the white sari there is a border of this red, about two inches wide, and above it tiny red triangles, placed very close together. Anjali has seen this pattern ever since she was born. She has seen her grandmother wear it and then her mother.

Gauri is a small woman, young, and looks even smaller at the large wooden loom. She is slim, but now, in the sixth month of her pregnancy her stomach is becoming rounded out. Her face is delicate, the bones prominent. Under her bright eyes there are two or three slim folds of skin that give her face an unexpected vulnerability. She is wearing a light yellow sari, with rust coloured stripes on it, faded now.

"I had better check the rice," Gauri says, and gets up.

In the kitchen the rice is cooking in a huge aluminium vessel, an imitation of a traditional curved shape, with a very wide bottom, the rest of it gradually narrowing as it goes up. The vessel is bent and dented. Gauri lifts the lid and checks the rice by taking out a few grains and pressing them with her fingers, like Anjali's grandmother used to. She lifts the pot off the coal fire.

"It's done," she tells her old mother-in-law, who is sitting in a corner. The kitchen is a tiny room whose walls are completely black with soot, though all the pots and pans are shining clean. The mother-in-law is wearing a plain sari which was once white. In all these villages Anjali has never seen anyone wearing a fresh white sari or dhoti, anywhere. The only bright white is the sari that Gauri is weaving on her loom, which will be taken to the city and sold.

"You can eat now," Gauri says, serving the old woman her lunch on a large aluminium plate.

Anjali steps out of the small house with its two tiny rooms and a kitchen, made of brick and covered with a corrugated tin roof. In front of the house is a tiny patch of mud and weeds. Across this is the weaving shed. She stands outside and sees Gauri's two children, a boy of three and a girl of seven, playing. She has been back in this country for a few years now and spent much time travelling, going to villages for the first time, to small towns, crossing the landscape back and forth by train, things she had never done before she left.

As soon as the children see Anjali they run up to her, their little brown bodies bare except for the faded underwear they both wear, made from the same printed cloth. On their chests and back there are tiny boils from months of endless perspiration.

"Didi," the children cry, happy to see her. The boy runs little circles around her. The girl stands and stares at Anjali. She examines at leisure Anjali's light blue kurta and churidar with its delicate chikan work.

"Didi," she asks, "why do you dress like a man?"

Anjali laughs. "Well…because it's…convenient. I can run in this, and jump and do all kinds of things."

"You can do that in a sari too, my mother does it all the time."

"True, my little one."

Gauri's husband is a fisherman and he sells fish in a market far away. Gauri says it is a three hour walk. She has lived here ever since she was married eight years ago.

"Will you eat?" Gauri comes out and asks her.
"I'm not hungry yet," Anjali says.
"All right, let's go to the loom then."

The weaving shed is a room with brick walls and a roof of corrugated tin. There is one small opening, high enough for a man to go through. It is dark inside, all shadow and no light, and the heat is stifling. Sweat pours from the skin, endlessly. Anjali keeps wiping her face, and even her head is wet with perspiration. Gauri sits at the loom, bent over, and Anjali sits behind her, on the floor. Gauri's blouse is stuck to her back, completely wet. At the loom, while she continues her work and the loom makes its regular wooden sounds, Gauri says, "You are very beautiful. How are city women so beautiful? Look at me, old and in my rotting sari." There is no heaviness in her words. Her coral and conch shell bangles, a pair on each arm, hit against each other constantly as she works, making tiny sounds under the large sounds of the loom. Suddenly she turns around and smiles. The folds under her eyes look even more prominent.

"Anyway, you have your life, and I have mine."

"It's a gift, an ability to create this, an art," Anjali says.
For a long time there is silence. Anjali looks at Gauri's back.
"Are you trying to make me feel better?"
"Do you think I am?"
For a moment Gauri takes her hands away from the loom. She puts them on her lap, but they become uncomfortable there, and restless, as though not used to being idle even for a moment.

"I don't know about art, about gift. I learnt this from my mother and it's something I do, that's all, and it earns me some money and it keeps me from being even poorer. I haven't met too many people from the city. But there are two kinds. The ones who just want the work by giving you as little possible, or the ones who talk about art and craft and greatness. But you know what it is for me? A place to think."

"What do you think about?"

"Is it so easy to talk about where the mind travels?"

Anjali smiles. She gets up and goes towards the opening of the shed to get some air. But outside the air is thick with moisture and without movement. Against the brick wall of the weaving room there is a broken plastic bucket, a broom, and two rags sitting in the weeds. A small papaya tree hangs over them.

Anjali walks back in and stands at the loom. Gauri is beginning something new on the fabric. She is in the middle of the white cotton cloth now, beginning something with red.

"What is that?"

"This? A buti, I'm doing the butis now. Small flowers."

"How much do they give you for each sari?"

"One hundred. It will be sold in the market for about five hundred."

"And if a sari has butis you get extra?"

"No."

Anjali is amazed.

"Why do you do it then? It's so much more work!"

"For the beauty, I do it for the beauty."

On the white, half of a red petal has been formed.

They eat lunch sitting in the kitchen. On Anjali's tin plate there is rice, dal, and two kinds of vegetable, and a pabda fish cooked in mustard paste. She looks over at Gauri's plate and sees only rice and dal.

"Gauri, no, I'm not going to eat this if that's all you're going to eat." Anjali takes out some vegetables and some rice and tries to put it on Gauri's plate. But Gauri will not listen. She pushes Anjali's hand away.

"You're pregnant," Anjali says.

"Please. You don't know how much it means to me," she says.

"All right then, at least half the fish. Which side do you like, the head side or the tail side?" Gauri does not answer and Anjali decides to give Gauri the tail side which has more flesh on it. She puts it on Gauri's plate.

Gauri begins to weep, very silently. She eats the fish first of all, before the dal and rice. She does not stop weeping as she takes the bits of flesh off from the central bone. When she sucks the tail for any remaining flesh, it is without the pleasure it is meant to give, she does it mechanically, and in the same way she sucks the central bone and then chews it. She brings up the end of her sari and wipes her eyes.

Anjali cannot understand. She keeps looking at Gauri, but Gauri does not look at her. Anjali begins to eat. She eats till every single morsel of food on her plate is finished, though she is not very hungry. When her plate is empty, she hears Gauri say, "A little more rice and dal?"

Anjali shakes her head. She looks up and their eyes meet. Her eyes filled with tears, Gauri takes both their plates, washes them and stands them up to dry.

When she finishes, her eyes dry now, Gauri says, "Didi, you lie down for a while and when you've rested I will take you to see something."

It is late afternoon when they start out.

"Where are we going?"

"You'll see," Gauri smiles.

Sweat streams down their backs and down their legs. Gauri sometimes stops and puts her hand on the small of her back.

"Does it hurt?" Anjali asks.

"A little."

They reach a place filled with large ponds, banyan and mango trees on their banks. When they get very close Anjali sees, under the bright blue sky, on the clear water of the ponds rise hundreds of red lotuses, a thick blood red, lit up by the late afternoon sun. She stands still, breathless. She has seen the red lotus long ago, in her childhood, and then only one or two. They had been brought for a special puja. Here they sit on the waters of these ponds, so many of them. Anjali and Gauri walk on a thin embankment between two ponds, balancing themselves by holding out their arms, like children. Anjali sees that the red of the lotus is the same red as the border of the sari Gauri is weaving. The flowers rise just above the water, protected by their large green leaves.

"Do you know how the lotus flower became red?" Gauri asks.

"No."

They find a square of embankment at the corner of one pond. Gauri makes herself comfortable on the hardened earth of the embankment, folding her legs on her right side, supporting herself by resting her left hand on the earth.

Anjali puts her legs into the shallow water. Beneath her feet she can feel loose, flowing mud, and weeds cling to her toes. She reaches out and touches a lotus, the flower as soft as human skin.

"One day," says Gauri, "the sky darkened suddenly at noon. It was the colour of an eclipse sky, the same silver grey colour, although the sun was still whole somewhere behind it. Then there came dark clouds, almost black, and among them one blood red cloud, larger than all the others, throwing a dark red shadow on the earth. The cloud was made of the blood that gets spilt here from our wounds, from childbirth, from slaughter, from war. It became darker and darker red, and then it began to rain down on the earth in large drops. When it fell it was red only on the lotus flowers. Everywhere else, it became clear and transparent like water. Only a flower can take blood and turn it into beauty for its life is not so very long, only as long as it's blooming. So the rain of blood spared everything else, human beings first of all because we can never forget. Nothing is forever gone with us. It spared the birds which began to shriek when the sky darkened unexpectedly, for birds must live much longer than flowers, and the trees which must live much, much longer than birds. And do you know why the lotus, of all flowers, could absorb this rain of blood? It is the flower that has been since the beginning of time, on the dark waters, before the world began. After all it could take the weight of a god and not break. Look."

What appears on Gauri's face is a ferocity that Anjali has not seen before.

"Do you see the colour of the red? It is the colour of being awake."

Anjali has been in this little village for a few weeks. One afternoon as she walks on the soft mud road, past ponds filled with the water hyacinth, it begins to rain lightly. On the road, under the trees, are fallen gulmohur petals, making the ground orange, and further on little fruits of jamun which have fallen in the rain, some completely crushed, staining the ground purple with its flesh and juice. *A few feet away from their window was the boundary wall of the house,* and on the other side of the wall began a vast jungle of weeds. Sitting at the window, what meets the eyes are the crowns of wild trees forming waves in a green sea, myriad creepers hanging from the trees, where the top of the bamboo trees have bent over with age covering the shondali and bonchalta trees and the yellow wildflowers, under that on the dark soil dances the wagtail. Beneath the large trees, the holud, bonkochu and kotuol plants are pushing desperately through the deep green jungle to catch the light of the sun; in this struggle for life, the plant that is not strong and capable and has been overshadowed by its more powerful, arrogant neighbour, the leaves of that plant are pale and lifeless, the stalks jaundiced and dying—before this death struck gaze there is the shining sunlight of winter's end filling the forest, the world wrapped in the tender smell of wildflowers is disappearing slowly with all its beauty, mystery and vastness.

This forest near their house reaches till the field of a big house on one end, on the other it stretches unbroken till the river. For Apu this forest is endless, he has wandered very far in this forest with his sister, he has never seen its end—only paths under tittiraj trees, and the heavy, swollen chalta fruit hanging everywhere, swaying the gulancha creepers near it. A narrow path runs till the mango grove, then begins again after it under this tree and that, through flowers and creepers and mynah thickets, and comes out who knows where, and in what direction, to a place where there are only wild creepers swaying in the air and parasite plants climbing onto the moss covered branches of ancient raintrees.

This forest has touched his heart and his sister's with its deep green newness. Since they were born they have been deeply familiar with this forest, every second, every moment, with a quiet joy it fills their eager hearts with so many different, so many wonderful *emotions. On top of the bushes made green and strong by the rain there are the yellow stamens of fragrant wildflowers, in the falling light and gathering shadows of the coming sunset the squirrel goes lazily back and forth over the thorn tree's branches, the profusion of leaves and flowers and fruits, above everything when on the farthest bent branch of this thick forest an unknown bird sits alone, then he cannot describe the various, mystery filled, deep joys of his heart to anyone. It is as if a dream, Maya, the birds sing all around, flowers drop from trees, the light of sunset becomes even more filled with dark shadows.** Apu, who had seen so little of the world, and she who has seen so much of it, how are they the same?

That afternoon a few village people walk by with baskets on their heads, going to market or returning. Rain drips from banyan and gulmohur trees. A young woman sits under one of them and strings small garlands of yellow wildflowers. Among these people, suddenly she sees a man, taller than the others, walking in her direction. When he comes closer and they are about to cross each other, she sees that it is her father. He is wearing a long, black cashmere overcoat, one that he wore when he was alive and had to go to a cold country.

He has not seen her and is about to pass her by when she runs up to him. When he sees her a smile of incredulous surprise appears on his face. They embrace each other. It is long, endless this embrace, as endless as the reality of their separation, and Anjali loses herself in it, all her joy, all her sorrow lost, till there is nothing left, yet a nothing protected by his incredibly tender alertness.

"I was looking for you," he says.

---

*   From *Pather Panchali*, by Bibhutibhushan Bandopadhyay

"You...were looking..."

"Why should you be surprised my golden one?"

Then, very quietly, looking at his fingers and lining up the tips as he always used to, he says, "I thought you might need me."

Anjali is surprised but she does not ask why. She only wants to hold him and hold him and hold him. She reaches up and kisses his face, wet with the rain falling on it, but the skin firm like she has always known it. He looks very well, not at all older, and his large black eyes, the same eyes as hers, shine as they look at Anjali.

"You are all right aren't you?" he asks. "You're happy?"

"Yes," she says. "Yes. Let's sit somewhere."

They begin walking. He looks down at her as they walk, watches her for a while.

"Your body has changed, the way it moves, the way it holds itself. Confident," he says.

"Perhaps."

"I like it."

They come to a thatch roofed shelter by a pond. Inside the shelter is a rough wooden bench. They sit down. Her father takes off his overcoat, and Anjali sees he is wearing a shirt and trousers of almost the same dark colour as the coat. The shirt is long sleeved, buttoned at the collar, with a pocket on the left side of his chest, the trousers slightly loose, a little pleated at the waist and turned up at the ankles, like they wore them in her father's days. Anjali does not ask him why he is wearing an overcoat in this weather. She doesn't know why but she is afraid of the answer.

"You should have a child," he says, smiling.

"There's nothing like that," she says, "*should* have..."

"There is, something like that..." he says, stroking her head. "Can you forgive me?"

Anjali cannot speak, so she bends her head just the slightest bit, instead of saying, "I've already forgiven you, a long, long time ago."

He looks at her, opening his eyes completely, the same way in which he had looked at her many years ago when he had turned away from her. This time the look is in reverse, and everything that he had taken away and more is now being returned to her with an energy she has never felt before from anyone. Anjali holds the edge of the bench so as not to be pushed back by its tremendous force.

Though the sky outside is overcast, the pond before them shines in the little light there is in the sky. The pond is overflowing and as they watch it they see a small silver fish jump out of the water and back again.

"You know, when I was very small, I used to go fishing in ponds like this one."

"I remember you telling me about it," she says. Another fish jumps out of the water and in, followed by two more. Then one. Then three, all from different places, in different directions. They watch the fish, almost indulgently.

"Parshey," he says.

"Why did you never take me to the villages, to the countryside?"

He takes his time to answer.

"I suppose I didn't think it was necessary."

"But it's such a large part of this land."

"It was the past for me. It was where I played and fished and ate fruit from the trees, but after that it was past. I never wanted to come back again. I'm surprised to find you here."

"It was necessary for me to come."

"I always thought that what was necessary was to take you

outward, to show you the world. And you, you always wanted to see it."

"Yes. I did. Why did you never want to come back to these parts?"

"It had nothing left to give. Are you not more my golden one, are you not so much more because of what you have seen and how far you have travelled and how much you know?"

"I'm not sure."

Her father reaches out and takes Anjali's hand in his.

"How is your mother?"

Anjali shakes her head.

His face darkens and she feels she should tell him it's all right but he begins to speak.

"There will come a time," he says. "There will come a time when…the flow of your life will be impeded. There will be causes for some of the impediments, the welling up of your own mistakes, your own inabilities, and of those close to you. There will be other impediments which appear to have no causes at all but must be lived all the same. There will be effects which will outlast their cause. Do not be afraid. Accept the impediments, for they will come to stay a long time."

A single drop of rain falls through a hole somewhere in the thatch.

"Why do they have to stay a long time?"

"They have to. For years. What passes by too fast cannot leave anything behind. You will be filled with residues, with debris. Your breath will change its course." He strokes her head slowly, and closes his eyes. "Inaction prevented me. From becoming an individual, becoming myself. And when the resistances came I was unable to let them speak, completely. Perhaps I was slow and life went by too fast." There is no regret in his face, no disturbance.

Anjali listens to him carefully.

"And I will be there always to look after you. As you can see I am healthy and well," he says with a smile. "But you, my golden one, are already more than I could ever have been."

Anjali is amazed. How can she be more than what protects her? "I…"

"Ideas have few contradictions, emotions have many," he says.

The fish continue to come out of the water and make arcs in the air. The rain falls harder.

"I never thought I would be able to live without you," she says.

"I never thought I would be able to live without you either," he replies.

It is so silent that they can hear each other breathe.

Anjali turns to her father. She puts her head on his shoulder and begins to weep, to cry all the grief she has amassed in her life and not been able to live or abandon, even the grief he himself had brought her, like a little girl she weeps, because he will always hold her, protect her, and it is only with him that she has ever been and always can be a child. Her father is silent as she weeps, and undisturbed. As she weeps she notices the dark cloth of the shirt under her face changing colour. She raises her head, thinking it must be her tears. But the entire shirt is slowly becoming lighter, turning from a charcoal grey into a dark blue, then to a blue of the sky. She looks down and sees the fabric of his trousers also changing. She sits up and looks at him. Now the blue becomes lighter and lighter, the sky colour leaking out till finally the shirt and trousers are a glowing white.

He pushes her hair back from her forehead and cheeks, hair sticking to her damp skin.

"It's all right," he says. "It's all right. Remember, when your reality is unbearable or insufficient there are other worlds, other images. The universe is very, very vast." His white clothes shine in the silver monsoon light that falls inside the shelter.

"Don't ever go," she says.

"Now that, my little one, would not be real in any world." He smiles tenderly, indulgently, like father to daughter, like a person of greater knowledge to a genuine beginner.

"Tell me, now that you have seen so much world, what is it that you would like to do?"

"I'm writing. I'm going to be a writer."

"Stories?"

"Yes."

A look appears on his face of great fulfilment and pride, with regard to himself and her, and as if the difference between them mattered very little.

"My only child, a writer...I used to love literature too, but I loved cinema even more. If I wasn't an engineer, perhaps I could have made films...Bergman, I loved Bergman."

A middle aged village man walks in and, seeing them, sits down on the damp ground. With him he has a large basket filled with spinach.

"Do you remember which ones?"

"The Virgin Spring...the Seventh Seal...those were my favourites."

"Those are the only two I haven't seen."

The village man watches them talk. He is square faced and thin, with a dirty white vest and a dhoti of a similar colour. He sits with one leg folded down on the floor, the other leg folded up, with an arm resting on it. The man watches them with his large, dark eyes,

eyes which so closely resemble hers and her father's, without even a hint of self consciousness. His mouth is slightly open, revealing the ends of teeth that are sharp, uneven and stained with paan. He watches them with an amazed curiosity merged with complete resignation as if they are people very close to him and at the same time very far away. It makes her uncomfortable but her father doesn't seem to notice. He is looking at the rain and the jumping fish.

"Did you ever really love my mother?" Anjali asks.

He is quiet for a very long time, so long that she thinks he will not answer.

"I don't know, yet." He is lost in thought.

She looks at him. She cannot take her eyes away from his face. The glowing white clothes throw onto his face a new kind of light.

The village man has made several bundles from the spinach, tying every bundle with a tiny, thin rope. He holds up one and asks, "Like to buy a few? They're fresh, I picked them this morning."

"I thought spinach was a winter vegetable," her father says.

"Used to be," the villager says, almost authoritatively. "Nowadays, Babu, everything grows in every season, everywhere."

"We live far away," says Anjali, "that spinach will wilt by the time we get home."

"How far is far? I'll pack it so that it stays fresh, I promise. Only two rupees a bundle."

"No," says Anjali, "another time maybe."

"All right," he says with resignation, and goes back to making his bundles.

Anjali begins to feel sleepy, not out of tiredness but as if something is lulling her to sleep. She feels her father's hand on her back.

"Come, lie down with your head on my lap and try to sleep. Everything will be all right when you wake up."

"That's exactly what you used to say to me when I was a child," she smiles.

"Did I?" he says, surprised.

She falls slowly asleep, looking at the diminutive points of light that the natural little holes in the thatch let in. She hears the rain falling. Perhaps she sleeps for a long time, she doesn't know. When she wakes her head is not on her father's lap but on the wooden bench. She sits up and sees her father is not there. Next to her she sees his glasses, the frame a dark brown tortoise shell, the glass thick. He was not wearing them when they were together. She picks them up, surprised, and they are heavy as a block of stone. The spinach seller, who has been dozing quietly in a corner, wakes and sees the glasses in her hand.

"Did he leave them behind?" he asks.

"Yes."

"Give them to me."

Anjali hands them over to him slowly because they are so heavy, but as soon as the man takes them she can tell they become light, because he opens them with a casual flick of the wrist and puts them on.

"Will he be needing them?"

Anjali shakes her head.

"I'll keep them then," he says, "I can't see too well anymore."

Anjali leaves him looking around the hut in his new glasses and walks out under the twilight sky and sees no one anywhere. After a long time there comes an old woman in a white sari walking through the large puddles, her anchal held over her head.

Anjali has been back in this country for a few years now, and she has been travelling. She has gone from place to place and there is much that she has found. Now she knows that entire countrysides have lain dormant inside her, together with ancient tales and ways of being. *Apu comes often here to the riverbank to sit under a large chatim tree and fish. He loves this place, so solitary, so many kinds of trees bending over the river water on both sides, on the other bank a thick forest of reeds, kadam and silk cotton trees with creepers hanging from their branches, bushes filled with purple wildflowers, in the distance the bamboo grove of Madhabpur village, the call of birds, the shadows of the forest, the green of the reeds, all merge and blend together to create a quiet solitude.*

Since he had first come here to these fields in his childhood he has been enchanted with this field, forest and river. As soon as he sits under the shade of the chatim tree and casts his line in the water and looks around him, his heart fills with wonder. Whether the fish come or not, when the deepening shadows of late afternoon are filled with the smell of ripe dates from the date palm grove, on the cool wind comes the call of the papiah and the nightingale, the sungod spreads a sky red from branch to branch and slips behind the banyan tree at the edge of the fields, the river water darkens, the hornbills call out on their way back to their nests, that is when he feels overwhelmed, he looks around at everything with wonder in his eyes... Her travels have brought closer the thing inside and the thing outside, to her the most necessary of all encounters.

On the train back to the other coast Anjali looks out of the windows from morning to sundown. The journey begins with the green, thick vegetation of the eastern coast, with its banana, date palm, coconut and mango trees, its houses on the banks of brimming ponds. She has been back in this country for a few years, she has been on this journey many times before, and she can anticipate what she will see on the ride. And she will see those things but they will never repeat themselves, they will recur. The landscape and everything in it, will unfold like a tale from the myths of this land, always known but each time differently told, different in its details, depending upon the teller.

These are the things she always sees.

The ruins of a large, ornate building, with arches and domes, perhaps a modest palace or a humble fort. Small white temples with conical roofs, not even large enough for a man to enter through its doorway. Equally white mosques, much larger, but always silent, never a namaz going on. Rivers that have now run dry or changed their course, rivers that are now beds of yellow sand. A bullock cart moving on a dirt road with a man and a woman sitting in it, and the road curving away into a thick grove of trees. Where are they going? Do they love each other? As they near a city, rows of small one or two roomed houses, next to open drains clogged with garbage, and children standing looking at the train passing by. Then again, after the city is left far behind, perhaps an ancient stone bridge with large arches below, rooted deep in the ground. Far away, blue hills, with a single house at the highest point. Who lives there? What do they do? A huge river with simple blue boats carefully moored at the shore but not a single person anywhere in sight. In the middle of a landscape, suddenly, a half constructed house, with empty spaces in the brick walls for doors and windows, but no ceiling and through the empty windows some hills passing by on the other side. Nothing anywhere near, no village, not even a settlement. Who builds these houses in the middle of emptiness and then abandons them half done? A goat running away, frightened. A few minutes later a shepherd, with a gaze that looks not at the train but through it to somewhere beyond. From all these things that recur there emerges a great sense of survival, resilience, life. There also emerges a curious melancholy, a weight, or is it inside her, born of a very old civilization. Sometimes this melancholy hangs from the branches of passing trees and springs up in the paddy fields. Does it come from a changelessness, from a need for the new that has never been understood or fulfilled? Whatever it may be, all these things in the landscape are intimate, close, for Anjali, and vast only in a way that the known can be vast. You can only take further what you know, she thinks, what you, in some way, love.

Anjali goes to sleep that night on the upper berth. She falls asleep almost immediately wrapped in a sheet and a blanket to protect her from the severe air-conditioning. In the middle of the night she is awakened by something. She is so deep in sleep that at first she does not realize what it is. She opens her eyes and sees that her sheet and blanket have been thrown off, and there is a hand on her right hip, moving swiftly, and with a violent roughness into the place between her thighs. She jumps up and all she can see in the darkness is a man's figure disappearing. By the time she arranges her clothes again, jumps down and looks around, there is no one anywhere to be seen. In anger, victimized, and most of all, violated, she walks up and down the long, dark compartment. There are only sleeping bodies wrapped in sheets and blankets. No one to accuse or punish, no one to even suspect. She looks for the train attendant just outside and finds him snoring loudly. Not a single person seems to be awake except a young man leaning his head on a window pane and sobbing softly. Anjali stands looking at him for a few moments and then returns to her berth. She gets up again and goes to the bathroom to wipe her entire body with a wetted towel. She returns and sits up. Who could it have been? She has spoken to no one on this ride, lost in her thoughts. She has not even met anyone's eyes, except those of the woman on the berth opposite her. She stays awake for the rest of the night, struggling with her feelings. Outside, the passing landscape is a complete darkness unrelieved by even the faintest light. It is difficult to even see that there is a landscape. At dawn the sky reappears, a misty white and blue. Then a little later, the land shows itself, a darkened green, sometimes interrupted by dark water. Anjali falls asleep slowly, exhausted.

When she gets up the train is passing over a river of clear emerald through which she can see rocks and stones and mud. Where the river meets the shore is a place of great tenderness. Here the soft muddy sand, light brown, is ridged and wrinkled, like human skin. In this world a riverbank can have the colour and texture of skin, a river the colour of a stone, and a sky where the river ends can be the colour of fire. Slowly, the night falls away from her as she watches. There is a praise, she thinks, a praise which can cross the idea of balance, of the good and bad always carefully weighed against one another.

Anjali returns from her journey to the place where she and Riaz now live. The apartment is old, but with large, bright rooms. Towards the left the road slopes up and there is a large house, at least a hundred years old, made of stone and wood. No one can ever be seen there, but as soon as evening comes someone inside turns on a light. The light falls on one of the stained glass windows, always the same one. The window has a geometrical pattern, with a long, dark yellow oval in the centre, and two dark green triangles on either side, bordered by a row of small yellow squares on the top and bottom of the triangles. When they look at the house from across the street in the darkness of evening, this window with its muted stained glass light makes them quiet. Next to it there is a small white church, standing at the top of the slope. People come regularly for the services, a few early in the morning, many more in the evening, and most on Sundays. Anjali watches how they climb up the slope and then the steps to the door of the church, passing by the small stone grotto with the figure of Mary in it, some touching the lower part of the grotto as they go by, in the way people touch the steps of a temple. After the service, when they walk down, their bodies seem lighter. Is it just the downward slope, or has something been released? Sometimes in the evening the grotto of Mary is lit by candles that burn late into the night.

The road leading to the church, the old house, and the building in which they live, is lined by trees of gulmohur, mango, coconut and tamarind. To the right of their building are other tall apartments, but they are further away. What is close are a few vacant lots in which grass and weeds grow wild. Nearby, there is the ocean, which cannot be seen from here but always felt, in its breeze, its dampness, its salt smell.

Some astonishing fate always brings them to living places of great beauty and quietness. Here, when they come out of their bedroom in the morning, two sparrows fly and chirp in the living room, and often a pigeon sits on the inside ledge of the window. Perhaps it's the quietness that brings them in and makes them lose their sense of inside and outside. The koel calls, not only in the spring, but all year round. Bright green parrots dart out in pairs from the trees. Pale yellow butterflies hover in the air.

In the kitchen, there is Chacha, Riaz's old family cook who has been sent here to be with them. He lives with his son, who works in this city, and comes here every morning by eight. Chacha is almost seventy, thin, with a white beard and white cap. No one can slice onions like him. He holds the onions in his left palm and sends the knife through it, parallel to the floor. The knife rests against his thumb, which he has tied with cloth, while going through the onion. The slices that emerge are the lightest and finest possible. "Like air," says Chacha. He cooks with one pointed attention, starting with the spices which he grinds on the stone, the meat which he selects carefully at the market. Chacha says he has cooked for the nawabs of Lucknow. He mutters to himself as he cooks and whenever he sees either of them, a smile spreads over his face. "Bismillah," he says when taking the lid off the meat he has cooked. The kitchen gleams in the morning with the shine of bell metal, copper and brass. Riaz and Anjali have bought plates, glasses, bowls, pots and pans with care, from their makers, from a long tradition. The man at the bell metal shop tells them that very few things are being made now from this metal, and soon he will have to close down the shop.

"I will be all right, I have some money, I just wonder what will happen to those who make these things, so beautifully, how will they survive?"

Anjali uses the small inheritance her father has left her to travel and to write. Her life in the house is very quiet, full of watching, the outside, and herself. She sees how vast the self is. So vast that it is capable of including the trees, the birds and the sky, not only in their large gestures, but in their infinite details. How each tree moves in the wind differently, depending upon the shape and size of its leaves and branches, the length of birdcalls and how some rise up and some fall downwards. And of course, this outside in turn includes her. There is not that much she knows, but what she knows is what she can look into clearly and far, trees, skies, people.

She also knows that she needs beauty around her. She does not know whether that means it would be hard for her to live with ugliness.

It is always a joy for her to be with Riaz again when she's back. They talk late into the night and she tells him about Gauri, the weaving, the villages. When they make love she is moved by the familiarity of his body. She is moved by the great spaces in what is already known. She wonders sometimes if everything she is doing, her calmness and joy, have Riaz as their hidden anchor. It comes as a question and passes by, because till it is tested there can be no real answer.

Where Anjali lives she is often awakened while it is still dark, by the azan from somewhere nearby. In a strong voice the azan comes, with its long, stretched syllables rising upwards, travelling through the dawn. She does not really understand the meaning of the words, but she understands the cadences, the upward rising, the slow falling, the longing which goes far beyond words. A little later the church bell rings with its deep resonant sound and almost immediately after she can hear hymns being sung, softly.

"Lord make me a channel of your peace
Where there is hatred let me sow your love..."

Out on the street there are temples she passes, large and small, with bells for the puja ringing inside, or a chant going on. She passes also small alcoves where a Devi sits, with oil lamps and flowers at her feet. Often, in the twilight, the lamps and the flowers move her, especially the lamps. She does not participate in any of these things. None of it has to do with her any more, but she finds their presence near her, their existence, absolutely necessary.

In the temple of Shiva at Puttur in Karnataka, Anjali watches the flames in the oil lamps rise and fall, each time revealing aspects of the black bodied Shiva. The temple priest comes by and offers her some prasad. Her body knows exactly what to do, how to behave, remembers even things she had thought she had forgotten. But something else has happened. When she walks around the temple she sees the amazing sculptures, the incredible pillars, each one different, she sees the brilliant beauty of thousand oil lamps, the idol carved by a master's hand. She has become now a watcher, receiving everything through the eyes and ears, keenly, but the body no longer bends without thought, without reason, naturally.

Why does she need these things around her? Is it their beauty, their detailed, careful aesthetics from another time? Is it the need for differences to live, together, for the world to not become singular, for it to keep offering its varied realities? Or is it the need for the existence of belief, in whatever form, close to oneself?

Anjali meets someone who has a different answer for this.

It is only when the man asks, "Are you married?" that Anjali begins to lose her ease in talking to him.

"Yes," she says.

"How many years?"

She doesn't feel like replying.

"How many years?" he asks again, a little more loudly, perhaps thinking she hasn't heard him over the loud sound of the autorickshaw's engine.

"A few," she says.

It is very dark outside. Many of the street lights don't seem to work in this part of the city. She keeps looking at the back of the driver, straight and not even a little bit bent, in a white shirt, but how much can a back reveal?

Late at night, nearing midnight perhaps, she has hailed this autorickshaw at a local station. She has about a twenty minute ride to where she is going.

"Will you go to Palm Gardens?"

He had nodded his head.

When she got in he asked, "Which way do you want me to take? The long way under the bridge, which is a better road, or the short way through the milk colony, which is full of potholes?"

"The better road."

Anjali leans back. A golden disc hangs near the front window, with the name of Allah written on it. A few minutes into the ride the man says, "Tired? Looks like you've had a rushed day."

"I have," Anjali says, surprised.

"That's how this city is, finishes you off completely. I've been all over. Bangalore, Delhi, Madras. But this is the mother of all cities. It can raise you up and throw you down all in the space of a few months."

They go past large warehouses with corrugated tin roofs, innumerable shops crammed together, all closed at this time of night, buildings being constructed with piles of metal and concrete near them, where sometimes a solitary worker is still doing something under a very bright light.

"You're from Bengal, aren't you?"

"How could you tell?"

"The way you look, the way you speak. I lived there for a long time. In the old days you could always tell where a woman was from by the way she dressed, now that's not so easy."

He swerves the auto so suddenly that she falls forward.

"What happened?"

"Huge pothole. I used to love going to the Durga Pujas over there. So many lights, so much celebration, so much joy. And the rhythm of the dhaks."

Anjali is surprised but she doesn't remark on it.

"Yes, it's a happy time," she says.

"You don't say it like it means anything to you."

"You're very, very perceptive."

"Don't believe?"

"I...I don't know."

"You do know, but it's too complicated to discuss?"

Anjali laughs. "Well, I don't feel close to pujas, to rituals."

"Or feel close to religion as it is usually practiced, or even the idea of God. I understand. What you have is a different kind of belief."

"Well...yes, perhaps."

"But I want to ask you something. Don't you think that we need at least a few things outside ourselves that are symbols of the soul's aspiration, of something beyond ourselves? Otherwise, everything would have to be held inside our bodies."

They are passing by a huge cattle shed filled with buffaloes. Then a large, dirty pond.

"And if there were no rituals, nothing outside ourselves, then great compassion and understanding would have to take its place."

They are both silent for some time and there is only the sound of the autorickshaw.

"I loved those pujas. I used to watch the rituals carefully, they were so different. I'm a Muslim."

"Yes, that's why I was surprised when you spoke of the Durga Pujas."

"I wasn't the only one. There were plenty of other Muslims, Christians too. There's a small church near where I live. I often go and sit inside it. I think the songs they sing are beautiful, even though I don't understand the words."

They are going through a rather lonely stretch of road. It is then that he asks her if he is married. Then he asks her is she has children. He asks her if her husband is her age or older than her. She looks out to see if they are coming the right way. It seems to be taking a little longer than usual.

Anjali is quiet. She no longer feels like carrying on the conversation.

"Did I tire you?" he asks, almost tenderly, like a man to a woman. It makes Anjali uneasy.

"No," she says, in a voice she knows is very final.

He does not say anything else.

They reach Palm Gardens sooner than she had expected. They stop in front of the tall, white building she is going to and Anjali steps out and opens her bag for the money.

"You misunderstood me," he says, very quietly, but very firmly. "I have a wife at home, whom I love, and two young children. I was just enjoying talking to you that's all."

Anjali suddenly realizes she hasn't seen his face. When she got in, as happened very often with autos and cabs, she only saw the face quickly, in passing. And it had been so dark that she had hardly seen this man's face at all. Just as she realizes this, he turns around.

He is a man of about thirty five. He has thick eyebrows over large eyes, a long, high nose, a thick moustache over full lips. On the left side of his face, from chin to forehead runs a thick scar.

"I started talking to you because there was something in your voice, the way you said, 'Will you go to Palm Gardens,' that moved me. Not just the respect with which you said it, that is rare enough, but something else, which I can't so easily name."

Anjali is completely taken aback.

"I don't want your money. Keep it."

"Please," she holds out the notes. "You brought me a long way."

"You heard me, didn't you?"

She wants to say she's sorry. Instead she says, "What happened? To your face?"

"I would have liked to tell you. But now, you'll never know." He drives off before she can say anything else, with a loud autorickshaw sound, which now sounds like anger.

What Anjali sees first is only the dark. Slowly from this darkness emerges the stone walls and the stone floor with sudden curves and undulations that the eyes cannot see but the feet can feel. Only the entrance is a space of brilliant light. She moves forward. Near the entrance the sunlight falls inside in one large uneven patch and two long rectangles of unequal length. The light illuminates the undulations in the stone floor and the large round craters created by who knows what corrosions. This cave at Ellora is large and empty, its walls bare. It opens at one end to a courtyard, and at the other end to a small opening leading to steps. She walks to the steps and sees that they go down a steep drop to a small lake, shining in the bright light. Deep inside the cave, far from all three openings, the light is unsure, sometimes showing itself tenuously, sometimes collapsing into darkness.

Suddenly, with that abrupt change of sky that only occurs in the monsoons, the brightness outside is wiped away and the rain begins to fall, heavy and fast. It is only then that her eyes move to the courtyard and stay there, watching the rain fall into it. She walks towards this unexpected opening in the cave. Standing before it she watches the sudden rain fall and splash over ancient stone. As she looks around she notices something on the wall adjacent to the courtyard. In this changed light, more slow, more hesitant, there emerge two large stone feet with anklets on them, above them the legs, the right one bent with the knee pushing outwards, the left also bent at the knee, but straighter, the knee pushing out only slightly. At the thighs the light begins to fall away even more and everything above that is only darkly lit. Anjali has to go very close to discern the rest of the body, and the face. It is Shiva, enormous on the wall, a corpulent Shiva, unlike any she has seen before. Shiva is always broad shouldered, the torso narrowing from the shoulders to the waist, the stomach smooth and taut. Never like this, with heavy, fat arms and a swelling torso, round, swelling thighs and calves. It is a simple Shiva, not carefully adorned like many of the ones in the other caves. The simplicity leads the eye to what the body is made of, to the texture of the stone, grey brown, with little holes in it. The holes make the stone vulnerable. Anjali sits before Shiva, on the stone floor which was burning hot outside but here is almost cold. For once she wants to touch the life that the stone has created, perhaps for the first time in a life where deities could only be seen through the eyes. Here there is no one, and this is not a temple. She touches the bent knee of Shiva's right leg. It is cold and rough to the touch. She moves her hand down the leg to the protrusion of the anklet with its round stone beads, to the foot. She touches the five toes, separately, and then the sole. And the sole is the smoothest of all to the touch. She keeps her palm there, caressing the sole.

Does something happen when she touches? This is not a god for her, the touching not a ritual but a personal gesture. Is it then a coming closer for her to history, these caves, these sculptures wrought so gracefully from stone? No. What she has entered here and what she touches is a space before history was invented, and which has always been there, waiting, revealing itself only to those who do not use history to navigate the past. If Shiva is not a god for her, neither is he only a shape in stone, a sculpture. For her a god has always been remote, untouchable, and a sculpture too ordinary, carelessly accessible. No this Shiva is neither god nor sculpture, neither remote nor ordinary. All that she has heard and read and seen of Shiva returns lightly, to surround her. So does something happen when she touches? Yes, and it flows from the sole of Shiva's foot to Anjali's hand as from blood to blood and leaves nothing behind as evidence.

What happens outside is the beating of wings and she turns to see a bird disappearing towards the steps and the lake. She had thought the cave was as silent as this Shiva. Now she can sense underneath the silence a life that is only holding itself back and will emerge as soon her presence no longer prevents it. So that is what the smell is here. Nesting birds, ancient stone, dampness, bits of sunlight, moss, bird droppings, insects, and perhaps even wild animals that rest here for the night. To her it is the smell of time, not history, but time, and are these not all the life that time includes?

Perhaps it is fortunate that these caves are not preserved the way ancient monuments should be, and the passing of centuries can still be felt in the craters and the cracks, the holes in the stone, the faces of eroded, unrestored sculptures. It is perhaps fortunate that few people come here. She has seen only five or six people in the main cave, far from here, people looking for something to do with their holiday, people throwing their chocolate wrappers and drink bottles wherever they want, people wanting to leave a mark on the caves rather than be marked by them in any way.

She leaves the cave of the corpulent Shiva, knowing this is only her first time here. Outside the rain is now a drizzle but without a break, and the sky dark with clouds. Anjali walks in the rain and sees cave after cave on her left, carved out of the gigantic hillsides. Here the caves are Hindu, behind her the Jain caves, and much further ahead to where she can't yet see, are the Buddhist ones. The rocks and stones are wet and shining in the rain, the hillside blooming with fresh grass, little waterfalls everywhere rushing down to form brimming pools in countless craters and crevices. Every cave is set back into the flank of the hills and beyond them it is a climb up to the top of the hillside. Anjali walks up a small path between two caves. There are countless birds in the trees all around, making their different sounds which stand out from the steady drizzle of rain. When Anjali has almost reached the top and can see the sky spreading out above her she slips on a very wet rock, and begins to fall. She falls all the way down the slope, tearing the skin of her hands on the bushes and thorns she tries to grasp but cannot, face down on the wet soil she keeps on falling, the taste of damp soil inside her mouth, till she reaches the road, her face and hands bruised and bleeding, her body afraid.

An old man comes to help her as she tries to get up, stunned by the fall and bruised, but otherwise unharmed. He is wearing a small dhoti and a turban, and has a sickle in his hand. He puts the sickle down, takes off his turban and wipes Anjali's face with it carefully and then her arms and hands. Bunching up the cloth he stops the blood from her many wounds. Carefully he takes out a large thorn from her upper arm. The cloth of his turban smells of damp earth.

Neither of them speak. After he is finished he says, "Be careful, little mother, all alone."

"Thank you," she says.

He looks puzzled.

He takes a large mango that he had wrapped in the upper part of his dhoti, slices it with three sure strokes of his sickle into three equal pieces and gives her two. She eats the mango, which is sweet and overripe and pungent. Before she finishes, the man is already on his way, his thin shoulders sloping downward, and the sickle dangling from his right hand. As he walks the sickle swings back and forth, sometimes catching the monsoon light.

Durga emerges from the gathered shadows at the end of a long corridor of carved arches. Going closer over the uneven floor with its countless holes and craters, Anjali stands before Durga in her manifestation as Mahisasuramardini. Durga stands with her body bent to the right, in her right hand a long spear piercing, bloodlessly, the back of the mahisasura below her. Her right foot is firmly on the back of the demon, a little away from where the spear enters. Her left hand is on the upraised mouth of the demon, as if holding it closed. The mahisasura is illuminated completely by the sun. Above it hangs Durga's waistband, curving in a half circle. The light becomes fainter as it moves up over her wide pelvis, her full round breasts, her neck, and dies away almost completely on her face. Often in these caves, it is the face which is the least illuminated, the sun not finding its way from the entrance all the way in and up to the height of the head. The darkness on Durga's face is broken only by her smile, which has constantly to be found. It is sometimes there, sometimes not. While watching, Anjali feels in turn something watching her. Among Durga's other weapons and the smaller figures that surround her there is a small white owl, sitting near the hind legs of the demon, watching her. As she watches it, the owl flies up and positions itself on the hand of Durga that holds the piercing spear and begins to stare at Anjali again.

So this is the Durga, the Mahisasuramardini of her childhood, changed here in these caves, or changed perhaps by Anjali's own new sight.

From where Anjali stands, directly before the image, Durga has a stance that seems fixed, settled. But when Anjali moves to the right of the image and looks at it from the side, things change. From here Durga seems so much more in an action, thrusting in the spear, pressing down her left hand on the demon's mouth. Even the smile seems more alive, with its own life, perhaps even indifferent to the watcher. Only the hand on the demon's mouth seems the same from whichever angle one looks at it. That hand, though it grips so firmly, and grips a demon, that hand seems filled with affection. This hand of affection and the smile on the face speak to one another. Here, in these empty, ancient caves, without the endless rituals, it is possible to receive these images. Here, the craft and intention of the makers leads to a very vast consequence.

Days and days spent in these caves, spreading out one after another beneath the large hillside. There are numberless Durgas like this one, with a different look on the face, a new stance of the body, yet so much the same. Countless Shivas, Vishnus, Buddhas. And yet never repetition, only recurrence. In the same cave perhaps, Shiva dancing and Shiva as Kala the skeleton. Visnu blessing or killing the demon Hiranyakasipu. Is there everything here? Killing, lovemaking, dancing, dying? These caves that make stone speak as much as it can possibly speak, are like the hillside from which they were wrought, as natural and gracious and without denial as the trees, the waterfalls, the rain, the moving sky, and almost as necessary.

There is birth everywhere in this season. In her rooms large black ants are born from a white nest that looks made of froth, thousands of them. Anjali has to wait for them to leave before she can enter again. Outside, she sees small new snakes moving among the grasses. At a large pond there are enormous lime green frogs croaking under the monsoon sky. Everywhere wetness, birdsong and renewal. Walking up on another day to the top of the hillside, Anjali sees again the village man she had met after her fall. He has climbed up a coconut tree and with one sharp movement of his sickle he cuts off a large coconut frond. He slides swiftly down the straight trunk, puts the frond on his head and walks away, his sickle swinging from his hand.

Anjali reaches the top and looks around. At first there are only rocks, made darker by the rain, almost black, and amidst these dark rocks everywhere little flowing streams of the brightest, uninterrupted white, waterfalls like milk dropping from one level to another in thick white foam and ponds of craters filled with silver water. There is one tree, just one, springing up from these rocks, with a small silver pond next to it on which the tree can meet its own dark reflection. Climbing even higher she finds a flat expanse of the softest, newest grass. The valley falls away from these hills with its small white houses, its many trees. A shepherd walks by with his flock of sheep, silently, looking at her. Underneath her are the caves, stretching as far as her eye can see, from the Jaina caves to her right, the Hindu caves in the middle to the Buddhist caves at the other end. Time also stretches here, unbroken, from the days when they began building the first caves, in the sixth century, till this moment of her present. Inside the caves time speaks not only in the numberless holes and craters and undulations, it also speaks in the often eroded bodies in a broken arm, a chipped foot. Most of all it speaks in the often eroded faces where the nose is broken, the eyes destroyed, but nevertheless the tendency of the face is still retained–a specific strength, or stillness–like an endlessly resonant overtone.

Standing at one end of a cave, the face at the other end is never visible clearly. In the merging of light and shadow, what shows itself from a distance is the primary gesture of an image. Shiva dances often here in Lalitha. In one particular cave he dances with his left shoulder raised high, his left arm coming across his body and pointing downward towards the right. Always these gestures, these profound curvings and leanings of the body in one direction, the bending of the head, the suspending of an arm in the air, the legs and feet bent or crossed in a stance or dance.

Anjali remembers Rilke's words:

> "Weren't you astonished by the caution of human gestures
> on Attic gravestones? Wasn't love and departure
> placed so gently on shoulders that it seemed to be made
> of a different substance than in our world? Remember the hands,
> how weightlessly they rest, though there is power in the torsos.
> These self-mastered figures know: 'We can go this far,
> this is ours, to touch one another this lightly; the gods
> can press down harder upon us. But that is the god's affair.'"

Here, in these caves, no caution, no restraint. These gestures, throwing themselves out, expressing things not expressible in any other way. Every gesture profoundly human but perhaps forgotten or ignored in living.

Days spent walking in and through these caves, standing still, sitting on a step or the stone floor, looking with much more than the eyes, feeling with much more than the body. The first experience is of brilliant light at the threshold, and then an immediate darkness, both completely the opposite of each other yet both stopping the sight. Then the emptiness of the caves and the volume of the images, the heaviness of the image and the lightness of its gestures, the profound movement in the body and the absolute stillness on the face. And for Anjali the existence of the present and the past. But in these caves it becomes clear that opposites are only a way for the mind to grasp the fact that everything exists, at the same time. It is now that Anjali feels that the past is never gone and over, it is something that is always living, something that can bring things of great use and great solace to her at this very moment. What is the past really? It is the deep shadows that move in the wake of the light, it is the half expressed part of the present. Even though the past has already committed itself, it is full of doubt, and hesitation and tremulousness. It may be that these caves, these images, need her as much as she needs them.

The day she is leaving she goes to the cave of the corpulent Shiva one last time. This is one of the least ornate caves, she likes its simplicity and its great empty spaces, she likes the courtyard that lets in the light, the birds and the rain. She stands before the Shiva today, without touching it. There is bright light outside and many more parts of Shiva's body and face are illuminated. Every day is different here. The courtyard today is a well of light. Next to the courtyard in one corner there is a very black crow eating some grain. This time she feels no need to touch. Sometimes the eyes are enough. She has already claimed these images, these caves, as her own, she has claimed what they have given her, not a way, but ways of being, more multiple, more perilously poised and more divergent than she has ever known.

As she is leaving and begins to walk towards the entrance she sees at the threshold, exactly where the light and darkness meet, a boy, standing there looking at her. The brilliant light behind him leaves him completely in darkness, so all Anjali can see is a shape. She sees the thin boy, sees most of all the way his upper body leans towards the right, perhaps to see her better, and his two feet firmly planted on the stone. Behind him in the open light and framed in the entrance there is a large mango tree, leaning even more to the right than the boy, almost protecting the boy with its greater leaning, its upper branches moving lightly in the wind.

Outside, she walks down the silent road just below the caves. At the end of this road, where the central road begins, there is a small crowd of people. Approaching closer, Anjali sees that in the centre of the crowd is a man lying on the ground. She looks more closely and sees the old man who had helped her after her fall, the man with the sickle. He lies there with his eyes closed, his arms and legs spread out. In his right hand he still clutches the sickle.

"What happened?" she asks the people gathered around.

They look at her curiously.

"He's dead," someone says. "Yes, dead," says another. "Dead," says someone else.

When Anjali looks at the dead man again she sees a trickle of blood coming out of his mouth. The blood runs down his chin but also lodges in the many wrinkles around his mouth. His left hand is kept palm down and Anjali looks closely to find that it is holding a half eaten mango on which there is a large patch of blood. Some blood and mango juice have run together onto the surface of the road next to the hand, forming a pattern of orange and red.

"He hadn't eaten for days," says the man standing next to her.

Anjali has travelled to so many parts of this country by now. She has seen the incomparably green coasts of Kerala, the chatai makers in the villages of Tamil Nadu making chatais from grass they find on river beds, chatais as soft as silk. She has been along the banks of the Ganga in the north, to the ancient cities. She has seen hundreds of diyas afloat on a dark river as a tribute to the ancestors. But it is the mountains and the hills that draw her most, give her yet another sense of home. Only in the hills does everything seem to come and go, not having more substance than necessary.

Anjali is in a little town in the foothills of the Himalayas, where a friend has an empty house. This house is at one end of the town, away from the shops and the road where cars entered from the highway, and in front of the house the entire valley opens up, with mountain ranges on the other side. It is an April afternoon, warmer weather for these parts, and Anjali sits outside on the porch directly above the valley, watching the tall evergreen and fir and pine, and the continuous movement of light and shadow, so different than on the plains down below. She has a notebook in her hand and once in a while writes down a few things, descriptions, thoughts. The gate of the house is quite far, and a long gravel road comes to where she is sitting, all the way from the gate.

Bent over her notebook, Anjali hears the sound of gravel crunching under feet. She looks up and sees a very tall, slim man, in his sixties probably, standing near her, surprised.

"Forgive me," he says. "I didn't know anyone was here."

"It's all right," she says.

He has skin burnt by the hill sun, as most hill people do, and he looks strong and healthy, with sharp hill features. His gaze is very direct.

"I'm here for some time, maybe a month," Anjali says. "The person who owns this house is a friend of mine."

"Jo bhog karta hai, usika hota hai," he says.

Anjali smiles.

"Look at me, I live over there." He points to a large house at the other end, on the same side of the hill. "The owners never come. They have quite a large outhouse where I live. I herd the sheep and goats and wander. The place is all mine."

"How long have you lived there?"

"Many years."

He notices her notebook and says, "You're writing, are you a writer?"

"Yes."

"What language, not English?"

"Yes, English."

"Woh to ghulami ki zaban hai."

Anjali smiles.

"I hope you're not offended memsahib."

"No, not at all. What else do you do besides herding sheep and goats?"

"I used to be a schoolteacher long ago, gave it up. Did a couple of other jobs, gave them up. Since then this is all I do. Mai azad kism ka aadmi hu memsahib." He is dismissive of his past, and doesn't seem to want to talk about it.

"You're here by yourself memsahib?"

"Yes."

A slow smile appears on his face. "It's good to see a woman here alone."

As he is standing there a storm begins, suddenly, like on many afternoons in this season. The tall pines and firs begin to sway, the sun slowly disappears. There are clouds over the mountains on the other side and they slowly begin to cross the valley. They both turn to look at the valley and the mountains.

"Please sit down," Anjali says.

The man sits quietly, on the paving of the porch, his knees drawn up, his arms around his knees. The loose white pyjamas he is wearing begin to flap in the wind. This wind also throws open doors and windows, it rushes between the hills and through the valley making a great sound. The clouds, not quite black, but very dark grey, slowly keep coming towards them. The man makes not a sound and sits quietly watching. When the clouds have reached overhead, they are so close that she feels she can almost touch them. She bends her head back and looks up, above her. The clouds continue to move beyond them, beyond the house, they cross the hills behind and go towards the valley on the other side.

In front of them now there is more light but still no sun. In the empty space that is the valley the air is filled with blowing pine needles and small hill flowers. The man stands up.

"Khul jao memsahib," he says.

She looks at him.

"Khul jao," he smiles. He turns around and walks, not back up the gravel road but directly down from the fairly steep slope that begins at the edge of the porch, through the brush and the bushes and the flowers, down into the valley.

Later, Anjali asks Dayal, the caretaker, about this man.

"He's been here ever since I can remember," Dayal says. "The whole town respects him. Everyone. When there are disputes between people he is often asked to settle them. The rest of the time, he lives in that house, looking after the sheep and goats."

The day after this she receives a telegram from Riaz saying her mother is very ill. She leaves immediately.

"Eat something," Anjali tells her mother, standing near her with a plate of food in her hands.

"I'll eat with your father when he comes home from the office," her mother says.

Anjali is quiet.

"He won't be home very soon."

"I'll wait."

Anjali puts the plate on the table by the bed.

It is evening and the nurse sits in her white nurse's cap and white starched sari at the head of the bed. She is young and cheerful.

Anjali's mother had a fall where she hurt her left leg. Part of the leg became blue and since then she has had a fever and not been able to get out of bed. Sometimes she loses her sense of physical reality, but only sometimes. The doctors don't know what it is and ascribe it to her long illness of the mind. They say she fell because her bones are decaying. Her need to bathe and keep herself clean and wash her hands constantly is still unabated. That will not change at this age of seventy three the doctors tell her, locking an already firmly shut door. The house seems abandoned by everything except misery. Dust lies thick on the furniture and cobwebs hang from the ceiling. Anjali does nothing to clean it up. She lives in her father's study, free from termites now and the only room without cobwebs and dust, as though someone had been cleaning it everyday though no one has. To clean the house, to repair it, would mean at least some hope, some desire to keep it standing. Anjali has none.

The illness goes on for months. Anjali is there because she cannot abandon her mother. One day she goes to visit a friend. She leaves in the morning and returns late at night. She finds the doctor in her mother's room and the nurse doing a cold compress.

"What happened?"

"Your mother's fever shot up to 105," the doctor says. But I've given her medicine and it should come down soon."

"I was away all day…"

"You can't be here all the time, don't blame yourself," he says.

"We're taking care of it Didi," says the nurse, with a smile.

The doctor leaves and the nurse goes out of the room. As soon as they leave, Anjali's mother opens her eyes and looks at Anjali.

"See what happens when you leave me here alone?" The nurse returns and she immediately closes her eyes again. Anjali is amazed at how acute her mother's sense of reality sometimes is. She is amazed at her cleverness. Anjali wishes her mother were insane, so completely beyond reality that she couldn't hurt anyone. But no. From her mother there would never be any relief. The pain of madness would always be made knife sharp by the presence of reality.

Anjali decides to sell the house. On the surface it is a decision born of practicality. The walls are flaking, the ceilings are damp, the water pump breaks down every other day, the pipes in the ancient kitchen are continuously clogged. With her mother so ill it will be impossible for her to take care of it in any way. But perhaps the real reason, and how can one ever be absolutely sure of these things, perhaps the real reason is the anger that is pushing inside her now, ceaselessly, refusing to be suppressed. There is anger at her mother for being what she is, anger at her father for letting it be that way, anger at the house that has held all this for so many years to finally become a house of utter lovelessness, what is more, a lovelessness she now has to protect. But rage, for her, is a new emotion, and she is only slowly learning how to express it.

She begins to look for buyers, and many come to bid for this large house, well situated at an intersection of quiet streets. They come and walk down the corridors, stand on the balcony and peer down into the street, knock on the thick Burma teak doors in appreciation, and walk up the stairs to the roof to check the waterproofing. Anjali watches them. She cannot really imagine other people living here.

Some of them look at the house only casually. They say they will break it down and build an apartment building in its place, sparkling, with granite floors and large plants in the lobby. That seems best to Anjali. As the blows come and the house caves in, she can see clearly the grief of years getting released. Her father's heart speaking its regret after a lifetime of being married, realising what a monstrous mistake he has made. A daughter's heart, her own, mystified, still trying to understand why she had to go away. Her mother's hideous insides of empty gestures and rituals, and perhaps even the horror they tried to hide over a whole life, being set free. And the joy? Yes, the joy. She forgets there was joy also, once upon a time, long ago. That could also come finally out, from under the rubble, the joy between her and her father, the love between her grandparents, the love between them and their only son, the very unusual love between grandmother and granddaughter. All of this would then become part of the air, because the air allows all things to pass through it.

"Sit by me," her mother says one morning.

Anjali sits near her thin body, the ends of the legs and feet showing under her sari.

"You always loved your father more than me, didn't you?"

Anjali is surprised at this asking of the obvious. She takes her time to reply and finally says, "Yes."

"Why?"

It is very hard for her to speak now because she can only speak the truth. There is a constriction that begins around her chest. The blood throbs in her head. She makes a great effort to gather herself. After some time passes, she says, "Because you... are not capable of love."

"Close the windows, there's a chill in the air. Where's the nurse?"

"Did you hear what I said?"

"I heard you. Can I have some water?"

Anjali gets up, gives her a glass of water and closes the windows. It is winter and there is in fact a chill in the air.

Her mother drinks the water and shuts her eyes.

"I'll take a nap, I'm sleepy," she says. She shuts her lips tight and closes her eyes.

There is absolutely no hope when words mean nothing between people, when the truth will never be looked at. Anjali has read novels about a parent in madness, moving novels, by Bruno Schulz, by Danilo Kis. She has read of fathers or mothers with delusions, with abnormal dreams, people who had crossed the border into madness, but still fathers and mothers, whose dreams and delusions were born of feeling, who would hold their child's hand, even if rarely, and show them something, or kiss the child before he went to sleep for the night. For her, this mother was only physical, someone who years ago had opened her legs and given birth to her, and nothing, not one thing more. Here, between them, there was nothing but pain. It is only when she would know that completely and no longer hope for change, wish for a miracle, that she would be free of this woman lying here before her. Sometimes, at very long intervals, she would search the years for something she had perhaps missed or forgotten, a true gesture of love made by her mother, an indulgent remark. Anjali was a person of rigour, and she wanted to be sure. Could there perhaps have been love that she didn't see, or love that had been covered over by something she did not understand?

One night, the nurse knocks on her door.

"Come quickly please."

Anjali's mother is sitting up in bed and weeping, the tears wrenched from inside her. She looks at Anjali and says, "They rang the bell for so long, for hours. Why didn't you open the door? Why?"

"Who Ma?"

"My father. My father and my brother, your uncle. They rang and rang, they called out my name. I asked the nurse to open the door and she didn't, I called for you and you didn't come."

It is difficult for her to hold her mother because she knows where she wants love there will be hardness, and holding her is like wanting the feel of human skin and its softness and reality but instead feeling an artificial limb of wood or steel. But Anjali holds her nevertheless, the thin body racked with tears.

"They must have been cold out there on a winter night."

As Anjali holds her she calms down slowly. In the bright eyes of the young nurse she sees a hint of fear.

People come to visit her mother, aunts, nephews, cousins, family friends. The older ones heave with exhaustion after walking up the stairs. They carry boxes of sweets in their hands. They sit in chairs next to the bed and talk and laugh with her mother. Her mother is on her best behaviour, wearing her public face. She thanks them for the sweets, and for coming, asks after their children and old parents. As they are leaving the guests ask Anjali what the doctors say. If Anjali talks only about physical ailments, they listen, but the minute she mentions her rituals, the mind's illness, the heart's weight, they begin to look uncomfortable. "No, no there's nothing like that. She'll be all right when she gets out of bed." Or they change the subject abruptly, "How is Riaz?" they might ask. "Is the house sold yet?" The only people who will talk about it directly are her aunts. And they say, "He spoilt her, you know, your father did. She should have been slapped a few times, that would have straightened her out. These things cannot be indulged."

The doctor tells her that her mother must be forced to get out of bed and walk, even for a short while. He suggests a physiotherapist whom he knows well. The physiotherapist comes on the first day and sits in the living room. He is a broad, strong, stocky man, about fifty years old, with a large moustache. Anjali, as always, feels it a necessity to tell any doctor or nurse who come to her mother, about the true nature of her condition. This man listens to her and says in the end, "It's just loneliness. You live far away. The poor thing." Anjali says nothing.

Her mother has sessions with this man every day. He holds her around her fragile shoulders and walks her, very slowly, up and down the long inside corridor of the house. The corridor is dark because it has rooms on either side and no windows. Long ago, in her grandfather's time this was open on one side. The wind came straight in, passed through the rooms and left from the balcony on the other side, opening doors and windows on its way. The sunlight fell in large rectangles, drying the thinly sliced mangoes her grandmother had laid out on white muslin on the balcony floor. Later, new rooms were built along the free side of the corridor, among them the large living room, and the wind and light were shut out forever.

On the fifth day of walking along this corridor, while Anjali is sitting in the study and reading, she hears her mother scream. By the time Anjali comes out the nurse has led her mother to the bedroom and the physiotherapist stumbles into the living room, and collapses on the sofa, holding his right hand, his face twisted in pain.

"What happened?"

"Your mother, your mother," he says.

"What is it?"

With great difficulty he says, "She bent my right thumb all the way back. A little more and it would have broken."

The doctor is called, the thumb is bandaged, and when the pain is a little less, the physiotherapist gets up to leave.

"I don't think I can continue with her," he says.

Anjali nods her head and sees him down the stairs.

After he has left, she asks her mother, "What happened? Were you angry with him?"

"He's not a good man," her mother replies sternly.

"But what did he do?"

Her mother does not reply.

The nurse signals with her eyes that Anjali should leave the room. She leaves and waits outside the open door where her mother cannot see her.

"Tell me Auntie," asks the nurse, "what did he do? Maybe you don't want to say it in front of your daughter."

"Of course I can't. How can I say these things in front of my daughter? I did that to him because he tried, he tried to destroy my honour. You know, as a woman."

After this Anjali moves her mother to a new apartment where she will now live.

"Let me die here, this is where I live, this is where they brought me as a new bride," she had pleaded.

"The roof will fall down soon Ma."

"I don't care."

But as soon as she moves to the new apartment full of air and light, and a small terrace filled with flowers, her health begins to return. But her mother carries the darkness of the old corridor, of the old rooms, inside her, and even in this new place that darkness will slowly emerge and begin to counter the light.

On her last night Anjali lies down on the empty terrace of the house she has sold, on an old chatai, smooth as silk, made thirty years ago in Medinipur where it was once an art. Above, there are stars.

The next morning she prepares to give away the keys to the new owner. She walks through all the rooms to make sure nothing has been forgotten. At the end of the inside corridor, at the head of the stairs, there is a blackboard fixed on the wall. It had been put there in Anjali's childhood. On it, in a scrawny child's handwriting, with awkwardly linked letters, was written, "Today we are going to". At the word "to" the length of the blackboard had ended and for some reason the child Anjali had not continued the sentence on the next line. Since the sentence was in white pencil instead of chalk, it had never been erased. The board too had for some reason never been removed. Above the board there was the face of Durga, with the black eyes, a round pearl nose ring in the perfect nose, and a touch of a smile. Anjali decides to let these things be.

On a second round through the house, she discovers in her mother's room, in a corner closet, a pair of forgotten red clogs her father had brought her from Holland when she was thirteen. She had never worn them, she couldn't remember why, and the clogs were still shining and new. In the same closet there is a photo album she had never seen before. Here, the first page has a round, cameo shaped photograph of her father in his twenties, with thin gold rimmed glasses, looking young and happy. The album is filled with happy family photographs, her grandparents smiling, her aunts young and beautiful, her father. But she does not look at them. The album, which for some reason she has never seen before, increases her anger. So much happiness and joy, all before her time, she thinks, for this, ending in this? She takes the clogs and the album to a huge garbage can at the head of the stairs, near the board and the Durga, and throws them in.

As Anjali walks down the stairs time ebbs and flows inside her in the only way it can, without a beginning, middle and end, the years all standing together in the same place. She walks down quickly, without lingering, leaving her anger to spread through the rooms. Downstairs, the new owner is waiting in a grey suit and tie. He is a manufacturer who makes steel parts for the railways. He smiles at her. She cannot tell him that he will inherit grief, that every enclosed space retains for a long time the lives of its former owners. She smiles back at him and hands him the keys.

"I can't believe it," Riaz says softly, "I absolutely cannot believe it."

"Well that's the way it is," Anjali screams.

"What about Richard, what was that?"

"But it didn't hurt you, did it, you said so yourself."

"What are you saying Anjali, what are you saying to me?"

"I'm saying I can't accept this, your seeing this woman," Anjali screams again.

"Are you asking me to stop seeing her completely?" Riaz's face begins to harden.

"Yes, yes that's what I'm asking."

Riaz looks away from her and out of the large windows. The church bell rings for evening prayers. He gets up, comes and holds her. His face has changed. She sees that his eyes are wet.

"Give it some time," he says. "You'll be all right."

Anjali pushes him away so violently that he almost falls backwards.

"I have given it time, and this is the way I feel," she shouts.

Riaz picks up his car keys. "The core of my life is lived here, with you, and that will never change. This other thing is only a part of my life, just as Richard was for you, or am I wrong?" He does not wait for an answer. He leaves the house. Anjali goes into her bedroom and shuts the door.

For the last two months this room has been her shelter. She lies in the darkness, doing nothing, sometimes even thinking nothing, watching the trees and birds outside without receiving their beauty. After she returned from selling the house Riaz told her one day that he had become close to someone at his research lab. He would like to bring her over. The noise in her heart was like the crashing of a house. But to Riaz she said, "All right."

All day after that there was an actual physical ache in her chest. She tried to reason with herself, but the feeling of danger, of Riaz going away from her, of her fear of being alone because his attention would now be concentrated somewhere else, all of this piled up inside her. She could do nothing else but think about this. But she was unable to express any of these fears to Riaz. How could she? What would he say?

The woman came over for dinner. She was from the North East, with high cheekbones and flattened features, very beautiful, and with a full, almost plump body. She had with her a little child, her son, three years old. The child did not look like her, had much sharper features and a thick mop of hair on his head. Anjali was polite and surprised at her own ability to make conversation when the only desire she had was to be silent. The woman, she found out in the course of the conversation, had returned six months ago from Princeton, where she did her Ph.D. Over dinner, in gaps in the talking, and when the other was not watching, they looked at each other with an intense curiosity. When unexpectedly one of them raised her head and their eyes met, it created a moment of great discomfort. Riaz was the only one completely at ease, almost joyous, looking after everything. The woman was divorced, she said, as she fed the child who sat on her lap throughout dinner. Sometimes the child, with bright black eyes, large like in all small children, gave Anjali a happy smile. Anjali found it difficult to smile back. That was the only time she met this woman to whom her husband was so drawn.

"Why didn't you tell me before?" Anjali had asked Riaz.

"You weren't here, and besides I've only known her for a couple of months."

"That's a long time."

"I don't think so," Riaz said firmly. Anjali was quiet.

Two months went by, with her life at a standstill, her life closed up in a darkened bedroom. When Riaz tried to touch her she turned away. She did not feel like touching him. When he said he was going to meet the woman, to spend the day with her, all she could say was, "all right," and go back to her bed and her daily increasing pain. Riaz noticed how she was living but he said nothing. I should be able to take this, Anjali told herself, I must, it's the only right way. But the will, she found was not always strong enough to change the heart. For two months she struggled, against her own darkness, she told no one because she knew for most people these things are a matter of right and wrong, and that is not how she and Riaz lived. What happens when you may want to do something, but the heart cannot, will not, do it? She thought of nothing else. Only when she slept did she rest, but the waking to each new day was painful, reluctant, and she opened her eyes only when she could not keep them shut anymore. Riaz continued to live his life, spending more time with the woman, less at home, with her.

After these two months something turns inside her. An anger begins, a new emotion. Till now, everything has been going into her, and all of it has been retained there, becoming a weight of grief, creating the dull pain in her chest. Suddenly a day comes when Riaz arrives home in the evening the anger rushes out, unpremeditated, from the depths of the body and she tells him he cannot see the woman any more. It is after that conversation that he picks up his car keys and leaves. Anjali realizes that her fear has diminished. The fear of conflict with the one she loves most, the fear of loss, of acting wrongly, fears she did not even know she had. It is the growing sharpness of the pain that diminishes the fear. As the fear decreases there is room for the new, increasing anger.

That night, after the evening's fight, he comes back late. In the dark bedroom he turns on a bright light.

"Turn it off," Anjali shouts.

"I want to talk," he says. "Get up, stop lying in bed all the time." He is angry now.

Anjali sits up.

"Why don't you go out, start your work, and stop this?" he shouts.

Anjali pulls at his shirt and tears it, some buttons fall off. She takes his hair and pulls it, pushes his face. He is shocked, but he doesn't do anything, just watches her.

"Because I can't stand it," she screams. "Because you're hurting me, and forcing me to do something I can't do."

"Why can't you? Have you even tried?" he shouts.

"Yes, yes, yes, but I can't. You could but I can't."

"You have to."

"I don't have to at all."

"Well I'll have to go away then Anjali," he says, his voice suddenly calm.

"Leave, leave right now then."

"No. I'm going to leave when I want, in the morning."

They lie next to each other on the bed, unable to sleep even for a moment, waiting for dawn to come.

When it does come it is slow and golden. Riaz is crying. He turns around and holds her, but she feels hard and stiff. He buries his face in the space between her neck and shoulder.

"How can I go away? I don't want to leave you."

Anjali stays still, without a word, her heart like an iron door.

"Anjali why is this so difficult? Why are you taking away my joy?"

Anjali is quiet for a moment. The presence of joy in him, and the complete absence of joy in her, how strange, she thinks.

"I don't know why this is so difficult for me, just this."

"What else will be difficult between a man and a woman, what else, this is the biggest difficulty of all, isn't it?"

They both become silent. Outside, there is the sound of the birds waking.

"Give me some time. I don't want to leave today."

"All right," she says, again that word, so often repeated, but this time said with a hope entering her heart.

From that evening onwards when Riaz comes home, he smiles, and she feels a happiness after a long time. For five days, and she will always remember that it was five days, they eat together, make love, walk by the ocean before sunset. Everything is like before, the way it always used to be between them, the sharing of a great love, an immense joy, amazing peace. As they walk by the ocean, Anjali sees couples sitting and watching the waves, so many, of so many ages, so differently dressed, sitting close together, arms around each other, heads on each other's shoulders. For the first time she wishes that none of them would ever have to suffer in their love. An unreal wish, she knows, but not any the less stronger because of its unreality.

"I can't do it," Riaz said at the end of the fifth day.

Anjali looked at him.

"It's false what I'm living. I need to live my life fully. I can't do this. If you don't accept my life I'll have to go away, for a while at least."

"You're so harsh," she says.

"No. It's you who are harsh."

She goes out of the bedroom to sleep on a chatai in the living room. There, of course she cannot sleep and she watches the shadow of the palm fronds on the wall as they move in the night wind. They have never had bad times, Riaz and her. This feels like it doesn't belong to their life, but to someone else's. Exactly at that moment Riaz appears in front of her, as if he had heard her heart.

He stands there also looking at the shadow of the palm fronds. The outside, filled with night and sky and trees has so much beauty. At this moment, Anjali knows they are not part of it. Why not? Why do things always have to change? Can not even one thing, just one, remain the same? Riaz stands there looking at the shadows and at the outside. Anjali lies on the chatai, and because she is lying down she can see the whole sky and a few stars. Hours pass and they do not speak. In that silence is all their love, all their pain, all the night's beauty, all their questions. When the koel begins to call, and it is the hour before dawn. Riaz turns around and goes back to the bedroom.

"If you really love..." Anjali has heard. "If you really love someone..." she has read. What does it mean? She does love, and she knows, so also does Riaz. Anjali falls asleep suddenly and before she is up in the morning Riaz is there with his things packed, ready to leave. His face has changed and become hard again. He does not say even one word. Till the end she keeps hoping he will not leave, that he will change his mind, he'll come and hold her. But none of these things happen. When he is ready to go it is she who runs up to him and says, "Don't go."

"It's too late," he says. After a few moments he says, "I've always, always been there for you ever since you left your father's house."

"I have no one else."

"How can I be everyone to you always?"

"I've never asked you to give up anything before."

"Is it valid, is it all right because it is one thing? Perhaps it is for me a most important thing."

Anjali feels her rage coming up again.

"Just go," she shouts.

He stands near the door for a few minutes.

"You've changed. Look at you, your face, so hard. What happened to all your tenderness, your femininity?" He picks up his bag and leaves.

That day, when Chacha comes, she tells him to go away for a while, that she will not be needing him for now. He does not look at all surprised. All these days he has been hovering around, cooking, feeding them, taking care of them, without making a single remark on what he so obviously sees.

"If you wish, beti," he says. "But whenever you need me, you know I'm there."

"Yes Chacha," she says and forces herself to smile.

Anjali is finally alone, as alone as she has never been. She brings down all the bamboo blinds in the house, keeping out much of the light. It is winter, and the evening comes quickly. She is grateful for that because she finds the darkness more bearable than the light of day. Things lose their incredible sharpness in the dark. Only the blunt contours remain, the shapes of things.

That evening, as the light is falling, at twilight, which used to be her favourite time of day, she sits looking at the things before her.

She sees the ceramic pitcher with a broad round base and a narrow neck, painted with simple stripes of blue and yellow ochre, and an elegant curved handle, from which they pour water every day. She takes the pitcher, half full of water, and hurls it across the room. The water splashes out as the pitcher flies across. The pitcher falls and shatters below a miniature painting of Ragini Todi hanging on the wall. She sees the painting shake slightly. She goes over to the painting and smashes the glass that covers it. Blood runs from her hand and onto the pale green grass in the painting. She smashes a large pane of a tall bookshelf. More blood runs down her hands, her arms, falling in bright drops on the floor. The glass shatters into tiny pieces, falling on her and on the books inside. She opens the small glass doors of the shelf and takes out rows and rows of books and scatters them on the ground. The books lie on their spines, open and helpless, or buried awkwardly under one another, their pages bent and smashed. Nothing, nothing can protect her now. She weeps and weeps and they are tears of anger and tears at the unexpectedness of life's pain. There are so many choices. You can hurt yourself, you can hurt another, or both, and you can even hurt the things that surround you. It is eight in the evening. Anjali is exhausted. She falls asleep with the blood still on her hands and some very fine bits of glass on her hair, her face.

I am in a car, driving into the mountains of the lower Himalayas, on a road that curves and slopes and rises. For eleven months I have been inside myself. It is often difficult for me now to distinguish between inside and outside. The silence on these mountain roads is different from the silence on the plains. It is more detached, more serious, more alert. Or is that the silence of my own self?

This rented car, with its old driver, keeps going up the roads, leaving the cities and plains further and further behind. I notice that large parts of these hills are brown, without trees or any kind of green, destitute, melancholy. This brown stops the sight because the sight cannot accept here this unexpected colour. I remember then that this is where the British felled trees, the great deodars, in order to build sleepers for the railways. Sometimes they replaced it with pine, a tree whose acidic cones fell into the soil and destroyed it. I know now that life will no longer bring me unrelieved beauty, it will bring me beauty with a presence of its opposite, to remind me of the true nature of things.

There is no one on these roads for miles. Rarely, someone collecting firewood, or a child dragging along a mountain goat. It is spring, too early yet for the travellers. I know the seasons very well now. They have been my companions, changing and moving and protecting me, stepping in where those other things fell away, books, language, people. It is only in these eleven months that I have understood the need for at least some things that never change.

I began these eleven months with my eyes growing accustomed to darkness. I could feel my way around the house without turning on a single light. I could see the shadows of trees, I saw how sharp the tips of the palm fronds were, I saw on a moonlit night the shadow of the banyan's leaves reflected on its own broad trunk. When I looked at these trees I wanted to uproot them, to maim and mangle them, tear the leaves, and break the branches so that their white insides would show in sharp, jagged pieces. If I saw flowers I wanted them torn, smashed. I wanted to pluck the grey feathers off the pigeons that came and sat on the awnings, to break one of their delicate legs so they could not fly. The plane of life had been disrupted and no longer retained its uniformity. Fear, desire, love, ugliness, beauty, violence, these things were no longer separate.

For months I lived nothing but loss. Had I not lost everyone that I had loved, or whom I had even the possibility of loving? Why?

What a living, thriving, growing thing loss can be. It penetrated everywhere, taking over even the strongest of presences to which it was in no way directly related. It stripped me of everything I had, in all my life's aspects. Even language, my other self, my instrument of understanding, disappeared. I became a collection of absences. I was desperate, only to stay alive.

One night there was a storm, a winter storm, unexpected, with thunder and lightning. I watched the storm from my bed, watched the lightning light up fragments of the room, fragments of my hands and legs. It lasted for a few hours and then faded away. After the storm was gone I saw a bird come and rest on a corner of the window sill, a dark bird, the colour of the night. It did not move at all, as if it had been frightened by the storm and was taking shelter here. But why after the storm was gone? It sat at my window for hours, one more of life's imprecisions. I watched the bird from my bed, and could only see it because my eyes were accustomed to darkness. Against the night it was barely discernible. Its colour was darker than the sky. As I watched, for a long, long time, the bird moved only once, to turn its head up towards the sky and back down again. A small thing began in me. That was when I moved, I know now, into another time inside myself.

The driver tells me we have an hour and a half more to go. I reach for my bottle of water. He says, "Memsahib, don't drink that. There are many springs up ahead."

I turn my eyes to the road in the late afternoon sunlight, clear and thin in the mountains. The forests have become thick and green as we have climbed up, with trees of pine, fir, deodar, chestnut and rhododendron. Up above there is a clear sky. After a few more bends and turns, the driver stops the car and parks it on the side of the winding road. We come out and there is water rushing out from an opening in the dark brown rocks above the road. At the opening the water is thick and milk white, and by the time it reaches down to where we are it has become absolutely clear. I cup my hands and drink the water, cool to the touch, cool inside my throat, and then I splash my face with it and my arms. With the water comes one small leaf and a tiny twig.

"It's good," I say.

The driver has had his drink of water and is sitting on the rocks. He has a dark, burnt face, and his hair is completely white. I also sit, on the other side of the flowing spring. In front of us there is the road, a steep drop at its edge, then the valley below and the mountains on the other side. As I look at this I feel as I always do when I go up into the mountains. I feel as though I am leaving the known world behind, I feel, along with this vast beauty, a sense of apprehension.

"There will be things waiting for you up there," says the driver suddenly. "There always are." He lights a beedi.

"Do you live up here or in the plains?" I ask.

"I used to live up here, somewhere near where I am taking you. But I moved down to the plains so my son could go to a better school. Now he's in college. He's very intelligent. But I don't like living down there. I'll move back up in a couple of years. What is your work Memsahib?"

"I'm a writer."

A very subtle light illuminates his face.

"I can't read," he says. "But my son can. He reads many, many books."

A sudden wind comes and shakes all the pine and chestnut trees we are under. We both look up immediately. Here, the wind is not just part of the air, it is a vital presence, it always speaks, to everything around and to the thoughts of those it passes near.

"Do you think a man must know how to read and write?" the driver asks.

"No."

"I thought so. My son says everyone should go to school, read books, but I'm not so sure. The only thing a man has to know is himself. And then he can know the whole world, Germany, England, Sweden…"

I smile at the way he says these names.

"I take foreigners up and down quite often. They have such shining hair, like gold." He pulls at his beedi, and then begins to cough. The cough goes on and on. He gets up and takes another drink of water from the spring.

"Are you all right?"

"Yes, yes." He clears his throat several times. "I'm all right Memsahib, it's you who are not."

I look at him, surprised. He is looking at the mountains on the other side, not at me. "And the mountains will not let you forget."

In the car, as we climb higher and higher, I admire the skill with which this man negotiates the bends and turns, and the old car begins to assume a rhythm of its own. We do not speak once we are in the car, he concentrating on the road and I looking only ahead of me. The car tilts right with one turn, left with another, and with each bend the sight meets something different, either a hill which blocks everything beyond, or the landscape opening up to show the valley and the far mountains.

After another hour, the driver says we are almost there. I am going to a place that is not a town, not even a village. As we approach, I see a little tea stall with an old man standing behind it. His skin is wrinkled and folded and thick. He looks at us without curiosity. Next to the stall there are two men, sitting on a boulder, drinking tea and eating pieces of bread. Nearby, there is a tiny post office with a verandah and a red door. It is closed now. Further up is a large house in wood and stone, where the car stops. This is a Christian ashram run by an American woman who has lived here for over thirty years. The ashram is a group of cottages, of which I will have one to live in for a few months.

Inside I meet Sarah, the American woman, and her assistant, an older Indian woman named Alika. Sarah is probably in her late fifties. She wears a sweatshirt and pants and looks very capable. Alika is in a long skirt and blouse, a slim, serious woman. They welcome me warmly. I am grateful for the American way of not prying, not asking too many personal questions.

"Dinner is at seven," Sarah says. "Do join us."

There are more people at dinner. Besides Sarah, Alika and myself there are two men, an American who is a friend of Sarah's and a very tall, very blonde Swede, who does not speak English very well. There is steak, potatoes and sweet peas grown in Sarah's garden. I am quiet, very quiet, in spite of the effort of the two men to make me speak. I have lost my ability to meet new people, to be interested in their lives. Sarah and Alika leave me alone. I feel from them a strange unspoken understanding.

"I'll show you to your cottage tomorrow," Sarah says. "It'll be dark soon and it's best to move your things and set you up there in the day. Tonight you can sleep in the spare room upstairs."

"Thank you," I say.

"The leopard has been down near here the last couple of nights," Sarah says to us all. "So carry a torch if you want to go for a walk and don't go too far."

"There's a leopard here?" I ask.

"More than one," Alika says. "They've begun to come down for food. The forests are so denuded now. They come down looking for dogs. Last year they even took away a little baby."

"But isn't there a security force or something that patrols the area to prevent this?" the American asks.

"No," says Sarah, amused, and continues eating. The Swede looks a little alarmed.

"Not your first time in the mountains, right?" Sarah asks me.

"No," I smile.

"I thought not," she smiles back.

After dinner I come outside and stand on the wide porch, the mountains behind me and ahead of me. It is dark now and there is a sky crowded with stars. I sit down on the steps of the porch. It has been very, very long since I have looked at a sky like this one, since I have sat under anything so vast.

The two men come out with a bottle and some glasses.

"Would you like some cognac?" the Swede asks me.

"No, thank you," I say. I turn around and walk into the house and as I walk away I can hear the Swede say, "To come near an Indian woman, not so easy," and the American says, "Well I'll be damned if..." and then his voice drops and I can't hear what he says.

My room for the night is in the attic, in what is actually Sarah's study. It has a sloping roof and is filled with books. There is one window through which, if I bend down, I can see the outside and the stars. With my eyes used to darkness I can discern the outlines of the mountains and the trees that stand close to the road, and the road going further up beyond the house into the wilderness. I can even see where it begins to curve.

After the bird came, I passed over into living again. There was as yet no joy, but there was living, there was the beauty of the trees and the night coming back into me. I could see loss as loss, despair as despair. I could face things. I saw that to face something meant just that, to stand firmly before it and not look away. As I looked I saw that only what had not been understood kept on repeating itself. I thought of everyone I had loved, so deeply, for so long. I thought of my father, my grandmother.

From somewhere in my younger years a gesture came back to me, an ancient gesture. I remembered that as a young girl, I resisted touching the feet of elders. I examined everything for worthiness. I looked for wisdom on the forehead, strength in the eyes, grace on a face, compassion on the lips, ease in the hands. These things I did not find. My body resisted bending. The years passed by and more people grew old around me. Now, so far away from everything, I see them again, deeply attached to every pain, clutching the wooden edges of tables and chairs, sometimes with both their hands. Their eyes are faded, uncertain, and with these eyes they watch everything that cannot stand its ground, as if to say, "Look, we have always known that things are transient, unsure, that it is difficult for people to be strong." My body wanted to bend now, now that no one was near me, to go down slowly, lovingly, before my eyes the face, the crumpled neck, all the cloth covered body and finally the aged feet on which I would rest my palms for a moment before taking them to my head. I now knew what it meant just to endure.

The days slowly became easier to live through. I listened carefully to the birds calling and noticed how unfinished their calls were, always upward rising, or falling downward, but never resolved. I looked closely at the trees all around and watched how they moved in the wind, each one with a different rhythm. The gulmohur had slim branches bearing large leaves. Each leaf had a central stem with tiny leaves growing from it. When the wind came, the branches moved in broad gestures, up and down and sideways. The leaves, while being pulled along in these larger movements of the branch, also responded to the wind by themselves, through a controlled trembling of different intensities. When I looked even more closely I saw that the trembling never really stopped, except when the air was absolutely still. Because the gulmohur had light branches and leaves, they all went down and up gently in the breeze, and if I watched long enough I felt the tree was breathing. I knew, with an intimacy that bordered on love, the response of many trees to the wind, the tamarind, the mango, the coconut, the palm. I knew that when there was a high wind and all these trees rustled together, it sounded exactly like rain.

At night my heart was pulled, without reason, towards the yellow lights. At the windows of homes a yellow light by which people read and ate and laughed. On the steps of the church yellow lamps, in the grotto outside so many candles, on the street the streetlamps. These lights were a warmth, a kind of home. Most of all, through the dense group of trees, when I inclined my head, or when wind stirred the leaves and parted them, suddenly a yellow light far away. The desire to live must come back from things other than people and relationships and circumstance.

One evening, when it was almost dark, I saw reflected in the open window the gulmohur tree and the sky. As it grew darker and darker, the tree and the sky were joined by the reflection of my books, papers and pens, just behind the window pane. As all these things came together, I was amazed. I recognize that, I said to myself, that is the peacefulness of what used to be my life.

The windows were being opened once again. I cleaned up the house and dusted it every day. One day as I dusted the three miniature paintings on the wall, one with drops of blood on it, I saw the sunlight illuminate them completely, brilliantly, all three paintings placed diagonally one on top of the other. Every day is not the same, I thought, even for a painting.

The first painting, the lowest one, was of Ragini Todi, a woman holding the veena, with three deer looking up at her, two on the right, one on the left. Beyond her was a pale green landscape, sparse, with small undulations. The woman was wearing a lahenga on which there were the tiniest flowers. It was a painting from 1649. The second was of Radha and Krishna in the centre of a grove of banana trees. Radha was dressed in red and gold, looking up at Krishna. Krishna held her face in his hands. They were both reclining on an ornate diwan. It had been painted in 1800. The third painting was a meeting of three Sufis, two young and one much older with a white beard, all with turbans. The older Sufi held a book in his hands though the book was closed. They sat on an expanse of green grass, with a small white dargah nearby, under a golden sunset sky. The painting was from 1657.

I looked at the colours in each one. In Ragini Todi, the pale green of the lahenga and the pale green of the landscape, exactly the same. My eyes cannot stop moving between the two, they have been made so inseparable.

In Radha and Krishna, Krishna's body is dark blue. In the grove of banana trees which are light green, suddenly a few leaves, only a few, are the same dark blue as Krishna's body, connecting them forever. My heart moves when it sees these blue leaves, moves unstoppably between the grove and Krishna.

In the meeting of the Sufis, one of the Sufis holds a book that is golden, the same precise gold as part of the sunset sky above him. Here, the movement of my eye and heart traverses the greatest of spaces, that between the tiny book and the vast sky.

Is everything so closely related then, the near and the far, that which man has made and that which he has not? Is nothing to be denied?

I felt the need to leave the house, to go out into the world, after eleven months. I dreamt of the mountains.

I sleep well in Sarah's attic. In the morning, after breakfast, she takes me to my cottage. We cross the road in front of the house and walk through dense bushes and trees. There are langurs overhead, swinging from branch to branch, leaping across impossibly large spaces. The forest is filled with the hum of insects and the cries of birds, most nearby the regular beat of the woodpecker. There are no human noises besides our footsteps on the leaves. A few minutes from Sarah's house, inside the forest, the trees and undergrowth suddenly clear to reveal a lake such as I have never seen before. The water is the colour of transparent emerald, silent, unmoving, untouched.

"There are three lakes like this one," Sarah says. "Your cottage is by the second."

My cottage is on the banks of a lake identical to the first except in size. This one is a little smaller. Sarah shows me the cottage, essentially a large room, built of stone, with a bed and a small kitchen counter on one side.

"There you go," says Sarah. "Let me know if there's anything else you need." She touches me lightly on the arm and walks away with sure, confident footsteps.

I unpack the few things I have brought along. Clothes, a notebook, and the three miniatures. For the first time I have been courageous enough to not bring along a single book. Or perhaps I know only too well that this is not a time for reading. After I have unpacked I go out and sit by the lake. It has an alert serenity, a quiet vigilance, and is unsurprised by a leaf that suddenly falls on its surface, or by the being who comes speechless to its shore.

A month passes by. My notebook is still empty, but the three miniatures hang on the wall. It is spring changing into early summer, and when I touch the water in the lake with my hands, it is still cold, but not ice cold. There are even more birds in the trees. I go walking one morning beyond my lake to the one further on, the third. There are two more cottages, at what seems like the edge of this forest, where the higher mountains begin, but they are all empty. I walk with the knowledge and freedom of being alone. When I reach the banks of the third lake I stand quietly. Beyond the lake is the mountains and beyond that the sky. I look around at all the trees, the thick vegetation. Under a tree, very near the lake, I see a man sitting on a small rock, looking ahead of him. I walk closer to him and see that he is not much older than I am, has shoulder length hair, uncombed and windblown, an unkempt beard, a leaf brown shawl wrapped around his bare chest, and thick, rough, dark brown trousers ending in bare feet. He does not notice me, though any human sound is very easy to distinguish here. I go even closer. He looks up at me suddenly. The light through the trees falls such that only a part of his face is in the light, the rest of him is in the shade. The light falls on a broad forehead, the right eye, most of the high, broad nose, and on the deep fold from the nose down around the mouth on the right side. The right eye is in the light, the left completely in the shade, but both eyes have the same question in them, the deepest question of all, whatever that is for him, they have the same receding pain, a pain in farewell, so that I can see that the question and the pain have been separated, perhaps very recently. As he raises his face to look at me I know that these are not eyes that are seeing only what is before them. We both look at each other, and do not speak or move. He stands up and, still looking at me, raises his hand as if to run it through his hair. But the hand is quite far from his head and when it moves up, the man spreads his fingers, and moves the hand through empty space. Slowly, after he completes the movement, he brings the hand down again. I stand there. The man turns around, with his body slightly bent towards me, as if to say he is not turning his back on me, but taking my leave. He walks away, deeper in, towards the edge of the forest.

I do not ask Sarah who this man is. I want to keep myself from curiosity. But in a few days when I meet Sarah at the post office, she tells me.

"There's a man living in one of the cottages by the third lake," she says. "You might have run into him."

"Yes. I have."

"He's come down from the mountains."

"We are in the mountains."

"No, from much higher up," she gestures towards the mountains rising ahead of us. "From where you can't go much further."

That is all that Sarah says. I like her reticence.

In the evenings it is difficult to be outdoors, although I do sometimes go down to the lake at night. Inside, I sit in silence, or cook my evening meal. Otherwise I look and look at the three miniatures, which I have arranged in exactly the same way, on the wall opposite the door. I have looked at them so much, in the day, by the yellow light in the evenings, that they have become a part of myself now. When I close my eyes I can recall with absolute precision the angle at which the woman holds the veena, or the distance between the sufis on the grass.

Today my watching reveals yet something else, unseen till now. I see how what is close in these paintings, and what is far, foreground and background, have almost the same weight. The foreground is only to anchor the eye, to give it a point of return. What happens inside me and what happens near me, are they on the same plane?

That night, very late, as I am about to fall asleep, the dogs begin to bark. There are not many in these parts, and they rarely bark at this time. From the barking the dogs move to whining, almost weeping, in a way I have never heard before. I wake and sit up in bed, looking out of the window. There is one single light outside my cottage but beyond that everything is completely dark. Soon, the langurs begin to screech, a rough, shrill sound, that merges something of the human, the animal and the bird in it, and the forest is filled with this sound. Then there begins a scratching on my door, a desperate scratching. I do not open the door for a while, but the scratching goes on and on and then I hear the whimpering of a dog. I open the door and there is the furry mongrel that I see near my cottage every day, shaking and rolling its eyes in fright. As soon as I open the door the dog darts inside. Almost immediately I see the caretaker of the ashram, an elderly man, with a lantern in his hand.

"Memsahib, stay inside and lock your door. The leopard has come down. My son saw the footprints, and now you can hear the animals, can't you?"

"All right," I say.

I close the door and lock it. Inside, the dog shivers and looks around but makes not a single sound. I pet it and stroke it, and then it calms down, but only for a few minutes. I listen, and now the entire forest seems filled with fear, birds, langurs, dogs, jackals, goats, insects. The darkness is of unknown depths. I sit on my bed, the dog shivers on the floor. Time passes very slowly. A jackal lets out a long cry. This is only the beginning. Soon after the forest becomes absolutely silent, but it is the silence of the forest holding its breath, a forest in waiting, with every being, from the smallest to the largest, completely, incomparably, alert. Every sound stands out clearly, when and if it comes. Is that the rustling of leaves, or an animal running to hide? Far away somewhere there seems to be a commotion of human voices. Have they seen it?

The leopard, I remember from books, and suddenly I realize that my knowledge from books is so much more than my knowledge in any real world, the leopard is a solitary animal, living in forests, or forested mountains. It is a nocturnal animal. It is an agile climber. I understand the screeching of the langurs. The leopard often stores what it kills in the branches of a tree. It feeds upon any animal it can kill, and has a special liking for dogs. I feel a fear rising inside me, a primal fear. I know that inside the cottage I am safe from harm, but the fear does not go away. Very soon it brings along with it all my other fears of loss and pain and aloneness, a terrifying fear of all that I have yet to live. I also realize that I am not afraid of what I do not know, for it has no form. I am afraid of the known, of what has made me suffer before, or the suffering I have seen in others. I despise myself for feeling like this, but the fears do not decrease. I sit in the dark with myself and the shivering, soundless dog, for what seems like hours.

After that long time, there is a knock on the door. I open the door a little and see standing outside the man I had met a few days ago.

"I came because I thought you might be afraid."

"Come in," I say.

He comes in and sits on the floor. The dog looks at him and looks down again. He begins to stroke the dog's head. He is wearing the same shawl on his bare body, the same thick trousers. I stand there looking at him.

"I think the leopard will stay awhile," he says. I nod my head, and go back and sit down on the bed. Far away a bird shrieks. The dog goes into an even more intense bout of shivering. The man takes the dog on his lap and holds it close.

"Once I was in the upper forests," he says, "and a hunter, while lifting his gun towards a leopard, grazed a tiny twig. The leopard lifted its head in the direction of the gun, and then slowly walked away. A leopard can hear everything."

We sit like that almost all night, in the darkness. Sometimes, I look at the man. But he never looks at me, except when he speaks.

"Do you know that the leopard comes down not only to hunt but also to drink from these lakes? There is not enough food or water up there nowadays for him to survive."

He has just finished saying this when we hear the very shrill and long cry of a dog. The cry goes down and up, then down and up again and then stops with the sudden abrupt quality of a switch being turned off. The leopard has made its kill.

The dog now stops even his shivering and sits still with a stillness I have never before seen in any animal. The man holds him tight. The forest seems as motionless. At least an hour passes before the dog moves again, it stretches slowly, tentatively. There is no sound from the forest, from the monkeys, the birds, the insects. It is a forest still holding its breath, making sure the leopard has gone. Then slowly the silence changes. I had never known there could be so many kinds of silence. This one is the silence of relief, of the forest closing its tired eyes to sleep. It is still quiet but underneath there are small rustlings, a few quiet, unfinished calls, drones of insects, the last few sounds before sleep comes.

"It's gone back up," the man says, not looking at me.

I realize that all this time my body had been taut and tense. Now, it relaxes again. The man lifts the dog off his lap. It is the time just before dawn. The man walks up to me and sits next to me on the bed. He takes my face in his hands. The hands are amazingly rough. I look at him in surprise. He takes his rough hands and begins touching my face. From these rough hands there emerges the lightest touch. With his eyes shut, his hands move from the forehead, through my eyebrows, eyes, the slight hollows beneath them, the nose, the space between the nose and the mouth, the cheeks, the lips, the corners of the lips and finally the chin. All the while his eyes are completely closed and he is concentrating. Only when he stops and takes his hands away does he open his eyes.

He says, "In this," he moves his head towards the forest outside, "or in anything else. There is nothing to be afraid of, ever."

"I'll go now," he says. At the door, he smiles. It is a smile which holds nothing back.

We become friends. Often, we sit by the lake, or on the verandah of the closed post office, drinking tea made by the old man at the tea stall. But the man rarely speaks beyond the barest of necessary sentences. It is a friendship of silence, of watching things together. After a few days I ask his name.

"Amar," he says.

He does not ask me mine.

I sometimes cook a meal for him. He eats quietly, looking out of the open door towards the lake. One day he sits before the miniature paintings on the wall.

"They're very beautiful," he says.

I tell him that they have taught me a great deal. I start talking about what I have seen in them. He listens carefully.

Then after a long time, still looking at the paintings, he says, "But what about the absence?"

I look at the paintings.

"Can't you see it? There, in the paleness behind Ragini Todi, in the sky above those Sufis, all around Radha and Krishna in the banana grove."

When I look closely now, at these paintings I know so very well, they begin to become new and unfamiliar again.

That night after Amar leaves I open my notebook for the first time since I have been here. It is a large black notebook, with blank, cream coloured pages. I sit on the floor, with my back against the bed. I hold my pen over the paper for a long time. I think of Amar, of the forests, the lake, the leopard. Finally, I write:

"The mountain lake, in the dense woods, an extreme serenity. The leopard comes to drink, dipping its thick tongue in the silent, emerald water. It goes away stilled. The lake becomes disturbed, filled with ferocity. It wants to leap outside its shores. Where the water meets the land is no longer the place of tenderness. The lake trembles here with rage."

I know this has come from inside me, but I cannot name the place of its origin.

The next time I meet Amar, we walk on the road next to Sarah's house, following the road into the forest. The road slopes down and up with the forest on either side. I begin to tell Amar about myself, my life. I keep talking as we walk, but talking carefully, because when I speak I must give form to things very precisely. So I speak slowly, turning the words over in my head, I speak with gaps and pauses. Amar listens with an incredible attention, waiting at the pauses, or saying, "Yes?" When we sit down at the edge of the forest with our back to the road, his eyes look steadily at mine while he listens, only turning away when I myself look down to find a word or a phrase. So I tell my life, as much as I can, because in the end a life is not really expressible. We sit there for hours. I realize there is a desperation in me to be understood. I end abruptly with my coming here, to the mountains.

Amar says nothing for a long time. But this is one moment when I cannot bear his silence. He stands up and faces me, and then sits lightly on his haunches so that his face is looking directly at mine.

"The universe is not casual," he says.

Sudden tears spring to my eyes and remain there.

We walk back through the edge of the forest. The langurs watch us with their alert black faces as they swing from branch to branch. Walking next to him that evening, for the first time I feel the rising of desire. It has been so long that the body has almost forgotten the feeling. It takes me by surprise. When I am very near him there is a smell of skin and hair, as if freshly washed. Now, it makes me want to touch him. That evening, as we part at my cottage door, Amar says, "I understood."

Amar almost always speaks things in one sentence, one phrase. He never describes things at length, or explains them, or takes them apart. Slowly I begin to understand the importance of this. The one sentence contains everything. I listen to it, it goes inside me, and if I have understood, it expands and fills me completely. If I have not, it remains there whole, waiting till it is understood. It is a new way of exchange, without explanation, argument, or discussion.

In the mountains each day is different, unlike in the plains. Sometimes there is sunlight, and sometimes none. Large clouds often pass over the sky, casting half the mountains in shadow. The clouds may rain or may not. Some days are so clear and bright that the blue of the sky seems almost transparent. There may be a high wind, there may be an almost frightening stillness. And so it is inside myself. No day is the same any more, as it used to be in my old life, before these eleven months, ever since I left my father's house. Things happened, of course, new things, changes, even very hurtful ones. But even through pain, the deepest inside had a kind of evenness, only slightly undulated by the outside. Now everything inside is shifting, changing, turning over, every day, even if the outside remains the same.

I understand now why the mountains, and perhaps these mountains, are the place where many people have seen through their pain, lived through their transformations, walked through the vast spaces of their own selves. This is a detached landscape, but always watching, alert, never allowing anything to be lulled into forgetting. Perhaps these mountains are the other, the stranger to our tropical landscape of rain and heat, rising suddenly out of the earth, to help us recognize ourselves.

Sarah invites me to dinner one evening. We sit in the large living room near a window that looks out onto the mountains. She tells me that she came to these mountains as a young woman from Boston, and decided to stay on. This ashram was already there, being run by an Englishman. When he died, she took it over. They have prayer meetings, in a large hall at the edge of the woods, and run a school, and a small clinic a few miles away.

"So, how have you been?" Sarah asks.

"Very well," I smile. "I love these mountains and forests."

"And Amar? You two have been spending some time together haven't you?"

"Yes." I am aware that my face changes as I answer, but of course, I am not sure how. I also know that Sarah sees the change. She smiles at me. Then she looks at the mountains.

"There aren't too many people like him," she says. Still looking at the mountains, she asks, "Are you married?"

"Yes."

She is quiet, thinking.

"That's my only regret," she says, "that I didn't get married. In those days, I didn't think it was important. Now..." She turns around to look at me. "And it's not only loneliness I'm talking of.

I feel now that you need another, very near you, to understand yourself."

I look at her and think of her entire life, a life that I know nothing of. But I know this, what she has just told me, something so lived, so felt.

"You convince me of something I have been thinking about for a while," I tell her. "The importance of honesty lies not in its being a virtue, or being the correct thing. It is profound because it is capable of taking us very far inside things."

As we eat dinner Sarah says, "I always wanted a life where I would never regret anything. Now I realize that regret is also a presence. Every true regret is real, tender, filled with life."

"I think I understand."

We continue to eat, passing each other the bread or the spinach. Neither of us speaks for quite a long time.

"I had to come to this country to learn how important silence is between people," Sarah smiles. "Tradition knows how to interpret different kinds of silences, or to just let them be. Modernity does not."

I continue eating, thinking about what she has said. Before we finish dinner I tell her, "I have been alone for eleven months."

Sarah looks up at me, but she does not look surprised. She does not ask me anything more, and that is all that I want to say. After dinner, when I am leaving, she puts a hand on my shoulder.

"Take care," she says.

Early one bright, clear morning Amar comes to my door. He says, "Come, I'll take you to see the giant deodars up above."

We stop first to drink tea and the old man gives us two steaming glasses. This morning he sings, as he makes his tea, in a broken old voice,

"Naina katoriyan zulfan kale dang,
it sade bag me koi tota bole rang
kunj kurlaiyan koi nage chhori kanj
kini bo musafare koi chupi suttea amb
bhaya bo lalariya koi gudha karea rang
suhi meri cholari sabaz lahariya band...

Eyes like small lotus buds and dark curls of serpentine form
in my garden a parrot calls alone
the herons wail and a snake has left its skin behind
like a wayfarer who sucks a mango and throws its stone away
O dyer, dye my clothes a fast colour
make my choli a deep red and its fastenings of green waves..."

We walk slowly up the mountain roads, and it takes us almost till noon. As we climb we see less and less people along the way, which in these parts means that where there were few there are now almost none. The last man made thing we pass is a not very large stone temple with the pujari ringing its bell inside. The sound of the bell here is not loud and echoing, it gets absorbed by the endless silence around it. When we reach the beginning of the forest I stop, amazed. There are deodar trees that are almost three stories high, standing crowded against each other. Their trunks are large and wide, so wide that it would take three people to put their arms around one of them. Amar leads me into the forest and we are plunged in the deepest of shadows. The sun does not penetrate very far, blocked by the massive, irregular crowns and the spreading branches. I have to sit down and bend my head completely back to actually see the tops of the trees so far up above.

It is a vast world here, with its own laws. Here, sight has very little meaning. In this silence which is as dense as the forest, it is sounds that lead, give a sense of direction, give rise to images of the unknown. There is a violent rustle in the undergrowth and I raise my head. What is it? It disappears as suddenly as it began. No sounds linger here, nothing remains behind. Again, further on, a sound like heavy breathing. Is it an animal or a human being? This dense silence, only sometimes broken by sounds, produces a kind of apprehension I have not known before. Amar keeps leading me further and further in, till it seems to me we have walked at least an hour from the edge. In the absence of sight's keenness it is the arms and legs that take over, and the grounding of the feet. Amar walks in front of me, and I behind him, hesitantly. In Amar's body there is no hesitation, nor is there an effort, or a purposeful going forward. He walks, bending and turning his body under the branches and leaves, like a river winding its way through, as if without even a knowledge of obstacles.

"This is the centre of the forest," he says.

Here the darkness has grown even deeper. No sunlight comes horizontally because we are so far from the edge of the forest. From up above, the sun falls only in small slivers of light. We have reached the centre of the forest but he still walks as if he is in search of something. There are barely any sounds here at all, not even the drone of crickets. After walking for what seems like a long time, at one point we find a gap in the crowd of trees where one deodar has fallen. There the sun, having found an opening, falls in a luminous column of light.

"Come, come here," he says.

I walk up and stand in the centre of the shaft of light which is wide enough to hold just me. From here, when I look, I can see almost nothing in the darkness around, and Amar becomes just a shape. I close my eyes and raise my face upwards. It is sunlight with a different meaning. With my eyes still closed I hold my hand out to Amar and say, "Come."

He enters the light as I step back a little, so that my back is now in the shadow. I open my eyes to look at him. His eyes are closed and he also has his face raised upwards, directly into the light. We are a breath away from each other. I can feel my desire rising, coming up from my body through my throat. Amar leans forward, both his arms at his side, and places his face next to mine, without touching it. We stand, with our faces resting on the air above each other's shoulders.

"I am not yet prepared," he says, very quietly.

The sunlight hits the ground at the fallen trunk, and there it breaks and spreads out, as much as it can. I sit on the fallen trunk, and I am covered in a pattern of sun and shadow.

"Where were you before you came here?" I ask.

He steps out of the shaft and says, "I was in a cave. For eleven months."

"Where?"

"In the upper ranges."

"What kind—" I begin to say, but Amar stops me.

"Don't ask me questions that are born only of curiosity."

"And suppose that I really wanted to know?"

"Why would you really want to know?" His voice rises for the first time. "Of what use would that knowledge be to you?"

"Sometimes—"

"Always!" Amar shouts. "Always a need for the experience of another. Why? And so little learnt from one's own self!"

He turns around and walks away through the forest, underneath his feet the loud sound of deodar needles disintegrating.

I am left alone on the trunk, with the insects and woodpeckers as companions.

Nothing is only correct, tender, comforting any more. I move through diverse worlds in a single hour. But because all of me is open, my wounds fresh, my griefs pulsating, my fears so alive, Amar's words at first come very near me as I sit there, and after I have sat there for hours looking down at the ground all the time as if something from above was forcing me, the words step inside. I look up at the sky after those hours to see that it is turning dark. I get up and begin to walk, looking straight ahead of me. When I have almost reached the edge of the forest I see Amar sitting on the ground at the foot of a tree. Only when I reach him does he stand up. He stands behind me and puts his palm, from behind, on my forehead, with the greatest lightness. The other hand he brings to rest, as lightly, on my upper arm.

"Anjali," he says my name for the first time. "The normal is only the old, the already lived."

We reach the road and walk back under the darkest evening sky. It is the night of no moon. I can somehow walk because there is a tenuous illumination, in spite of the moon's absence, of the sky giving light, however faint. But I soon begin to stumble. There is always something lying on the road, pebbles or a fallen branch, even an old milk bottle. Amar never stumbles, not even once. He also never looks after me, to make sure I don't fall, like another man would. As soon as this thought enters me I slip on something, fall backwards and down on the ground. Amar helps me up. Just as my body begins to relax in his arms, he moves away.

"Do you want to sit for a while," he asks.

"No," I say.

We continue walking down to the ashram. Suddenly I do not resent the lack of help from Amar. I feel that it is good like this, to stumble, to fall, to not be able to see everything, to take the work away from one's eyes. For months and months and months how tired my eyes have been. An exhaustion takes over me and a memory of the many, many things I have *seen* passes physically through my eyes. Words, so many, many words, books, so many, films in black and white and colour, breathtaking temples, airplanes, palaces, the colours of rituals, an old man's burning pyre, new universities sprawling over hills in a new country, old sculptures, caves, living cells moving under a microscope, faces of the most diverse people, animals in zoos and sanctuaries. As I see these things it comes to me that to take the work away from one's eyes means not closing them, but gazing very, very far as opposed to the near, even if it be in utter darkness, to ease the muscles of the eyes and not have them strain towards a certain point, and most of all, to keep the gaze unfocused.

Before I know it I hit something and fall again and my head lands hard on a rock.

When I open my eyes again, everything is unclear. As my eyes focus, I realize I am in Sarah's study, on the single bed. Sarah is leaning over me. She takes my hand in her's and says, "You're all right."

My head is pounding, and when I reach up I feel the rough cotton of a bandage.

"You hit your head on a rock and lost consciousness. There was some bleeding. We brought the doctor and he checked you. You're all right. Tomorrow we'll take you to the hospital and run some tests just to make sure."

"I don't feel too bad."

"Good. I'll go and arrange some dinner for you."

When Sarah leaves I look around. Light from a yellow lamp falls on the shelves filled with books. Further than the shelves, near the door, I see Amar. He looks at me. The yellow lamplight doesn't quite reach him so he stands in half darkness. Very, very slowly he raises his right arm. It takes its time, this raising of the arm, it takes a few minutes. The hand is raised, palm inwards, open. He brings this hand up to a few inches from the eyes. Then, with the hand he makes a diagonal, wiping gesture, but without touching anything. After this, the arm comes down again, as slowly. I try to raise my head up to see him better, but it is too painful, so I lie back down again. Amar comes to the bed and sits down on the floor, to my right, his face at the same level as my arms. A tear hangs at the edge of his right eye. His face is very calm but somewhere far inside a question is rising. I can see it and I know he can too. He takes my hand and kisses it and then he leaves the room. It is the last time I see him.

That night I cannot fall asleep. My thoughts have no end. I can see some night outside the one low window, and the spines of some of the brighter books, here and there a word in gold. The last thing that comes up in my thoughts before I sleep is that I have never loved a man who has not given me more than he has taken away.

Now I write in the mornings. I wake up early, drink a cup of tea and open my notebook. Only a few pages are full. What comes out of me are single lines, at the most two sentences one after another. The source of my writing has changed. What comes on the page is often something I do not know at all, and have never felt before. Today I write: "Inside the heart of something, anything, life holds itself in perfect balance."

Light rises early over this eastern edge of the country, this country that is nearly a continent, and has moved a long way over the water, raising mountains, covering seas. It rises early, the light. Travelling very near, very far, Anjali has reached this place in the eastern part of Bengal. The landscape comes first, perhaps to make ready, to prepare, to enable the heart. It is already hot and humid, even at the coming of the sun. In the groves she walks through this light and heat are ripening the mangoes on the trees, standing so close to one another that their curled leaves touch each other and sometimes merge. It can happen that the leaves of one tree sometimes hang from the branch of another. In these groves it is still not easy to see, the sun has not risen high enough. As she walks on there are bamboo trees and bokul, and further away she can see lines of the tall taal. As the light rises higher she emerges from this vast grove and comes upon a lake, on the banks of which banana trees stand, their large, broad leaves hanging over the water. She is standing, facing the lake, looking at the rising sun. As Anjali comes closer she turns around. Already the heat has brought sweat on her forehead, a dampness above the lips. She looks at Anjali with her large eyes.

"I am no one to you, no one," the woman says.

Anjali's heart twists in pain. This woman already knows what she desires.

"Not your mother, not a sister. Because no one is like anyone. Like a mother, like a sister, there is no such thing. Every relationship is only itself."

"Yes," Anjali says, because what else can she say? She is surprised to see her, but it is a surprise filled with inevitability.

She is middle aged, this woman, of course not old enough to be her mother, a sister perhaps. She has the still deep black hair of most middle aged women in Bengal, perhaps only a few strands of grey which can never be seen, and moist, shining skin that will age only many years later. And of course large black eyes lined with kajal that she has put there with a forefinger. In the deep green vegetation of these parts women do not age quickly, in the moist, warm weather, the face, the body and skin retain their shine, for years.

And of course, she is beautiful, like everything born of a pure and helpless desire. For that is the place from where this woman has come. Who is she? Perhaps she is from a hundred years ago, Anjali as she wishes to be, she is the far point of Anjali's sight, a herself that emerges from Anjali in the process of her becoming.

Sarajubala, for Anjali knows that is the woman's name, wears a black dhakai jamdani of the lightest, finest weave, with round golden butis, and a long, pale gold blouse. The sari is worn the way they used to wear it in those days, wrapped around several times, without any pleats, and the anchal hanging small over the shoulder. Her hair is tied behind her head, a silver comb at the centre of the knot.

"I've been waiting for you," she says, turning suddenly tender.

She smiles and her eyes first darken looking closely at Anjali, then turn lighter, suddenly almost transparent, looking through her, looking at no one. With the smile, the rounded, still youthful face swells a little, there is a bloating near the eyes, small wrinkles near the full lips, as the smile spreads she grows older, she ages ten years. When the smile is over, the face returns to its more youthful aspect again.

"Tell me then," she says, the way people do when they have known each other for years. Her face shines with the loveliest light. They begin to walk past this lake, past more trees of krishnachura and coconut, the light getting stronger now, past many small ponds and little streams. At some of them women are already up washing clothes. The sound of clothes being beaten on the shore comes together with that of the rising birds, and the rustling of Sarajubala's sari, it rustles as if fresh off the loom on which it was woven. The gold butis flash when they come in the path of the rising light.

"Do women still wait at windows and doorways?" she asks.

"Yes."

"And you?"

Anjali smiles.

"Yes. Even I, despite myself."

Beneath their bare feet small red berries get crushed and the red juice stains their feet before seeping into the moist soil. On the feet of Sarajubala it smudges the alta.

She looks sideways at Anjali and her eyes are afire with light for a moment. Then she looks away.

"There is such a feeling in window sills," she says. "A calmness, a grief, a security."

"And in awnings," says Anjali. "Of mud, or wood, or concrete."

"Built so firmly, to protect. Yet sometimes, it is they that need your care."

"Clothes drying by themselves in the sunlight. Free, lonely."

"And in the evening among the dense trees, and through the trees, when I incline my head—"

"or wind stirs the leaves, unexpectedly—"

"suddenly a golden light or two, far away from homes or streets—"

"revealed as the tree bends or wind parts the leaves, for a few moments..."

"Such gladness then—"

"These golden lights extending—"

"the range—"

"of the heart."

"Did they tell you much about these parts?" Sarajubala asks.

"Not really. Only little bits, about how much water there was, seeping out of the soil, the ponds, streams, lakes and the rivers wide as seas. The constant fertility of the land, the sweetness of the fish. The hilsa in the Padma. They never wanted to come back to visit, my grandparents, or my father."

"Of course. Why would they want to test memory?"

"But a place they had loved...that they were born in..."

"They knew it was not just the space they would need to go back to, but the time, and they knew that the two were inseparable."

Green parrots thrust themselves out of the mango trees. The mynah calls and calls.

They come to a large house sheltered by mango and jackfruit trees. It is at least a hundred years old, but in very good repair. The wooden shutters at the windows are all closed against the rising heat.

"Come," she says.

Inside, in the cool darkness, they walk through large rooms, no one in them, and all the furniture covered with white sheets. Anjali can see only the gold butis on the black sari and the faint gold of the blouse. She can smell breakfast being made somewhere, vegetables being cooked. They go upstairs and go into the only room where the furniture is not covered, and the wood gleams in the darkness. Sarajubala's room.

There is a four poster bed, an alna with nothing hanging on it, and a heavy dressing table with a shining mirror. On it there are combs, a silver sindur holder, a brass kajal lata. All of this shining and completely free of dust. Sarajubala opens one window and some light falls in. They sit on the bed, Sarajubala gathering up her sari, and Anjali her long skirt.

"I like it," Sarajubala says, pointing at her skirt and blouse.

"Are you curious about today's time?" Anjali says. "Do you want to know how people are living?"

"I don't know…in the end, not so much. The time that I am not a part of is only a kind of loose imagining, without rigour, and what emotion can that have? But what I and all that is around me have lived, that is overwhelming."

She gets up and brings an intricately carved silver box. Inside there are leaves of paan and whole nuts of supari. She begins to cut the supari, right hand on the handles of the jaanti and the left hand holding the supari in between the blades.

Anjali puts out her hand for some bits. She puts them into her mouth and chews them, at first bitter and then turning sweet. It brings back very long ago memories of dark, humid afternoons, the women lying on beds with their long hair spread out beyond their heads, their sari blouses loosened, their gold bangles making sounds as they turned, reading a novel, reading a newspaper and turning the pages with a rustling sound that disturbed someone else's coming sleep, and everyone chewing bits of supari, cutting the bigger bits noisily with their teeth, long ago when she was a little girl, and it was a time of great security with a sadness at its core, a sadness of limits, limits that she has now crossed.

"And your husband," Sarajubala asks. "How is he? He's the only one you really love, that you're in love with, the one you want to love again, in the next life."

"Why do men always want women to be tender?"

"Their need, as it is ours to be protected. But to understand that the two things are the same, it takes time. Tenderness is a kind of protection, and protection a kind of tenderness."

"You must eat something, you haven't eaten a thing since last night, have you?" she says and disappears. She comes back with a large bell metal plate that shines like the gold butis on her sari, and puts it in her hand. The plate has potatoes cooked with panchforon, green chillies and salt, just the way Anjali used to like it, and luchis thin and light as air.

What she eats is more than food. She eats a kind of time, a kind of love.

As she is finishing, Sarajubala says, "Let me bring you some more."

"No," she smiles. "This is more than enough."

"No wonder the girl is so thin," she says, with indulgence. "All right." She takes the plate away.

The heat is beginning to ripen now, to mature. Sarajubala sits in front of Anjali on the bed.

"Give me your palms," she says.

She touches Anjali's open hands, palm to palm. Her hands are cool as the evening breeze that will blow here when the sun goes down. They stay like that for some time. Then she moves up behind Anjali and puts her two hands on Anjali's head, the fingers towards the face. Her sari as she comes closer smells of old wooden cupboards and sandalwood. Anjali notices on the front of the sari, well below her chest, there is a large area that is brittle and brown, as if it is an ancient fabric. She looks to see, but the rest of the sari is crisp and new. Sarajubala brings her palms down on Anjali's eyes, the fingers pointing downwards. She feels the heat and sweat recede, a calmness coming, her breath slowing down.

Anjali can feel Sarajubala resting her hand on her eyes for a very long time, then the base of her throat, down to the centre of her chest, to her navel, the place between her thighs and then her two feet. She holds the soles of Anjali's feet with her hands.

Time passes.

Anjali sees before her a relaxed sky, of the deepest blue, so relaxed that over it anything can pass. She looks at it for as long as she can. It takes its leave of her, although she does not want to let it go.

After this she sees an immense field of snow, stretching infinitely. In the foreground of this field she sees on the left Riaz, directly behind him her father, standing by himself to the right, Richard, and towards the back of the field, Amar. They are all wearing long, black overcoats, like the one her father had, of the softest cashmere wool. They are silent, looking, saying nothing.

Time passes again.

She sees herself, standing in the middle of a vast green field, not of this land, shining in the sun, in a long white dress that moves in the wind. She sees herself from the back, she can see her neck and her bare arms. The grass grows long around her. She is as alone as she can possibly be, the fields stretch to the sky, and she is filled first with an abandon and then with an energy she cannot name, an energy that will make her capable of doing all that she ever needs to.

It is then that Sarajubala moves away, and Anjali begins to fall asleep. She hears the mynah calling, the regular beat of the woodpecker.

"You…" She tries to speak but her voice has become a hoarse whisper. She stops, she waits a few moments.

"Who were those men in the white field?" Sarajubala asks. "Men you have loved?"

"Yes…You cannot, cannot imagine how tired I am, how exhausted," Anjali finally says, her voice coming as if from a very far place.

"My golden one," she can hear Sarajubala say.

As she falls asleep Anjali knows this woman has emerged from a part of herself that has travelled through the oldest memories. This woman is her deepest wish, fulfilled.

When Anjali wakes up, it is late afternoon. She sees Sarajubala sitting near her, fanning them both with a palm leaf fan. Her wrist moves with the effortlessness of someone who can do this for hours.

"How long have I slept?"

"Four days."

"I was so tired." Anjali sits up. Everything in the room is as it was, the window open at exactly the same angle, the things on the dressing table untouched, free of dust, only the afternoon light falls differently.

"Come," says Sarajubala. "It is time to go up to the terrace. The evening breeze has begun."

They climb up dark, narrow stairs and out onto the huge roof. As she steps out Anjali sees that right below the house is a river, a river wide as the sea. Her heart moves in joy. She walks to the edge of the roof and watches. The river curves exactly at this point, curves towards the house and then away. Sarajubala looks at her and smiles. There are boats on the river, simple wooden boats with coarsest cloth for sails. There are fishing nets on the water. On the left of the river there are fields of paddy. She can see some men and women working in the fields, their bodies bent over. Sarajubala unrolls a golden madur for them to sit on. The ground is still warm.

Sarajubala strokes Anjali's back. Her two hands move alternately from the shoulder to the small of the back and begin again. The lightest touch, the firmest feeling.

"If your hair was long I would have combed it now, and tied it up," she says. She puts her fingers on the nape of Anjali's neck where the hair ends, in light wisps.

"Tell me about your hands," Anjali says.

"I smell a storm coming," Sarajubala says. Suddenly the harsh light seems to have become gentle. The sky hangs down on the crowns of the trees and the broad river, somewhere the wind throws open a window. There is, Anjali can feel, a watery taste in the air.

"My story begins when I left home at twelve to come to my husband's home, this home. My father, whom I loved very much, wept when I left. Our village was miles away from here. I came to this house, filled with light and people. I was not unhappy. They all loved me. My husband was twenty. We were happy together, and lived like that for five years. One day he left, from right here, from this riverbank, on the boat, to go to the city.

"I'm going Saraju," he said from the swaying boat.

"Don't say you're going," I said. "Say you'll be back."

But he smiled and said again, "I'm going."

"This river takes away, it brings back, all the time. How was I to know this would be different? He never came back. People were sent to the city to look for him. He couldn't be found.

"Of course, everyone called me abhagini. I had nothing, I would have nothing, not even a child."

"Don't look at me like that," she suddenly told Anjali with a certain roughness. "You do not yet know that fortune and misfortune are not easy to separate. You know, but you have not yet learnt it, the way you learn something forever, beyond forgetting."

"Are you turning away what I feel inside when you tell me these things?" Anjali asks, angered.

"I don't like sentiment," she says. "Stories must be told to those who can feel." She becomes quiet. "Sentiment is a story touched only from the outside. One has to look inside stories and not be full of greed, not be too eager to look into a person's life."

"You're wondering, did I know why he never came back? Did something happen to him, or did he leave me. The answer is that I don't know. There were no signs of him wanting to leave, but who can know what another's heart may desire? I merely and simply do not know, the way some things always remain unknown.

"A few years went by in great suffering. At twenty five, things began to change. I was beginning to touch aloneness, which has nothing to do with turning away from people. I watched things, the things that were given to me. The curve of this broad river, I watched. The movement of the coconut tree I saw carefully. While the whole large leaf sways up and down, the individual stalks often have a very different, small, delicate kind of movement, like an intense trembling. The crow crying out at noon I heard. I began to see that there were no straight lines except in what people created. That each thing is unfinished, the tree's movement, the birdcall. There is no finality to the things of this world. I saw the difference between repetition and recurrence. These were things I saw. Spoken, they are separate things and I do not have your gift of language to make of them a whole.

"The first person my slowly changing hands touched was a little child, my brother-in-law's young son, two years old, who was running a high fever for days and we all feared he would die. One day something moved me to touch the soles of his little feet, to hold them in my hands for a long time. That night the fever started receding and in a few days he was well. The next person was our cook, Jadu. Standing over the fire one day he had a fit which threw him to the ground, frothing at the mouth. This time something moved me to place my hands on his eyes. It took a long time, but he emerged to consciousness. Then I knew that I had been given something. Of course, they all stopped calling me abhagini," she began to laugh. "My heart goes out to people and their fickleness. They began to come, first from this village and then from villages all around. Suddenly, so much attention, so much praise. My hands, they said, were transforming not only the physical body, but also the energies inside, the heart."

"How?"

"That, my little girl, living in the age of speech, is not something that can be spoken. But I will tell you one thing. At first, I was full of purpose. I spoke to the person whom I touched, asked questions, and wished with everything I had that my hands would make him well. But slowly, and maybe because the heart cannot take so much wishing, the sense of purpose went away. As I grew older when I put my hands on someone I often did not know what disease they had, what grief of the heart. More often than not I did not ask. I looked at and touched a person the way I looked at the river and the sky, without purpose. Later I understood that purposelessness frees the gaze, and someone being healed, changed, transformed, is only a consequence.

"But there was one thing that needed to be fulfilled in me, the body's desire. I was brimming with it, and there was nowhere to go. I was helping others, but I could not help myself."

While they have been talking the wind has begun to blow in strong gusts. Dust swirls around them. The mango and jackfruit trees bend and sway, a few ripe mangoes fall to the ground. The wind gets stronger and the birds begin flying home with sharp cries, crows, mynahs, bulbuls. Sarajubala covers her head with her anchal.

"I'll go down and make sure all the windows are shut," she says.

Anjali bends her head and shades her eyes. The kalbaisakhi swirls above and around her. She suddenly hears music, as if someone is playing a tanpura. In the flying wind she looks all around. She sees, at the far end of the terrace, there are two small sitting areas under decorated concrete canopies. Inside one of them stand two tanpuras, one in an ebony coloured wood, the other, lighter and more golden. The wind comes and plays over the strings of the tanpura, and the notes begin to rise into the air, then as the direction of the wind changes, they abruptly stop. They begin again as the wind comes and stop as the wind turns away. Sometimes they are notes that are melodic, at other times, when the wind comes the opposite way, the notes are atonal. These notes which are otherwise long and continuous when played by a human hand become now little bits of unfinished tones, and a new kind of improvisation emerges from the relationship between them and the storm, surprising, unknown.

When Sarajubala comes back, they take shelter in the other canopy, but not till the dust has settled on their skin, entered their eyes and become a gritty taste on their tongues. From where they sit they can watch the sky darkening with kalbaisakhi clouds. "Do you sing?" Anjali asks.

"I used to," says Sarajubala.

The river swirls in its bed. Finally the rain comes, not heavy, but light, enough to make the dust wet and bring a feeling of great coolness to everything. They watch the rain, without speaking, till it gets completely dark and the broad river merges into the evening, and only the butis on Sarajubala's sari give off a faint light.

"Did you ever use your hands on yourself?"

"I tried, but it never worked. The days passed, but the nights were hard. Many years passed in this way and though I saw and understood many things, this one emptiness did not go away. I would look at almost every man and wonder how he kissed, how he made love, how he touched a woman's breasts. I also knew that I needed to feel tenderness for the man I would desire, because even though I saw so many men, I rarely desired any of them."

Behind the moving kalbaisakhi clouds there seemed to be the hint of moonlight.

"Years passed in this way. But no one is long permitted to remain what they are and why should I be an exception? I began absorbing things from touching the people I healed. This was a new thing. In the past, it was I who gave, and they went away. Now, they were also giving me, despite themselves, and giving me the dark and the light. Their fears, their joys, their desires. Their violence, their grief, their ecstasy. It was not my choice to take only what was expansive, to leave what oppressed behind in the air. They had all found an empty space through which to enter me and I was helpless. The balance of giving and taking had been upset. My hands became confused. I did not know what to do.

"One day, down by the riverbank, I met a man, visiting here from the city, a scholar. He was sitting on the banks and reading a book. I was thirty seven years old. What I had longed for had come to me. The body's passion, the heart's love. We went away to the city, we married, and a daughter was born to me. All this time I let my hands be. After my daughter was born, the power in the hands came back. I began to work again, on friends, neighbours, but I could never use them on my husband and daughter. When I did, nothing happened."

Her voice had suddenly changed. It was no longer the voice, which had told a story, full of memory, longing and empty spaces. It had become a voice which was grounded, definite and strong. The clouds parted and there was the moon, not quite full, but large enough to throw some light on the dark river and the trees.

"After a century I've used them on you. To slaughter your fears. To slaughter your fears and bring back your joy."

The night grew darker as they sat there and Sarajubala finally stood up and said, "You have to eat your dinner, come, come downstairs."

Downstairs there were tall oil lamps, throwing shadows on the walls and ceiling. Sarajubala went and got a plate of food. There was rice, a sour sweet dal with tiny mangoes in it, jackfruit cooked with garlic and onions, and hilsa in mustard paste.

"If you want to sleep upstairs we'll have to wipe the terrace clean of dust, and then take up some pillows and sheets."

"I would love that."

Anjali finished eating, the fish with its hundred tiny bones, the fish, silver and firm and sweet, the taste of which will always remain on her tongue, the thought of which will always remain in her imagination.

Upstairs it is cool under the open sky. Together they wipe the floor clean, they wipe the two golden madurs. They bring up fresh white sheets and pillows from Sarajubala's bed, and Sarajubala her silver box of paan.

"Oh," she suddenly says. "I forgot something."

She comes back up with a flame in a brass holder, a single, large flame. "From the puja room," she says. She passes her hand through the flame and puts the hand on Anjali's head very gently. Three times.

In the light of this flame so close to Sarajubala's face, she sees that Sarajubala has turned grey, the black hair almost invisible. Her face has grown older, more wrinkled, the eyes more moist. When she told her tale time entered her and showed its passing. The hands which blessed her were rough, the skin shrunken. Her feet as she sat down were the feet of an old woman. She passed her hand through the flame again, this time taking its heat and energy onto her own head.

"Tell me more about your husband. Were you happy? How was your daughter? Were you overjoyed?"

"My story is over now. You haven't said a word about yourself," Sarajubala says.

"You know everything."

"Not everything," she smiles. She lies down on her side, her head propped up on her arm. Far away somewhere, there is the cry of a jackal.

"I don't want only to be a teller of tales." Anjali says. "And when I am I don't want to speak only of strength."

"What do you want to speak of?"

"Of imperfections, what cannot be done, of helplessness. And..."

"And?"

"And yet, to always give life to aspiration."

Sarajubala looks at her. "For that, you will have to be careful. You will have to resist the desire to turn everything into language."

"Sometimes it is all I can do."

"Every gift exists because of an empty space somewhere else." Anjali looks at her.

The sky above them is filled with stars. The river makes its moving sound.

"What is joy?" Anjali asks.

"To open up things endlessly, and to know when to let them be."

Sarajubala takes the soles of Anjali's feet in her hands. This time her hands are warm, unlike the cool, gentle breeze that blows after the kalbaisakhi. She holds her feet, firmly. Anjali closes her eyes. Sarajubala moves up and touches her head, the same warmth, the same firmness. This time she can feel a stirring at the roots of her hair. After a long time has passed, she takes her hands away. Anjali opens her eyes. She sees Sarajubala bent over her, stroking the air above Anjali's face with both her hands, as if she is stroking the face but without ever touching it. Anjali closes her eyes.

She sees a room, in the house of her father that she has left long ago. It is as she remembers it, with the wooden Venetian windows closed to keep out the sun. Inside the darkened room she is packing a large suitcase. With her is a large, white skinned man, fleshy, too grounded, without anything fine about him. They are going to take a flight to another country, and the tickets that lie on the table are blue. The man wears a tee shirt in a dull, faded colour and her suitcase too is full of tee shirts, brimming with them, all a little old, a little used and in faded colours. On top of all of them lies a sari, bright and sparkling. It is a black jamdani, freshly made, with golden butis on it.

Only the air moves above Anjali's face. For a long time before her eyes, darkness, like the night.

Then she sees before her a very large bird, perched on a ledge, in daylight. Its body is grey and rough and has the texture of a tree bark. The large beak is blue, the deep blue of a day sky, and its large wing is of the same colour. The bird has only one wing, the one on the right, and it seems to be longer than the body. This bird is strong and wild, and looks at her with very sharp eyes, looks at her directly, without blinking, without turning away. She returns the look. The gaze they share is a gaze between two equals. In the air there is a wild animal smell.

When Anjali comes out of herself, it is the middle of night. She sits up and she sees Sarajubala on a corner of the terrace, painting a fish. As she goes closer she sees the fish, a rui fish, very large, perhaps three feet long and two feet wide, with its eyes dilated in death. Sarajubala paints the body of the fish with red paint, she makes a pattern of diamonds on its body. In the cool night breeze the odour of the fish is light, it disperses into the night air.

"I used to love doing this for weddings. It's been so long," she says. Anjali remembers the women in her family, painting fish like this one to be sent to the groom's home as a gift. The lamp Sarajubala sits by makes the scales of the fish shine.

"Such unending empty spaces," says Anjali. "Who else can I bring them to but you?"

"Imbalance can be the heart of a life, the secret of its magic. It will protect you."

"For so long I have thought of people as protectors, needed them as protectors. But it is never people, is it?"

"Never," she says. "Always only aspects of yourself."

"How," asks Anjali, "do you know so much?"

"I don't know so much," Sarajubala says, resting her brush on the broad tail of the fish. "There are things I don't know at all. I don't know for example, the world, is the world…is it…very, very large?"

"Would you like to see it?"

"Yes," she says with a light of expectation in her eyes.

"I would like to show it to you."

"In another life."

Anjali smiles.

"You don't believe in another life, do you?" asks Sarajubala.

"I don't know."

"Well, I'm here aren't I?"

Sarajubala picks up the brush again and finishes painting a row of small flowers just above the tail. After this she looks at her work, satisfied. She pats the head of the fish with its large eye and dilated pupil. They are about to turn away when the fish suddenly moves its tail up and then down with a thud. It begins to writhe, slowly, on the concrete floor. The eye, suddenly less dilated, seems to look around at the surrounding darkness that is not water. They watch the fish, surprised. It begins to writhe more violently, shifting from its place in sharp, small movements.

"We'll take it down to the water," Sarajubala says. A single tear drops from her left eye and passes down her face.

The sky begins to lighten and the koel calls. When the sun comes up on the river it is a red sun, brighter than normal, giving off an incredible heat. They gather up their madurs and go downstairs. In the room Anjali notices that Sarajubala has become a younger woman again. The greyness of hair has disappeared, as have the lines and wrinkles on her face. She stands at the mirror, takes out the silver comb, and shakes out her waist length hair, combing it carefully. Then she ties it up, using her hands to make a large, loose knot and puts the comb back. With her forefinger she lines her eyes with kajal. At the very end is the large dot of sindoor on her forehead.

When she is ready, they go up to get the fish. In the new risen light the fish writhes and moves in great fits and starts, its tail making the loudest noises as it hits the ground. Because the fish is so large it takes them some time to gather it up. They hold it in their arms, Anjali towards the head and Sarajubala towards the tail which hits her face from time to time. It is surprisingly warm to the touch, its scales brightening moment by moment and the red diamonds painted on it are brighter than blood.

They go down to the curve of the river. There both of them bend down and glide the fish back into the water. It immediately stops its writhing and begins to swim away, leaving behind a light red cloud in the water. Soon it has moved out of sight.

Anjali feels now the river filled with innumerable fish. The fish like this one, large and heavy, possibly swimming deeper in, the smaller ones closer to the surface, and the hilsa swimming upstream, unlike all the others. These fish caught, eaten with such gratefulness and savour, painted on, given in gift, brought home in all auspiciousness, given up for nothing except death. Fish the first avatar, painted on the floor at weddings, pujas, and celebrations, fish the moving anchor of a riverine people, carved on temple walls, woven on the borders and anchals of saris. When all things are related in this way, then nothing is lonely, ideas or things.

The fish enters the wide, wide river, his vast and natural home. He swims deeper in and faster, the water above, below and around him like joy. He sees near him aspects of other fish, most of them smaller, swimming by, limbs of people submerged in the water bathing the dirt off their bodies, the underside of a boat, the dangling hand of the boatman which he bumps into, the undersides of red lotus flowers, an image of Durga with the colours faded, a banana tree with large, wilted leaves, the body of a dead man in a white dhoti. He swims through all of this, suddenly loving everything, because he is not on that hardness of land and dying. He knows now the value of breathing. And he knows something else now that is completely new. For the first time the touch of a human hand has brought life to a fish instead of death. As he swims he knows that death will have to be met someday, but not now, not now, for now there is the joy of this vast water, this moving, clear thing that gives him his life.

Standing on the shore Anjali can feel the rui fish swimming away and being healed. She can feel, as if inside herself, the relief, the joy and the celebration of this fish as he moves through the water. The feeling disturbs her, because she does not know if it is her imagination only, or a new ability of her consciousness.

They walk, through groves thick with a multitude of trees. The koel calls, insistently, urgently. They walk past the krishnachura, the tree of Krishna, that signals the spring in these parts, and from whose bright red flowers the red powder of Holi is made. Everywhere there are banana trees, with dark mauve flowers hanging from the branches. Anjali remembers praying to the banana tree dressed as a bride, as Lakshmi. There is the bel whose leaves are an offering to Shiva, the tulsi that used to be part of every home. Every tree, every flower here has an existence beyond its vegetal self. Sarajubala stops under an enormous banyan, the tree of sages, of ancient wisdom, of forbearance. This one has a smooth light brown trunk, and a vast expanse of leaves, branches and aerial roots that create the coolest shade below. The hanging roots emerge from strong branches, but are themselves as frail as tendrils. They stand amidst these roots, and branches and leaves and Sarajubala places herself exactly in front of Anjali.

"Raise up your arms from your sides," says Sarajubala, "and then open your palms, very slowly, finger by finger."

Anjali looks down and sees that both her hands are closed into fists. She raises her arms, slowly. When they are almost at the level of her chest she begins to open her palms. First the thumbs, then the forefingers of both hands. Already she feels this is the most difficult thing her body has ever done. It takes a few minutes to open each finger. Her legs are trembling and under her feet there seems to be not hard earth but wet, shifting sand. By the time she comes to the third finger of each hand a broken wail emerges from her. A feeling of something leaving rises inside her, such as she has never known before, a leaving with a rush like a waterfall that becomes a river and flows away very far, to where she does not know. She knows only that this leaving is irreversible. Anjali is not able to open her hands fully, the fingers are still bent inward, and what emerges from her body and mouth are more sharp wails and acidic tears. Is it loss, this leaving, this flowing away? If so, it is not the loss of anything she has ever known, and therefore a loss that can never be replenished again, ever. Beneath her the ground moves and flows without cease.

When it has been long enough, Sarajubala comes from behind, reaches out, and holds her, arm to arm, hand to hand. Gently, she closes Anjali's palms. She brings down Anjali's arms, slowly, placing them by her sides. They stay like that, joined from head to hands to feet. Over them stretches the banyan, like a third, concerned.

"What…" asks Anjali.

"Let it be," Sarajubala says, very softly. She moves away.

Anjali sways, she reaches out to a hanging root near her to steady herself. She is amazed at the strength and hardness of the root.

"It is not from my life," says Anjali.

"Can there be anything that comes from within that is not inside? Let it be."

Sarajubala takes Anjali's hand and they sit at the enormous base of the tree. Anjali feels she is in a cave of branches, leaves, roots and shadows. Sarajubala stretches her legs out in front of her. Anjali puts her head on this stretched out lap, and falls asleep.

"May I go now?" Sarajubala asks, as soon as Anjali wakes up.

No, please stay, Anjali wants to say, but she knows she can't. Why can't she? She doesn't know why, but she knows she can't. Instead she says, "Already? I am still…I am still… too much myself."

Sarajubala smiles. It is a smile Anjali has seen before in old paintings, in frescoes, in sculptures at caves and temples. The lips are closed, the features composed. The smile lights the face tenuously, from the inside. On the face there is tenderness and strength, stillness and movement. A thousand Natarajas are behind this smile, Shiva and Parvati in embrace, Durga killing the Mahisasura, Visnu on the Sesanaga, the Buddha under the Bodhi tree. She knows that civilizations pass down gestures, now she sees that they also pass down the emotions that impel them.

"You…" Sarajubala begins to say, then stops. She places a hand on Anjali's head.

Anjali realizes that all this time she has never called Sarajubala by her name, because she is older than her and from another time, she has also not called her by a relationship, didi, mashi. There are some people you cannot address through any of these words. From long ago, from so long ago, a gesture passes through Anjali's body. She bends down, to a much older self, a much further way of looking. Her eyes take in Sarajubala's shining face, the sari with the gold butis, the place where the sari is torn and brittle, all the way till she reaches the two feet outlined in red. She touches both the feet with her right palm and takes her palm to her head.

When Anjali straightens up again Sarajubala says, "Let me look at you."

She puts a hand under her chin and looks her in the eyes. Then she walks away, slowly disappearing into a far grove of mango trees.

Anjali is sitting on the verandah of the post office one morning, when she sees Riaz walking up to her. She sees him and she knows the joy that enters her is incomparably real. "You look beautiful," he says. "The grey that was beginning in your hair is all gone." He says, "Your skin has such a shine." He looks older and thin, his face has new wrinkles and folds that she feels like touching. There are fresh strands of grey in his hair. She stands up and they hold each other. The tea stall owner looks at them while his tea boils before him. All their life together and apart is in that embrace.

"I've come to take you back," Riaz says, stroking her face.

"I'm not ready yet," Anjali smiles.

They drink tea at the stall, cupping and warming their hands around the thick glasses. Then Anjali takes Riaz towards her cottage, past the two lakes. When they enter her room Riaz seems not to belong there, in what has been only her space. As soon as he sits down on the bed he says, "I'm very, very tired."

Soon he is asleep with the sun falling in from the window on his face. In this bright light and with his face so still the large sadness that till now lay beneath his eyes, nose and lips, rises completely to the surface. It is, Anjali can tell, a suffering that has not yet understood itself. Evening comes and he does not wake up, and when it is night Anjali lies down next to him. In the darkness she can no longer see his face, but she can smell his skin, his hair and his sweat, all the smells that their love includes along with the smell of all their years together. One of them would have come to take back the other, it does not matter whom.

Lying next to Riaz this night, after so long, Anjali cannot fall asleep. The base of all fears is really the fear of completely inhabiting one's own self. She is no longer pushing against this fear. It is not that she is more certain, no, everything is even more tremulous now than before, more frail, more imperilled; earth and sky can collapse without warning, and a stranger or a shaft of light can suddenly appear and illuminate in the same trembling, uneven way.

Anjali extends her forefinger and places it beneath Riaz's nostrils. She remembers how when they were much younger Riaz would sleep so soundlessly and without ever moving that she would place her finger beneath his nose to make sure he was breathing. When she does it now it is to feel the flow of his breath, in and out, the flow of his life. In the morning they wake up, not holding each other or touching as they used to. An awkwardness has returned, as if their separation was more natural than their being together.

They talk, he of his work and the city, she of the hard and rigourous beauty of these mountains. But they do not ask each other any other questions.

The next day they go up to the deodar forest. It is already afternoon when they stop at the tea stall to drink two glasses of tea. It is the peak of summer in the mountains, the sun strong and sharp, but by the time they reach the edge of the forest it is beginning to set. Riaz hesitates but Anjali is confident, and she has a torch with her. They walk into the forest. As they walk a night rises from the forest floor to meet the night that falls from above. Anjali does not want to use the torch. They walk, using the little light around them, sometimes stumbling over the deodar cones that are strewn on the ground, sometimes crushing one underneath their feet. At first they walk almost blindly, but gradually the eyes get used to the darkness. They hear more than they can see. In the silence there are unpredictable rustlings. There is a sound like human footsteps, like theirs, on the forest floor. Suddenly, the sound of a bird flapping its wings, of something being dragged through the undergrowth far away. These sounds constantly appear, but without pattern or rhythm, so there is a sense that anything can happen, anything, in the very next moment.

Anjali wants to walk further in. It is Riaz who is more hesitant. He touches her arm and asks, "Are you sure?"

"Yes," she replies. "Here, hold my hand," she says. They can barely see each other's faces. Riaz takes her hand, but drops it in a moment, as if he has changed his mind.

The darkness is so different now than in the day. Then, there was a knowledge of the sun, being there, above everything, to be called upon when needed. Now the trees have no trunks, the dark brown almost invisible in the darkness, so that the branches above seem suspended in the night. Anjali and Riaz learn to separate dark from dark. The dark blue green needles of the trees form jagged shapes against the night, they are lighter than the darkness they stand against. In some places the needles give off a darkly silver hue. Standing in the middle of the forest they look up, far up above them. As always, in these mountains, even the darkest sky is infused with a faint light, whose source remains forever unknown.

A strong wind comes from nowhere, suddenly. The tall, tall deodars do not bend. The wind sweeps through the forest, like a long exhaled breath, with an undertow of longing. It stops as suddenly as it has come. Anjali and Riaz both stop walking and stand still at the same time. Just as they begin to move again, the wind returns, this time more slowly, creating a deep humming sound that takes its time to die down. Almost immediately it comes in one long sweep again, this time the undertow of longing grown more urgent. The trees still stand erect but the wind perhaps pushes some branches aside on its way, because a sudden uneven illumination travels down to the ground. In this light Anjali notices that the grey in Riaz's hair is lit. As she watches, praise comes back, with its edges frayed, with grey hair, aging skin, new lines around the mouth, a new roughness of the hands. She takes Riaz's hands and kisses them, her lips lingering over this unexpected roughness. Riaz does not respond. He looks at her. She can feel the sharpness of a grief pushing inside him but it is never easy to know the contours of another's pain. Two desires come to her, one following the other. First, the desire to protect him. And then, immediately, the desire to shake him, bend him, twist him, to make him wrench out all his confusion and grief, to force him back to life.

The next time the wind comes, it stays and stays and stays. It is not a wind that calms, it is a wind that raises questions. The great deodars of these mountains, patient, unbending, without doubt, and moving through them this mountain wind, probing, insistent, turbulent, unmooring who knows what on its way.

The wind stops and in the new silence, the deep darkness seems to return. Riaz is restless, walking up and down in a small clearing, sometimes looking at her. They see each other in parts, an eye, a suddenly raised arm, a fabric. They cannot see what passes over each other's faces. Is the space between them constantly changing? Is it sometimes as immense as that between the sky far, far above the tall deodars and the soil down below, and sometimes closer like the trees that stand so close but without touching each other through a single leaf or branch? It is hard to tell. But only love can enter the darkness of this forest and stand deep within it.

But when the sun has set, Yajnavalkya, and the moon has set, and the fire has gone out, and speech is hushed, what light does a person here have?

The atman indeed, is his light," said he, "for with the soul, indeed, as his light, one sits, moves around, does his work, and returns.

Only the crow can be both inside and above the deodar forest. From above, he looks at the spreading crowns of the trees, touching each other, for miles. He dives inside, and is amazed at the world he discovers there. In his flight he keeps moving from darkness into light and back again. It is delightful, this flying, unlike anything else he has known. He hovers in a shaft of sunlight, then flies through the shade. In the shade his dark body almost disappears. In the light it emerges again, black and shining. The crow flies and flies, for the sheer joy of seeing himself disappear and appear again and again. It is so quiet in the forest that there is only the sound of his wings against the air.

He flies only through the darkest shadow, avoiding all the shafts of light. He flies low, in the deepest darkness, near the forest floor covered by fallen leaves. He does this for hours. Then he moves upward where the shadows meet the light and he can see more clearly. Once up, he raises his left wing. He looks and sees that the deep darkness has wiped away the drop of blood.

The crow, he knows things from having lived, for what other way is there? He has lived countless lives before this one, but he has little memory of any of them. He forgets them all upon waking, but these lives have seeped into him, and his blood and body carry their essences, the changing knowledge within them, their rhythm of growth, flowering and decay, leading him to act in this, his present life. It is only when a life is over and he is preparing to sleep that some things may return to his conscious mind, a house with oil lamps in the night where a woman dies on her wedding bed, a solar eclipse near the riverbank of a river wide as the sea, a man opening the eyes of a god with chisel and stone, the god lying on the soil and the man standing above. And then he will sleep, which is all there is between lives. Perhaps the gods know more, but do the gods really exist? The crow flies up.

He will fly west and south to the cave that is his home, where he will sleep till time awakens him again, a sleep, which will heal, cure, and erase all conscious memories. He will awake with a new awareness of the present and the ancient past, of dreams that men have dreamed since the earth was, and because of all this, an unfailing knowledge of what will come to be.

On his way to the sky above, the sky always waiting for him, the crow moves towards the centre of the forest, to a fallen tree trunk above which light falls through in a brilliant shaft. He goes into the shaft and opens his beak. He releases the circle of light. It is absorbed in a moment by the shaft. These things, the crow feels, are no longer necessary.